THE MAN THAT CORRUPTED HADLEYBURG
& other stories

THE MAN THAT CORRUPTED HADLEYBURG

& other stories

Mark Twain

WORDSWORTH AMERICAN LIBRARY

This edition published 1996 by
Wordsworth Editions Limited
Cumberland House, Crib Street
Ware, Hertfordshire SG12 9ET

ISBN 1 85326 561 6

Typeset by Antony Gray
Printed and bound in Great Britain by
Mackays of Chatham plc, Chatham, Kent

INTRODUCTION

'The Man That Corrupted Hadleyburg' is the last published piece of major fiction by Mark Twain. It has a complicated and subtle plot about a town full of vigorously sketched characters surrounding the bank clerk Edward Richards and his wife Mary. Hadleyburg could be anywhere in America, 'the most honest and upright town in all the region round about it', whose citizens take pride in its reputation as being incorruptible.

The town had considered itself 'sufficient unto itself and cared not a rap for strangers or their opinions'; and because of this pride, Hadleyburg had in the past subjected a passing stranger to some unnamed offence. The stranger is revengeful and wishes to corrupt Hadleyburg's leading citizens. In retaliation he leaves behind a sack of gold coins (forty thousand dollars's worth) to be claimed by the person able to demonstrate that he once gave the stranger twenty dollars in charity. To prove himself to have been that person, the claimant is required to repeat the remark made at the time to the stranger.

Nineteen of Hadleyburg's leading citizens receive notes pretending to divulge the remark and all fall victim to the temptation of claiming the bag of gold. The stranger's reward has been advertised in the newspaper, and according to his instructions a public meeting in Hadleyburg is called. Candidates to receive the bag of gold are required to present themselves and correctly identify the advice that made the stranger's fortune. At the public meeting the claims of the citizens who have acted on the notes they have received are read out. They each submit an identical message, which turns out to be only a fragment of the 'real' message that is found in the bag.

Thus, a practical joke exposes the greed of the smug leaders of Hadleyburg – and Mark Twain reveals his mature view of human nature as innately corrupt, the most saintly among us being capable of deceit if offered the right temptation. Twain's interest in the nature of conscience is central to this story. When the bank clerk's wife, Mary

Richards, is confronted with her deceit, she admits that her conscience is not the result of inner strength:

> 'Oh, I know it, I know it – it's been one everlasting training and training and training in honesty – honesty shielded, from the very cradle, against every possible temptation, and so it's *artificial* honesty, and weak as water when temptation comes . . . God knows I never had shade nor shadow of a doubt of my petrified and indestructible honesty until now – and now, under the very first big and real temptation, I – Edward, it is my belief that this town's honesty is as rotten as mine is; as rotten as yours is.'

Readers who are already familiar with Mark Twain's tall tales and his ability to make us laugh out loud will find laughter in the public meeting where the Hadleyburg citizens are exposed. But generally his tone is detached in 'The Man That Corrupted Hadleyburg', which was written following a time of personal tragedy when he had struggled to overcome debts involved with bankruptcy and grief at his favourite daughter's death.

Some of the other stories reprinted in this volume also deal with moral questions, such as guilt and responsibility. For example, in 'My Début as a Literary Person' he recapitulates an earlier newspaper story about the clipper ship *Hornet*, which had been set on fire by a disobedient first mate. Twain reports how fifteen of the men on board survived hunger, delirium, exposure and the possibility of cannibalism and mutiny and arrived in Honolulu after 'a voyage of forty-three days in an open boat, through the blazing tropics on ten days' rations of food'. The men survived only because of the character of their captain, 'a bright, simple-hearted, companionable man'. Thus, as with the story about Hadleyburg, we see Twain expressing his understanding of the limitations of human nature.

The moral messages behind some of the other pieces, such as 'The Eskimo Maiden's Romance', are dealt with in a lighter way. Here we see the author's great skill with language, his mastery at distilling the rhythms of oral speech into written prose, his ability to identify with the deepest feelings of a variety of characters.

In his last years, Mark Twain's opinions on a variety of subjects – political, social, and artistic – were eagerly sought by the general public. Sometimes these opinions were controversial – see, for example, the burlesque of Sherlock Holmes and his ineffectual ingenuities in 'A Double-Barrelled Detective Story'. By this time in his career, what was important to most people was the fact of Twain, the skilful lecturer, exuberant humorist and creator of such enduring works as *The Innocents Abroad*, *Adventures of Huckleberry Finn* and *A Connecticut Yankee at King Arthur's Court*.

BIOGRAPHY

Samuel Langhorne Clemens (1835–1910), more familiarly known to us as Mark Twain, was born in Hannibal, Missouri, the St Petersbourg of his stories. His formal schooling ended early, and having learned the printing trade he became a journalist, writing for papers in Hannibal, St Louis, Philadelphia and New York. After four years he returned to the Mississippi where he became a river pilot and he took his *nom de plume* from the leadsman's call for two fathoms. From 1865 he began to establish his reputation as a storyteller and this was consolidated by *The Innocents Abroad* (1869), an account of a voyage through the Mediterranean, and *Roughing It* (1872), which describes his adventures as a writer and journalist in Nevada. He settled in Hartford, Connecticut, with his wife Olivia, and the 1870s saw some of his best work. However, the last two decades of his life were beset by financial and family problems. His son and two of his three daughters died, and the publishing house in which he was partner collapsed. The death of his wife in 1904 added to his store of bitterness and cynicism but in his last years he wrote some sombre and memorable works, including the remarkable moral fable 'The Man That Corrupted Hadleyburg' (1900) which attacks smugness and venality in a small town.

FURTHER READING

Everett Emerson, *The Authentic Mark Twain: A Literary Biography of Samuel L. Clemens*, 1985

Henry N. Smith, *Mark Twain:The Development of a Writer*, 1962

William M. Gibson, *The Art of Mark Twain*, 1976

James Cox, *Mark Twain: The Fate of Humor*, 1966

CONTENTS

The Man That
Corrupted Hadleyburg

It was many years ago. Hadleyburg was the most honest and upright town in all the region round about. It had kept that reputation unsmirched during three generations, and was prouder of it than of any other of its possessions. It was so proud of it, and so anxious to ensure its perpetuation, that it began to teach the principles of honest dealing to its babies in the cradle, and made the like teachings the staple of their culture thenceforward through all the years devoted to their education. Also, throughout the formative years temptations were kept out of the way of the young people, so that their honesty could have every chance to harden and solidify, and become a part of their very bone. The neighbouring towns were jealous of this honorable supremacy, and affected to sneer at Hadleyburg's pride in it and call it vanity; but all the same they were obliged to acknowledge that Hadleyburg was in reality an incorruptible town; and if pressed they would also acknowledge that the mere fact that a young man hailed from Hadleyburg was all the recommendation he needed when he went forth from his natal town to seek for responsible employment.

But at last, in the drift of time, Hadleyburg had the ill luck to offend a passing stranger – possibly without knowing it, certainly without caring, for Hadleyburg was sufficient unto itself, and cared not a rap for strangers or their opinions. Still, it would have been well to make an exception in this one's case, for he was a bitter man and revengeful. All through his wanderings during a whole year he kept his injury in mind, and gave all his leisure moments to trying to invent a compensating satisfaction for it. He contrived many plans, and all of them were good, but none of them was quite sweeping enough; the poorest of them would hurt a great many individuals, but what he wanted was a plan which would comprehend the entire town, and not let so much as one person escape unhurt. At last he had a fortunate idea, and when it fell into his brain it lit up his whole head with an evil joy. He began to form a plan at once, saying to himself, 'That is the thing to do – I will corrupt the town.'

Six months later he went to Hadleyburg, and arrived in a buggy at the house of the old cashier of the bank about ten at night. He got a sack out of the buggy, shouldered it, and staggered with it through the cottage yard, and knocked at the door. A woman's voice said 'Come in', and he entered, and set his sack behind the stove in the parlour, saying politely to the old lady who sat reading the *Missionary Herald* by the lamp:

'Pray keep your seat, madam, I will not disturb you. There – now it is pretty well concealed; one would hardly know it was there. Can I see your husband a moment, madam?'

No, he was gone to Brixton, and might not return before morning.

'Very well, madam, it is no matter. I merely wanted to leave that sack in his care, to be delivered to the rightful owner when he shall be found. I am a stranger; he does not know me; I am merely passing through the town tonight to discharge a matter which has been long in my mind. My errand is now completed, and I go pleased and a little proud, and you will never see me again. There is a paper attached to the sack which will explain everything. Good-night, madam.'

The old lady was afraid of the mysterious big stranger, and was glad to see him go. But her curiosity was roused, and she went straight to the sack and brought away the paper. It began as follows:

TO BE PUBLISHED – or, the right man sought out by private inquiry – either will answer. This sack contains gold coin weighing a hundred and sixty pounds four ounces –

'Mercy on us, and the door not locked!'

Mrs Richards flew to it all in a tremble and locked it, then pulled down the window-shades and stood frightened, worried, and wondering if there was anything else she could do toward making herself and the money more safe. She listened awhile for burglars, then surrendered to curiosity and went back to the lamp and finished reading the paper:

I am a foreigner, and am presently going back to my own country, to remain there permanently. I am grateful to America for what I have received at her hands during my long stay under her flag; and to one of her citizens – a citizen of Hadleyburg – I am especially grateful for a great kindness done me a year or two ago. Two great kindnesses, in fact. I will explain. I was a gambler. I say I *was*. I was a ruined gambler. I arrived in this village at night, hungry and without a penny. I asked for help – in the dark; I was ashamed to beg in the light. I begged of the right man. He gave me twenty dollars – that is to say, he gave me life, as I considered it. He also gave me fortune; for out of that money I have made myself rich at the gaming-table. And finally a remark which he made to me has remained with me to this day, and has at last conquered me; and in conquering has saved the remnant of my morals: I shall gamble no more. Now I have no idea who that man was, but I want him found, and I want him to have this money, to give away, throw away, or keep, as he pleases. It is merely my way of testifying my gratitude to him. If I could stay, I would find him myself; but no matter, he will be found. This is an honest town, an incorruptible town, and I know I can trust it without fear. This man can be identified by the remark which he made to me; I feel persuaded that he will remember it.

And now my plan is this: If you prefer to conduct the inquiry privately, do so. Tell the contents of this present writing to anyone who is likely to be the right man. If he shall answer, 'I am the man; the remark I made was so-and-so,' apply the test – to wit: Open the sack, and in it you will find a sealed envelope containing that remark. If the remark mentioned by the candidate tallies with it, give him the money, and ask no further questions, for he is certainly the right man.

But if you shall prefer a public inquiry, then publish this present writing in the local paper – with these instructions added, to wit: Thirty days from now, let the candidate appear at the town-hall at eight in the evening (Friday), and hand his remark, in a sealed envelope, to the Revd Mr Burgess (if he will be kind enough to act); and let Mr Burgess there and then destroy the seals of the sack, open it, and see if the remark is correct; if correct, let the money be delivered, with my sincere gratitude, to my benefactor thus identified.

Mrs Richards sat down, gently quivering with excitement, and was soon lost in thinkings – after this pattern: 'What a strange thing it is! . . . And what a fortune for that kind man who set his bread afloat upon the waters! . . . If it had only been my husband that did it! – for we are so poor, so old and poor! . . . ' Then, with a sigh – 'But it was not my Edward; no, it was not he that gave a stranger twenty dollars. It is a pity, too; I see it now . . . ' Then, with a shudder – 'But it is *gambler's* money!

the wages of sin: we couldn't take it; we couldn't touch it. I don't like to be near it; it seems a defilement.' She moved to a farther chair . . . 'I wish Edward would come, and take it to the bank; a burglar might come at any moment; it is dreadful to be here all alone with it.'

At eleven Mr Richards arrived, and while his wife was saying, 'I am *so* glad you've come!' he was saying, 'I'm so tired – tired clear out; it is dreadful to be poor, and have to make these dismal journeys at my time of life. Always at the grind, grind, grind, on a salary – another man's slave, and he sitting at home in his slippers, rich and comfortable.'

'I am so sorry for you, Edward, you know that; but be comforted: we have our livelihood; we have our good name – '

'Yes, Mary, and that is everything. Don't mind my talk – it's just a moment's irritation and doesn't mean anything. Kiss me – there, it's all gone now, and I am not complaining any more. What have you been getting? What's in the sack?'

Then his wife told him the great secret. It dazed him for a moment; then he said:

'It weighs a hundred and sixty pounds? Why, Mary, it's for-ty thousand dollars – think of it – a whole fortune! Not ten men in this village are worth that much. Give me the paper.'

He skimmed through it and said:

'Isn't it an adventure! Why, it's a romance; it's like the impossible things one reads about in books, and never sees in life.' He was well stirred up now; cheerful, even gleeful. He tapped his old wife on the cheek, and said, humorously, 'Why, we're rich, Mary, rich; all we've got to do is to bury the money and burn the papers. If the gambler ever comes to inquire, we'll merely look coldly upon him and say: "What is this nonsense you are talking? We have never heard of you and your sack of gold before"; and then he would look foolish, and – '

'And in the meantime, while you are running on with your jokes, the money is still here, and it is fast getting along toward burglar-time.'

'True. Very well, what shall we do – make the inquiry private? No, not that: it would spoil the romance. The public method is better. Think what a noise it will make! And it will make all the other towns jealous; for no stranger would trust such a thing to any town but Hadleyburg, and they know it. It's a great card for us. I must get to the printing-office now, or I shall be too late.'

'But stop – stop – don't leave me here alone with it, Edward!'

But he was gone. For only a little while, however. Not far from his own house he met the editor-proprietor of the paper, and gave him the document, and said, 'Here is a good thing for you, Cox – put it in.'

'It may be too late, Mr Richards, but I'll see.'

At home again he and his wife sat down to talk the charming mystery over; they were in no condition for sleep. The first question was, Who could the citizen have been who gave the stranger the twenty dollars? It seemed a simple one; both answered it in the same breath –

'Barclay Goodson.'

'Yes,' said Richards, 'he could have done it, and it would have been like him, but there's not another in the town.'

'Everybody will grant that, Edward – grant it privately, anyway. For six months, now, the village has been its own proper self once more – honest, narrow, self-righteous, and stingy.'

'It is what he always called it, to the day of his death – said it right out publicly, too.'

'Yes, and he was hated for it.'

'Oh, of course; but he didn't care. I reckon he was the best-hated man among us, except the Reverend Burgess.'

'Well, Burgess deserves it – he will never get another congregation here. Mean as the town is, it knows how to estimate *him*. Edward, doesn't it seem odd that the stranger should appoint Burgess to deliver the money?'

'Well, yes – it does. That is – that is – '

'Why so much that-*is*-ing? Would *you* select him?'

'Mary, maybe the stranger knows him better than this village does.'

'Much *that* would help Burgess!'

The husband seemed perplexed for an answer; the wife kept a steady eye upon him, and waited. Finally Richards said, with the hesitancy of one who is making a statement which is likely to encounter doubt,

'Mary, Burgess is not a bad man.'

His wife was certainly surprised.

'Nonsense!' she exclaimed.

'He is not a bad man. I know. The whole of his unpopularity had its foundation in that one thing – the thing that made so much noise.'

'That "one thing", indeed! As if that "one thing" wasn't enough, all by itself.'

'Plenty. Plenty. Only he wasn't guilty of it.'

'How you talk! Not guilty of it! Everybody knows he *was* guilty.'

'Mary, I give you my word – he was innocent.'

'I can't believe it, and I don't. How do you know?'

'It is a confession. I am ashamed, but I will make it. I was the only man who knew he was innocent. I could have saved him, and – and – well, you know how the town was wrought up – I hadn't the pluck to do it. It would have turned everybody against me. I felt mean, ever so mean; but I didn't dare; I hadn't the manliness to face that.'

Mary looked troubled, and for a while was silent. Then she said, stammeringly:

'I – I don't think it would have done for you to – to – One mustn't – er – public opinion – one has to be so careful – so – ' It was a difficult road, and she got mired; but after a little she got started again. 'It was a great pity, but – Why, we couldn't afford it, Edward – we couldn't indeed. Oh, I wouldn't have had you do it for anything!'

'It would have lost us the goodwill of so many people, Mary; and then – and then – '

'What troubles me now is, what *he* thinks of us, Edward.'

'He? *He* doesn't suspect that I could have saved him.'

'Oh,' exclaimed the wife, in a tone of relief, 'I am glad of that. As long as he doesn't know that you could have saved him, he – he – well, that makes it a great deal better. Why, I might have known he didn't know, because he is always trying to be friendly with us, as little encouragement as we give him. More than once people have twitted me with it. There's the Wilsons, and the Wilcoxes, and the Harknesses, they take a mean pleasure in saying, "*Your friend* Burgess", because they know it pesters me. I wish he wouldn't persist in liking us so; I can't think why he keeps it up.'

'I can explain it. It's another confession. When the thing was new and hot, and the town made a plan to ride him on a rail, my conscience hurt me so that I couldn't stand it, and I went privately and gave him notice, and he got out of the town and staid out till it was safe to come back.'

'Edward! If the town had found it out – '

'*Don't!* It scares me yet, to think of it. I repented of it the minute it was done; and I was even afraid to tell you, lest your face might betray it to somebody. I didn't sleep any that night, for worrying. But after a few days I saw that no one was going to suspect me, and after that I got to feeling glad I did it. And I feel glad yet, Mary – glad through and through.'

'So do I, now, for it would have been a dreadful way to treat him. Yes, I'm glad; for really you did owe him that, you know. But, Edward, suppose it should come out yet, someday!'

'It won't.'

'Why?'

'Because everybody thinks it was Goodson.'

'Of course they would!'

'Certainly. And of course *he* didn't care. They persuaded poor old Sawlsberry to go and charge it on him, and he went blustering over there and did it. Goodson looked him over, like as if he was hunting for a place on him that he could despise the most, then he says, "So you are the Committee of Inquiry, are you?" Sawlsberry said that was about what he was. "Hm. Do they require particulars, or do you reckon a kind of a *general* answer will do?" "If they require particulars, I will come back, Mr Goodson; I will take the general answer first." "Very well, then, tell them to go to hell – I reckon that's general enough. And I'll give you some advice, Sawlsberry; when you come back for the particulars, fetch a basket to carry the relics of yourself home in." '

'Just like Goodson; it's got all the marks. He had only one vanity: he thought he could give advice better than any other person.'

'It settled the business, and saved us, Mary. The subject was dropped.'

'Bless you, I'm not doubting *that*.'

Then they took up the gold-sack mystery again, with strong interest. Soon the conversation began to suffer breaks – interruptions caused by absorbed thinkings. The breaks grew more and more frequent. At last Richards lost himself wholly in thought. He sat long, gazing vacantly at the floor, and by and by he began to punctuate his thoughts with little nervous movements of his hands that seemed to indicate vexation. Meantime his wife too had relapsed into a thoughtful silence, and her movements were beginning to show a troubled discomfort. Finally Richards got up and strode aimlessly about the room, plowing his hands through his hair, much as a somnambulist might do who was having a bad dream. Then he seemed to arrive at a definite purpose; and without a word he put on his hat and passed quickly out of the house. His wife sat brooding, with a drawn face, and did not seem to be aware that she was alone. Now and then she murmured, 'Lead us not into t – . . . but – but – we are so poor, so poor! . . . Lead us not into . . . Ah, who would be hurt by it? – and no one would ever know . . . Lead us . . . ' The voice died out in mumblings. After a little she glanced up and muttered in a half-frightened, half-glad way –

'He is gone! But, oh dear, he may be too late – too late . . . Maybe not – maybe there is still time.' She rose and stood thinking, nervously clasping and unclasping her hands. A slight shudder shook her frame, and she said, out of a dry throat, 'God forgive me – it's awful to think such things – but . . . Lord, how we are made – how strangely we are made!'

She turned the light low, and slipped stealthily over and kneeled down by the sack and felt of its ridgy sides with her hands, and fondled them lovingly; and there was a gloating light in her poor old eyes. She fell into fits of absence; and came half out of them at times to mutter, 'If we had only waited! – oh, if we had only waited a little, and not been in such a hurry!'

Meantime Cox had gone home from his office and told his wife all about the strange thing that had happened, and they had talked it over eagerly, and guessed that the late Goodson was the only man in the town who could have helped a suffering stranger with so noble a sum as twenty dollars. Then there was a pause, and the two became thoughtful and silent. And by and by nervous and fidgety. At last the wife said, as if to herself,

'Nobody knows this secret but the Richardses . . . and us . . . nobody.'

The husband came out of his thinkings with a slight start, and gazed wistfully at his wife, whose face was become very pale; then he hesitatingly rose, and glanced furtively at his hat, then at his wife – a sort of mute inquiry. Mrs Cox swallowed once or twice, with her hand at her throat, then in place of speech she nodded her head. In a moment she was alone, and mumbling to herself.

And now Richards and Cox were hurrying through the deserted streets, from opposite directions. They met, panting, at the foot of the printing-office stairs; by the night-light there they read each other's face. Cox whispered,

'Nobody knows about this but us?'

The whispered answer was,

'Not a soul – on honour, not a soul!'

'If it isn't too late to – '

The men were starting upstairs; at this moment they were overtaken by a boy, and Cox asked,

'Is that you, Johnny?'

'Yes, sir.'

'You needn't ship the early mail – nor *any* mail; wait till I tell you.'

'It's already gone, sir.'

'*Gone*?' It had the sound of an unspeakable disappointment in it.

'Yes, sir. Timetable for Brixton and all the towns beyond changed today, sir – had to get the papers in twenty minutes earlier than common. I had to rush; if I had been two minutes later – '

The men turned and walked slowly away, not waiting to hear the rest. Neither of them spoke during ten minutes; then Cox said, in a vexed tone,

'What possessed you to be in such a hurry, *I* can't make out.'

The answer was humble enough:

'I see it now, but somehow I never thought, you know, until it was too late. But the next time – '

'Next time be hanged! It won't come in a thousand years.'

Then the friends separated without a good-night, and dragged themselves home with the gait of mortally stricken men. At their homes their wives sprang up with an eager 'Well?' – then saw the answer with their eyes and sank down sorrowing, without waiting for it to come in words. In both houses a discussion followed of a heated sort – a new thing; there had been discussions before, but not heated ones, not ungentle ones. The discussions tonight were a sort of seeming plagiarisms of each other. Mrs Richards said,

'If you had only waited, Edward – if you had only stopped to think; but no, you must run straight to the printing-office and spread it all over the world.'

'It *said* publish it.'

'That is nothing; it also said do it privately, if you liked. There, now – is that true, or not?'

'Why, yes – yes, it is true; but when I thought what a stir it would make, and what a compliment it was to Hadleyburg that a stranger should trust it so – '

'Oh, certainly, I know all that; but if you had only stopped to think, you would have seen that you *couldn't* find the right man, because he is in his grave, and hasn't left chick nor child nor relation behind him; and as long as the money went to somebody that awfully needed it, and nobody would be hurt by it, and – and – '

She broke down, crying. Her husband tried to think of some comforting thing to say, and presently came out with this:

'But after all, Mary, it must be for the best – it *must* be; we know that. And we must remember that it was so ordered – '

'Ordered! Oh, everything's *ordered*, when a person has to find some way out when he has been stupid. Just the same, it was *ordered* that the money should come to us in this special way, and it was you that must take it on yourself to go meddling with the designs of Providence – and who gave you the right? It was wicked, that is what it was – just blasphemous presumption, and no more becoming to a meek and humble professor of – '

'But, Mary, you know how we have been trained all our lives long, like the whole village, till it is absolutely second nature to us to stop not a single moment to think when there's an honest thing to be done – '

'Oh, I know it, I know it – it's been one everlasting training and training and training in honesty – honesty shielded, from the very cradle, against every possible temptation, and so it's *artificial* honesty, and weak as water when temptation comes, as we have seen this night. God knows I never had shade nor shadow of a doubt of my petrified and indestructible honesty until now – and now, under the very first big and real temptation, I – Edward, it is my belief that this town's honesty is as rotten as mine is; as rotten as yours is. It is a mean town, a hard, stingy town, and hasn't a virtue in the world but this honesty it is so celebrated for and so conceited about; and so help me, I do believe that if ever the day comes that its honesty falls under great temptation, its grand reputation will go to ruin like a house of cards. There, now, I've made confession, and I feel better; I am a humbug, and I've been one all my life, without knowing it. Let no man call me honest again – I will not have it.'

'I – well, Mary, I feel a good deal as you do; I certainly do. It seems strange, too, so strange. I never could have believed it – never.'

A long silence followed; both were sunk in thought. At last the wife looked up and said,

'I know what you are thinking, Edward.'

Richards had the embarrassed look of a person who is caught.

'I am ashamed to confess it, Mary, but – '

'It's no matter, Edward, I was thinking the same question myself.'

'I hope so. State it.'

'You were thinking, if a body could only guess out *what the remark was* that Goodson made to the stranger.'

'It's perfectly true. I feel guilty and ashamed. And you?'

'I'm past it. Let us make a pallet here; we've got to stand watch till the bank vault opens in the morning and admits the sack . . . Oh dear, oh dear – if we hadn't made the mistake!'

The pallet was made, and Mary said:

'The open sesame – what could it have been? I do wonder what that remark could have been? But come; we will get to bed now.'

'And sleep?'

'No: think.'

'Yes, think.'

By this time the Coxes too had completed their spat and their reconciliation, and were turning in – to think, to think, and toss, and fret, and worry over what the remark could possibly have been which Goodson made to the stranded derelict; that golden remark; that remark worth forty thousand dollars, cash.

The reason that the village telegraph office was open later than usual that night was this: The foreman of Cox's paper was the local representative of the Associated Press. One might say its honorary representative, for it wasn't four times a year that he could furnish thirty words that would be accepted. But this time it was different. His dispatch stating what he had caught got an instant answer:

Send the whole thing – all the details – twelve hundred words.

A colossal order! The foreman filled the bill; and he was the proudest man in the State. By breakfast-time the next morning the name of Hadleyburg the Incorruptible was on every lip in America, from Montreal to the Gulf, from the glaciers of Alaska to the orange groves of Florida; and millions and millions of people were discussing the stranger and his money-sack, and wondering if the right man would be found, and hoping some more news about the matter would come soon – right away.

🙖 2 🙔

Hadleyburg village woke up world-celebrated – astonished – happy – vain. Vain beyond imagination. Its nineteen principal citizens and their wives went about shaking hands with each other, and beaming, and smiling, and congratulating, and saying *this* thing adds a new word to the dictionary – *Hadleyburg*, synonym for *incorruptible* – destined to live in dictionaries forever! And the minor and unimportant citizens and their wives went around acting in much the same way. Everybody ran to the bank to see the gold-sack; and before noon grieved and envious crowds began to flock in from Brixton and all neighbouring towns; and that afternoon and next day reporters began to arrive from everywhere to verify the sack and its history and write the whole thing up anew, and make dashing free-hand pictures of the sack, and of Richards's house, and the bank, and the Presbyterian church, and the Baptist church, and the public square, and the town-hall where the test would be applied and the money delivered; and damnable portraits of the Richardses, and Pinkerton the banker, and Cox, and the foreman, and Revd Burgess, and the postmaster – and even of Jack Halliday, who was the loafing, good-natured, no-account, irreverent fisherman, hunter, boys' friend, stray-dogs' friend, typical 'Sam Lawson' of the town. The little mean, smirking, oily Pinkerton showed the sack to all comers, and rubbed his sleek palms together pleasantly, and enlarged upon the town's fine old reputation for honesty and upon this wonderful endorsement of it, and hoped and believed that the example would now spread far and wide over the American world, and be epoch-making in the matter of moral regeneration. And so on, and so on.

By the end of a week things had quieted down again; the wild intoxication of pride and joy had sobered to a soft, sweet, silent delight – a sort of deep, nameless, unutterable content. All faces bore a look of peaceful, holy happiness.

Then a change came. It was a gradual change: so gradual that its beginnings were hardly noticed; maybe were not noticed at all, except by Jack Halliday, who always noticed everything; and always made fun of it, too, no matter what it was. He began to throw out chaffing remarks about people not looking quite so happy as they did a day or two ago; and next he claimed that the new aspect was deepening to positive sadness; next, that it was taking on a sick look; and finally he said that everybody was become so moody, thoughtful, and absent-minded that he could rob the meanest man in town of a cent out of the bottom of his breeches pocket and not disturb his reverie.

At this stage – or at about this stage – a saying like this was dropped at bedtime – with a sigh, usually – by the head of each of the nineteen principal households: 'Ah, what *could* have been the remark that Goodson made?'

And straightway – with a shudder – came this, from the man's wife:

'Oh, *don't!* What horrible thing are you mulling in your mind? Put it away from you, for God's sake!'

But that question was wrung from those men again the next night – and got the same retort. But weaker.

And the third night the men uttered the question yet again – with anguish, and absently. This time – and the following night – the wives fidgeted feebly, and tried to say something. But didn't.

And the night after that they found their tongues and responded – longingly,

'Oh, if we *could* only guess!'

Halliday's comments grew daily more and more sparklingly disagreeable and disparaging. He went diligently about, laughing at the town, individually and in mass. But his laugh was the only one left in the village: it fell upon a hollow and mournful vacancy and emptiness. Not even a smile was findable anywhere. Halliday carried a cigar-box around on a tripod, playing that it was a camera, and halted all passers and aimed the thing and said, 'Ready! – now look pleasant, please,' but not even this capital joke could surprise the dreary faces into any softening.

So three weeks passed – one week was left. It was Saturday evening – after supper. Instead of the aforetime Saturday-evening flutter and bustle and shopping and larking, the streets were empty and desolate. Richards and his old wife sat apart in their little parlour – miserable and thinking. This was become their evening habit now: the lifelong habit which had preceded it, of reading, knitting, and contented chat, or receiving or paying neighbourly calls, was dead and gone and forgotten, ages ago – two or three weeks ago; nobody talked now, nobody read, nobody visited – the whole village sat at home, sighing, worrying, silent. Trying to guess out that remark.

The postman left a letter. Richards glanced listlessly at the super-scription and the postmark – unfamiliar, both – and tossed the letter on the table and resumed his might-have-beens and his hopeless dull miseries where he had left them off. Two or three hours later his wife got wearily up and was going away to bed without a good-night – custom now – but she stopped near the letter and eyed it awhile with a dead interest, then broke it open, and began to skim it over. Richards, sitting there with his chair tilted back against the wall and his chin between his knees, heard something fall. It was his wife. He sprang to her side, but she cried out:

'Leave me alone, I am too happy. Read the letter – read it!'

He did. He devoured it, his brain reeling. The letter was from a distant State, and it said:

I am a stranger to you, but no matter: I have something to tell. I have just arrived home from Mexico, and learned about that episode. Of course you do not know who made that remark, but I know, and I am the only person living who does know. It was GOODSON. I knew him well, many years ago. I passed through your village that very night, and was his guest till the midnight train came along. I overheard him make that remark to the stranger in the dark – it was in Hale Alley. He and I talked of it the rest of the way home, and while smoking in his house. He mentioned many of your villagers in the course of his talk – most of them in a very uncomplimentary way, but two or three favourably; among these latter yourself. I say 'favourably' – nothing stronger. I remember his saying he did not actually *like* any person in the town – not one; but that you – I *think* he said you – am almost sure – had done him a very great service once, possibly without knowing the full value of it, and he wished he had a fortune, he would leave it to you when he died, and a curse apiece for the rest of the citizens. Now, then, if it was you that did him that service, you are his legitimate heir, and entitled to the sack of gold. I know that I can trust to your honour and honesty, for in a citizen of Hadleyburg these virtues are an unfailing inheritance, and so I am going to reveal to you the remark, well satisfied that if you are not the right man you will seek and find the right one and see that poor Goodson's debt of gratitude for the service referred to is paid. This is the remark: 'YOU ARE FAR FROM BEING A BAD MAN: GO, AND REFORM.'

HOWARD L. STEPHENSON

'Oh, Edward, the money is ours, and I am so grateful, *oh*, so grateful – kiss me, dear, it's forever since we kissed – and we needed it so – the money – and now you are free of Pinkerton and his bank, and nobody's slave any more; it seems to me I could fly for joy.'

It was a happy half-hour that the couple spent there on the settee caressing each other; it was the old days come again – days that had begun with their courtship and lasted without a break till the stranger brought the deadly money. By and by the wife said:

'Oh, Edward, how lucky it was you did him that grand service, poor Goodson! I never liked him, but I love him now. And it was fine and beautiful of you never to mention it or brag about it.' Then, with a touch of reproach, 'But you ought to have told *me*, Edward, you ought to have told your wife, you know.'

'Well, I – er – well, Mary, you see – '

'Now stop hemming and hawing, and tell me about it, Edward. I always loved you, and now I'm proud of you. Everybody believes there was only one good generous soul in this village, and now it turns out that you – Edward, why don't you tell me?'

'Well – er – er – Why, Mary, I can't!'

'You *can't*. *Why* can't you?'

'You see, he – well, he – he made me promise I wouldn't.'

The wife looked him over, and said, very slowly,

'Made – you – promise? Edward, what do you tell me that for?'

'Mary, do you think I would lie?'

She was troubled and silent for a moment, then she laid her hand within his and said:

'No . . . no. We have wandered far enough from our bearings – God spare us that! In all your life you have never uttered a lie. But now – now that the foundations of things seem to be crumbling from under us, we – we – ' She lost her voice for a moment, then said, brokenly, 'Lead us not into temptation . . . I think you made the promise, Edward. Let it rest so. Let us keep away from that ground. Now – that is all gone by; let us be happy again; it is no time for clouds.'

Edward found it something of an effort to comply, for his mind kept wandering – trying to remember what the service was that he had done Goodson.

The couple lay awake the most of the night, Mary happy and busy, Edward busy but not so happy. Mary was planning what she would do with the money. Edward was trying to recall that service. At first his conscience was sore on account of the lie he had told Mary – if it was a lie. After much reflection – suppose it *was* a lie? What then? Was it such a great matter? Aren't we always *acting* lies? Then why not *tell* them? Look at Mary – look what she had done. While he was hurrying off on his honest errand, what was she doing? Lamenting because the papers hadn't been destroyed and the money kept! Is theft better than lying?

That point lost its sting – the lie dropped into the background and left comfort behind it. The next point came to the front: *Had* he rendered that service? Well, here was Goodson's own evidence as reported in Stephenson's letter; there could be no better evidence than that – it was even *proof* that he had rendered it. Of course. So that point was settled . . . No, not quite. He recalled with a wince that this unknown Mr Stephenson was just a trifle unsure as to whether the performer of it was Richards or some other – and, oh dear, he had put Richards on his honour! He must himself decide whither that money must go – and Mr Stephenson was not doubting that if he was the wrong man he would go honourably and find the right one. Oh, it was odious to put a man in such a situation – ah, why couldn't Stephenson have left out that doubt! What did he want to intrude that for?

Further reflection. How did it happen that *Richards's* name remained in Stephenson's mind as indicating the right man, and not some other man's name? That looked good. Yes, that looked very good. In fact, it went on looking better and better, straight along – until by and by it grew into positive *proof.* And then Richards put the matter at once out of his mind, for he had a private instinct that a proof once established is better left so.

He was feeling reasonably comfortable now, but there was still one other detail that kept pushing itself on his notice: of course he had done that service – that was settled; but what *was* that service? He must recall it – he would not go to sleep till he had recalled it; it would make his peace of mind perfect. And so he thought and thought. He thought of a dozen things – possible services, even probable services – but none of them seemed adequate, none of them seemed large enough, none of them seemed worth the money – worth the fortune Goodson had wished he could leave in his will. And besides, he couldn't remember having done them, anyway. Now, then – now, then – what *kind* of a service would it be that would make a man so inordinately grateful? Ah – the saving of his soul! That must be it. Yes, he could remember, now, how he once set himself the task of converting Goodson, and laboured at it as much as – he was going to say three months; but upon closer examination it shrunk to a month, then to a week, then to a day, then to nothing. Yes, he remembered now, and with unwelcome vividness, that Goodson had told him to go to thunder and mind his own business – *he* wasn't hankering to follow Hadleyburg to heaven!

So that solution was a failure – he hadn't saved Goodson's soul. Richards was discouraged. Then after a little came another idea: had he saved Goodson's property? No, that wouldn't do – he hadn't any. His life? That is it! Of course. Why, he might have thought of it before. This time he was on the right track, sure. His imagination-mill was hard at work in a minute, now.

Thereafter during a stretch of two exhausting hours he was busy saving Goodson's life. He saved it in all kinds of difficult and perilous ways. In every case he got it saved satisfactorily up to a certain point; then, just as he was beginning to get well persuaded that it had really happened, a troublesome detail would turn up which made the whole thing impossible. As in the matter of drowning, for instance. In that case he had swum out and tugged Goodson ashore in an unconscious state with a great crowd looking on and applauding, but when he had got it all thought out and was just beginning to remember all about it, a whole swarm of disqualifying details arrived on the ground: the town would have known of the circumstance, Mary would have known of it, it would glare like a limelight in his own memory instead of being an inconspicuous service which he had possibly rendered 'without know-ing its full value'. And at this point he remembered that he couldn't swim, anyway.

Ah – *there* was a point which he had been overlooking from the start: it had to be a service which he had rendered 'possibly without knowing the full value of it'. Why, really, that ought to be an easy hunt – much easier than those others. And sure enough, by and by he found it. Goodson, years and years ago, came near marrying a very sweet and pretty girl, named Nancy Hewitt, but in some way or other the match had been broken off; the girl died, Goodson remained a bachelor, and by and by became a soured one and a frank despiser of the human species. Soon after the girl's death the village found out, or thought it had found out, that she carried a spoonful of negro blood in her veins. Richards worked at these details a good while, and in the end he thought he remembered things concerning them which must have gotten mislaid in his memory through long neglect. He seemed to dimly remember that it was *he* that found out about the negro blood; that it was he that told the village; that the village told Goodson where they got it; that he thus saved Goodson from marrying the tainted girl; that he had done him this great service 'without knowing the full value of it,' in fact without knowing that he *was* doing it; but that Goodson knew the value of it, and what a narrow escape he had had, and so went to his grave grateful to his benefactor and wishing he had a fortune to leave him. It was all clear and simple now, and the more he went over it the more luminous and certain it grew; and at last, when he nestled to sleep satisfied and happy, he remembered the whole thing just as if it had been yesterday. In fact, he dimly remembered Goodson's *telling* him his gratitude once. Meantime Mary had spent six thousand dollars on a new house for herself and a pair of slippers for her pastor, and then had fallen peacefully to rest.

That same Saturday evening the postman had delivered a letter to each of the other principal citizens – nineteen letters in all. No two of the envelopes were alike, and no two of the superscriptions were in the same hand, but the letters inside were just like each other in every detail but one. They were exact copies of the letter received by Richards – handwriting and all – and were all signed by Stephenson, but in place of Richards's name each receiver's own name appeared.

All night long eighteen principal citizens did what their caste-brother Richards was doing at the same time – they put in their energies trying to remember what notable service it was that they had unconsciously done Barclay Goodson. In no case was it a holiday job; still they succeeded.

And while they were at this work, which was difficult, their wives put in the night spending the money, which was easy. During that one night the nineteen wives spent an average of seven thousand dollars each out of the forty thousand in the sack – a hundred and thirty-three thousand altogether.

Next day there was a surprise for Jack Halliday. He noticed that the faces of the nineteen chief citizens and their wives bore that expression of peaceful and holy happiness again. He could not understand it, neither was he able to invent any remarks about it that could damage it or disturb it. And so it was his turn to be dissatisfied with life. His private guesses at the reasons for the happiness failed in all instances, upon examination. When he met Mrs Wilcox and noticed the placid ecstasy in her face, he said to himself, 'Her cat has had kittens' – and went and asked the cook: it was not so; the cook had detected the happiness, but did not know the cause. When Halliday found the duplicate ecstasy in the face of 'Shadbelly' Billson (village nickname), he was sure some neighbour of Billson's had broken his leg, but inquiry showed that this had not happened. The subdued ecstasy in Gregory Yates's face could mean but one thing – he was a mother-in-law short: it was another mistake. 'And Pinkerton – Pinkerton – he has collected ten cents that he thought he was going to lose.' And so on, and so on. In some cases the guesses had to remain in doubt, in the others they proved distinct errors. In the end Halliday said to himself, 'Anyway it foots up that there's nineteen Hadleyburg families temporarily in heaven: I don't know how it happened; I only know Providence is off duty today.'

An architect and builder from the next State had lately ventured to set up a small business in this unpromising village, and his sign had now been hanging out a week. Not a customer yet; he was a discouraged man, and sorry he had come. But his weather changed suddenly now. First one and then another chief citizen's wife said to him privately:

'Come to my house Monday week – but say nothing about it for the present. We think of building.'

He got eleven invitations that day. That night he wrote his daughter and broke off her match with her student. He said she could marry a mile higher than that.

Pinkerton the banker and two or three other well-to-do men planned country seats – but waited. That kind don't count their chickens until they are hatched.

The Wilsons devised a grand new thing – a fancy-dress ball. They made no actual promises, but told all their acquaintanceship in confidence that they were thinking the matter over and thought they should give it – 'and if we do, you will be invited, of course'. People were surprised, and said, one to another, 'Why, they are crazy, those poor Wilsons, they can't afford it.' Several among the nineteen said privately to their husbands, 'It is a good idea: we will keep still till their cheap thing is over, then *we* will give one that will make it sick.'

The days drifted along, and the bill of future squanderings rose higher and higher, wilder and wilder, more and more foolish and reckless. It began to look as if every member of the nineteen would not only spend his whole forty thousand dollars before receiving-day, but be actually in debt by the time he got the money. In some cases light-headed people did not stop with planning to spend, they really spent – on credit. They bought land, mortgages, farms, speculative stocks, fine clothes, horses, and various other things, paid down the bonus, and made themselves liable for the rest – at ten days. Presently the sober second thought came, and Halliday noticed that a ghastly anxiety was beginning to show up in a good many faces. Again he was puzzled, and didn't know what to make of it. 'The Wilcox kittens aren't dead, for they weren't born; nobody's broken a leg; there's no shrinkage in mother-in-laws; *nothing* has happened – it is an unsolvable mystery.'

There was another puzzled man, too – the Revd Mr Burgess. For days, wherever he went, people seemed to follow him or to be watching out for him; and if he ever found himself in a retired spot, a member of the nineteen would be sure to appear, thrust an envelope privately into his hand, whisper 'To be opened at the town-hall Friday evening', then vanish away like a guilty thing. He was expecting that there might be one claimant for the sack – doubtful, however, Goodson being dead – but it never occurred to him that all this crowd might be claimants. When the great Friday came at last, he found that he had nineteen envelopes.

❧ 3 ❧

The town-hall had never looked finer. The platform at the end of it was backed by a showy draping of flags; at intervals along the walls were festoons of flags; the gallery fronts were clothed in flags; the supporting columns were swathed in flags; all this was to impress the stranger, for he would be there in considerable force, and in a large degree he would be connected with the press. The house was full. The four hundred and twelve fixed seats were occupied; also the sixty-eight extra chairs which had been packed into the aisles; the steps of the platform were occupied; some distinguished strangers were given seats on the platform; at the horseshoe of tables which fenced the front and sides of the platform sat a strong force of special correspondents who had come from everywhere. It was the best-dressed house the town had ever produced. There were some tolerably expensive toilets there, and in several cases the ladies who wore them had the look of being unfamiliar with that kind of clothes. At least the town thought they had that look, but the notion could have arisen from the town's knowledge of the fact that these ladies had never inhabited such clothes before.

The gold-sack stood on a little table at the front of the platform where all the house could see it. The bulk of the house gazed at it with a burning interest, a mouth-watering interest, a wistful and pathetic interest; a minority of nineteen couples gazed at it tenderly, lovingly, proprietarily, and the male half of this minority kept saying over to themselves the moving little impromptu speeches of thankfulness for the audience's applause and congratulations which they were presently going to get up and deliver. Every now and then one of these got a piece of paper out of his vest pocket and privately glanced at it to refresh his memory.

Of course there was a buzz of conversation going on – there always is; but at last when the Revd Mr Burgess rose and laid his hand on the sack he could hear his microbes gnaw, the place was so still. He related the curious history of the sack, then went on to speak in warm terms of Hadleyburg's old and well-earned reputation for spotless honesty, and of the town's just pride in this reputation. He said that this reputation was a treasure of priceless value; that under Providence its value had now become inestimably enhanced, for the recent episode had spread this fame far and wide, and thus had focused the eyes of the American world upon this village, and made its name for all time, as he hoped and believed, a synonym for commercial incorruptibility. (Applause.) 'And who is to be the guardian of this noble treasure – the community as a whole? No! The responsibility is individual, not communal. From this day forth each and every one of you is in his own person its special guardian, and individually responsible that no harm shall come to it. Do you – does each of you – accept this great trust? [Tumultuous assent.] Then all is well. Transmit it to your children and to your children's children. Today your purity is beyond reproach – see to it that it shall remain so. Today there is not a person in your community who could be beguiled to touch a penny not his own – see to it that you abide in this grace. ['We will! we will!'] This is not the place to make comparisons between ourselves and other communities – some of them ungracious toward us; they have their ways, we have ours; let us be content. [Applause.] I am done. Under my hand, my friends, rests a stranger's eloquent recognition of what we are; through him the world will always henceforth know what we are. We do not know who he is, but in your name I utter your gratitude, and ask you to raise your voices in endorsement.'

The house rose in a body and made the walls quake with the thunders of its thankfulness for the space of a long minute. Then it sat down, and Mr Burgess took an envelope out of his pocket. The house held its breath while he slit the envelope open and took from it a slip of paper. He read its contents – slowly and impressively – the audience listening with tranced attention to this magic document, each of whose words stood for an ingot of gold: ' "The remark which I made to the distressed stranger was this: 'You are very far from being a bad man: go, and reform.' " '

Then he continued: 'We shall know in a moment now whether the remark here quoted corresponds with the one concealed in the sack; and if that shall prove to be so – and it undoubtedly will – this sack of gold belongs to a fellow-citizen who will henceforth stand before the nation as the symbol of the special virtue which has made our town famous throughout the land – Mr Billson!'

The house had gotten itself all ready to burst into the proper tornado of applause; but instead of doing it, it seemed stricken with a paralysis; there was a deep hush for a moment or two, then a wave of whispered murmurs swept the place – of about this tenor: '*Billson!* oh, come, this is *too* thin! Twenty dollars to a stranger – or *anybody* – *Billson!* tell it to the marines!' And now at this point the house caught its breath all of a sudden in a new access of astonishment, for it discovered that whereas in one part of the hall Deacon Billson was standing up with his head meekly bowed, in another part of it Lawyer Wilson was doing the same. There was a wondering silence now for a while.

Everybody was puzzled, and nineteen couples were surprised and indignant.

Billson and Wilson turned and stared at each other. Billson asked, bitingly,

'Why do *you* rise, Mr Wilson?'

'Because I have a right to. Perhaps you will be good enough to explain to the house why *you* rise?'

'With great pleasure. Because I wrote that paper.'

'It is an impudent falsity! I wrote it myself.'

It was Burgess's turn to be paralysed. He stood looking vacantly at first one of the men and then the other, and did not seem to know what to do. The house was stupefied. Lawyer Wilson spoke up, now, and said,

'I ask the Chair to read the name signed to that paper.'

That brought the Chair to itself, and it read out the name,

' "John Wharton *Billson*." '

'There!' shouted Billson, 'what have you got to say for yourself, now? And what kind of apology are you going to make to me and to this insulted house for the imposture which you have attempted to play here?'

'No apologies are due, sir; and as for the rest of it, I publicly charge you with pilfering my note from Mr Burgess and substituting a copy of it signed with your own name. There is no other way by which you could have gotten hold of the test remark; I alone, of living men, possessed the secret of its wording.'

There was likely to be a scandalous state of things if this went on; everybody noticed with distress that the shorthand scribes were scribbling like mad; many people were crying 'Chair, Chair! Order! Order!' Burgess rapped with his gavel, and said:

'Let us not forget the proprieties due. There has evidently been a mistake somewhere, but surely that is all. If Mr Wilson gave me an envelope – and I remember now that he did – I still have it.'

He took one out of his pocket, opened it, glanced at it, looked surprised and worried, and stood silent a few moments. Then he waved his hand in a wandering and mechanical way, and made an effort or two to say something, then gave it up, despondently. Several voices cried out:

'Read it! read it! What is it?'

So he began in a dazed and sleepwalker fashion:

' "The remark which I made to the unhappy stranger was this: 'You are far from being a bad man. [The house gazed at him, marvelling.] Go, and reform.' " ' (Murmurs: 'Amazing! what can this mean?')

'This one,' said the Chair, 'is signed Thurlow G. Wilson.'

'There!' cried Wilson, 'I reckon that settles it! I knew perfectly well my note was purloined.'

'Purloined!' retorted Billson. 'I'll let you know that neither you nor any man of your kidney must venture to – '

The Chair: 'Order, gentlemen, order! Take your seats, both of you, please.'

They obeyed, shaking their heads and grumbling angrily. The house was profoundly puzzled; it did not know what to do with this curious emergency. Presently Thompson got up. Thompson was the hatter. He would have liked to be a Nineteener; but such was not for him: his stock of hats was not considerable enough for the position. He said:

'Mr Chairman, if I may be permitted to make a suggestion, can both of these gentlemen be right? I put it to you, sir, can both have happened to say the very same words to the stranger? It seems to me – '

The tanner got up and interrupted him. The tanner was a disgruntled man; he believed himself entitled to be a Nineteener, but he couldn't get recognition. It made him a little unpleasant in his ways and speech. Said he:

'Sho, *that's* not the point! *That* could happen – twice in a hundred years – but not the other thing. *Neither* of them gave the twenty dollars!'

A ripple of applause.

Billson: '*I* did!'

Wilson: '*I* did!'

Then each accused the other of pilfering.

The Chair: 'Order! Sit down, if you please – both of you. Neither of the notes has been out of my possession at any moment.'

A voice: 'Good – that settles *that!*'

The tanner: 'Mr Chairman, one thing is now plain: one of these men has been eavesdropping under the other one's bed, and filching family secrets. If it is not unparliamentary to suggest it, I will remark that both are equal to it.' (The Chair: 'Order! order!') 'I withdraw the remark, sir, and will confine myself to suggesting that *if* one of them has overheard the other reveal the test-remark to his wife, we shall catch him now.'

A voice: 'How?'

The tanner: 'Easily. The two have not quoted the remark in exactly the same words. You would have noticed that, if there hadn't been a considerable stretch of time and an exciting quarrel inserted between the two readings.'

A voice: 'Name the difference.'

The tanner: 'The word *very* is in Billson's note, and not in the other.'

Many voices: 'That's so – he's right!'

The tanner: 'And so, if the Chair will examine the test-remark in the sack, we shall know which of these two frauds' (The Chair: 'Order!'), 'which of these two adventurers' (The Chair: 'Order! order!'), 'which of these two gentlemen [laughter and applause] is entitled to wear the belt as being the first dishonest blatherskite ever bred in this town – which he has dishonoured, and which will be a sultry place for him from now out!' (Vigorous applause.)

Many voices: 'Open it! – open the sack!'

Mr Burgess made a slit in the sack, slid his hand in and brought out an envelope. In it were a couple of folded notes. He said:

'One of these is marked, "Not to be examined until all written communications which have been addressed to the Chair – if any –

shall have been read." The other is marked "The Test." Allow me. It is worded – to wit:

' "I do not require that the first half of the remark which was made to me by my benefactor shall be quoted with exactness, for it was not striking, and could be forgotten; but its closing fifteen words are quite striking, and I think easily rememberable; unless *these* shall be accurately reproduced, let the applicant be regarded as an impostor. My benefactor began by saying he seldom gave advice to anyone, but that it always bore the hallmark of high value when he did give it. Then he said this – and it has never faded from my memory: 'You are far from being a bad man – ' " '

Fifty voices: 'That settles it – the money's Wilson's! Wilson! Wilson! Speech! Speech!'

People jumped up and crowded around Wilson, wringing his hand and congratulating fervently – meantime the Chair was hammering with the gavel and shouting:

'Order, gentlemen! Order! Order! Let me finish reading, please.' When quiet was restored, the reading was resumed – as follows:

' " 'Go, and reform – or, mark my words – someday, for your sins, *you will die and go to hell or Hadleyburg – try and make it the former.*' " '

A ghastly silence followed. First an angry cloud began to settle darkly upon the faces of the citizenship; after a pause the cloud began to rise, and a tickled expression tried to take its place; tried so hard that it was only kept under with great and painful difficulty; the reporters, the Brixtonites, and other strangers, bent their heads down and shielded their faces with their hands, and managed to hold in by main strength and heroic courtesy. At this most inopportune time burst upon the stillness the roar of a solitary voice – Jack Halliday's:

'*That's* got the hallmark on it!'

Then the house let go, strangers and all. Even Mr Burgess's gravity broke down presently, then the audience considered itself officially absolved from all restraint, and it made the most of its privilege. It was a good long laugh, and a tempestuously whole-hearted one, but it ceased at last – long enough for Mr Burgess to try to resume, and for the people to get their eyes partially wiped; then it broke out again; and afterward yet again; then at last Burgess was able to get out these serious words:

'It is useless to try to disguise the fact – we find ourselves in the presence of a matter of grave import. It involves the honour of your town, it strikes at the town's good name. The difference of a single word between the test-remarks offered by Mr Wilson and Mr Billson was itself a serious thing, since it indicated that one or the other of these gentlemen had committed a theft – '

The two men were sitting limp, nerveless, crushed; but at these words both were electrified into movement, and started to get up –

'Sit down!' said the Chair, sharply, and they obeyed. 'That, as I have said, was a serious thing. And it was – but for only one of them. But the matter has become graver; for the honour of *both* is now in formidable peril. Shall I go even further, and say in inextricable peril? *Both* left out the crucial fifteen words.' He paused. During several moments he allowed the pervading stillness to gather and deepen its impressive effects, then added: 'There would seem to be but one way whereby this could happen. I ask these gentlemen – Was there *collusion*? – *agreement*?'

A low murmur sifted through the house; its import was, 'He's got them both.'

Billson was not used to emergencies; he sat in a helpless collapse. But Wilson was a lawyer. He struggled to his feet, pale and worried, and said:

'I ask the indulgence of the house while I explain this most painful matter. I am sorry to say what I am about to say, since it must inflict irreparable injury upon Mr Billson, whom I have always esteemed and respected until now, and in whose invulnerability to temptation I entirely believed – as did you all. But for the preservation of my own honour I must speak – and with frankness. I confess with shame – and I now beseech your pardon for it – that I said to the ruined stranger all of the words contained in the test-remark, including the disparaging fifteen. [Sensation.] When the late publication was made I recalled them, and I resolved to claim the sack of coin, for by every right I was entitled to it. Now I will ask you to consider this point, and weigh it well: that stranger's gratitude to me that night knew no bounds; he said himself that he could find no words for it that were adequate, and that if he should ever be able he would repay me a thousandfold. Now then, I ask you this: Could I expect – could I believe – could I even remotely imagine – that, feeling as he did, he would do so ungrateful a thing as to add those quite unnecessary fifteen words to his test? – set a trap for me? – expose me as a slanderer of my own town before my own people assembled in a public hall? It was preposterous; it was impossible. His test would contain only the kindly opening clause of my remark. Of that I had no shadow of doubt. You would have thought as I did. You would not have expected a base betrayal from one whom you had befriended and against whom you had committed no offence. And so, with perfect confidence, perfect trust, I wrote on a piece of paper the opening words – ending with "Go, and reform" – and signed it. When I was about to put it in an envelope I was called into my back office, and without thinking I left the paper lying open on my desk.' He stopped, turned his head slowly toward Billson, waited a moment, then added: 'I ask you to note this: when I returned, a little later, Mr Billson was retiring by my street door.' (Sensation.)

In a moment Billson was on his feet and shouting:

'It's a lie! It's an infamous lie!'

The Chair: 'Be seated, sir! Mr Wilson has the floor.'

Billson's friends pulled him into his seat and quieted him, and Wilson went on:

'Those are the simple facts. My note was now lying in a different place on the table from where I had left it. I noticed that, but attached no importance to it, thinking a draught had blown it there. That Mr Billson would read a private paper was a thing which could not occur to me; he was an honourable man, and he would be above that. If you will allow me to say it, I think his extra word "*very*" stands explained; it is attributable to a defect of memory. I was the only man in the world who could furnish here any detail of the test-remark – by *honourable* means. I have finished.'

There is nothing in the world like a persuasive speech to fuddle the mental apparatus and upset the convictions and debauch the emotions of an audience not practised in the tricks and delusions of oratory. Wilson sat down victorious. The house submerged him in tides of approving applause; friends swarmed to him and shook him by the hand and congratulated him, and Billson was shouted down and not allowed to say a word. The Chair hammered and hammered with its gavel, and kept shouting:

'But let us proceed, gentlemen, let us proceed!'

At last there was a measurable degree of quiet, and the hatter said:

'But what is there to proceed with, sir, but to deliver the money?'

Voices: 'That's it! That's it! Come forward, Wilson!'

The hatter: 'I move three cheers for Mr Wilson, symbol of the special virtue which – '

The cheers burst forth before he could finish; and in the midst of them – and in the midst of the clamour of the gavel also – some enthusiasts mounted Wilson on a big friend's shoulder and were going to fetch him in triumph to the platform. The Chair's voice now rose above the noise:

'Order! To your places! You forget that there is still a document to be read.' When quiet had been restored he took up the document, and

was going to read it, but laid it down again, saying, 'I forgot; this is not
to be read until all written communications received by me have first
been read.' He took an envelope out of his pocket, removed its
enclosure, glanced at it – seemed astonished – held it out and gazed at
it – stared at it.

Twenty or thirty voices cried out:

'What is it? Read it! read it!'

And he did – slowly, and wondering:

' "The remark which I made to the stranger [Voices: 'Hello! how's
this?'] was this: 'You are far from being a bad man. [Voices: 'Great
Scott!'] Go, and reform.' " [Voice: 'Oh, saw my leg off!'] Signed by
Mr Pinkerton the banker.'

The pandemonium of delight which turned itself loose now was of a
sort to make the judicious weep. Those whose withers were unwrung
laughed till the tears ran down; the reporters, in throes of laughter, set
down disordered pot-hooks which would never in the world be deci-
pherable; and a sleeping dog jumped up, scared out of its wits, and
barked itself crazy at the turmoil. All manner of cries were scattered
through the din: 'We're getting rich – *two* Symbols of Incorruptibility! –
without counting Billson!' '*Three!* – count Shadbelly in – we can't have
too many!' 'All right – Billson's elected!' 'Alas, poor Wilson – victim of
two thieves!'

A powerful voice: 'Silence! The Chair's fished up something more
out of its pocket.'

Voices: 'Hurrah! Is it something fresh? Read it! read! read!'

The Chair [reading]: ' "The remark which I made," etc.: " 'You are
far from being a bad man. Go,' " etc. Signed, "Gregory Yates".'

Tornado of voices: 'Four Symbols!' ' 'Rah for Yates!' 'Fish again!'

The house was in a roaring humour now, and ready to get all the fun
out of the occasion that might be in it. Several Nineteeners, looking
pale and distressed, got up and began to work their way toward the
aisles, but a score of shouts went up:

'The doors, the doors – close the doors; no Incorruptible shall leave
this place! Sit down, everybody!'

The mandate was obeyed.

'Fish again! Read! read!'

The Chair fished again, and once more the familiar words began to
fall from its lips – ' "You are far from being a bad man – " '

'Name! name! What's his name?'

' "L. Ingoldsby Sargent".'

'Five elected! Pile up the Symbols! Go on, go on!'

' "You are far from being a bad – " '

'Name! name!'

' "Nicholas Whitworth'."

'Hooray! hooray! it's a symbolical day!'

Somebody wailed in, and began to sing this rhyme (leaving out 'it's') to the lovely *Mikado* tune of 'When a man's afraid, a beautiful maid – '; the audience joined in, with joy; then, just in time, somebody contributed another line –

'And don't you this forget – '

The house roared it out. A third line was at once furnished –

'Corruptibles far from Hadleyburg are – '

The house roared that one too. As the last note died, Jack Halliday's voice rose high and clear, freighted with a final line –

'But the Symbols are here, you bet!'

That was sung, with booming enthusiasm. Then the happy house started in at the beginning and sang the four lines through twice, with immense swing and dash, and finished up with a crashing three-times-three and a tiger for 'Hadleyburg the Incorruptible and all Symbols of it which we shall find worthy to receive the hallmark tonight.'

Then the shoutings at the Chair began again, all over the place:

'Go on! go on! Read! read some more! Read all you've got!'

'That's it – go on! We are winning eternal celebrity!'

A dozen men got up now and began to protest. They said that this farce was the work of some abandoned joker, and was an insult to the whole community. Without a doubt these signatures were all forgeries –

'Sit down! sit down! Shut up! You are confessing. We'll find *your* names in the lot.'

'Mr Chairman, how many of those envelopes have you got?'

The Chair counted.

'Together with those that have been already examined, there are nineteen.'

A storm of derisive applause broke out.

'Perhaps they all contain the secret. I move that you open them all and read every signature that is attached to a note of that sort – and read also the first eight words of the note.'

'Second the motion!'

It was put and carried – uproariously. Then poor old Richards got up, and his wife rose and stood at his side. Her head was bent down, so that none might see that she was crying. Her husband gave her his arm, and so supporting her, he began to speak in a quavering voice:

'My friends, you have known us two – Mary and me – all our lives, and I think you have liked us and respected us – '

The Chair interrupted him:

'Allow me. It is quite true – that which you are saying, Mr Richards: this town *does* know you two; it *does* like you; it *does* respect you; more – it honours you and *loves* you – '

Halliday's voice rang out:

'That's the hallmarked truth, too! If the Chair is right, let the house speak up and say it. Rise! Now, then – hip! hip! hip! – all together!'

The house rose in mass, faced toward the old couple eagerly, filled the air with a snowstorm of waving handkerchiefs, and delivered the cheers with all its affectionate heart.

The Chair then continued:

'What I was going to say is this: We know your good heart, Mr Richards, but this is not a time for the exercise of charity toward offenders.' (Shouts of 'Right! right!') 'I see your generous purpose in your face, but I cannot allow you to plead for these men – '

'But I was going to – '

'Please take your seat, Mr Richards. We must examine the rest of these notes – simple fairness to the men who have already been exposed requires this. As soon as that has been done – I give you my word for this – you shall be heard.'

Many voices: 'Right! – the Chair is right – no interruption can be permitted at this stage! Go on! – the names! the names! – according to the terms of the motion!'

The old couple sat reluctantly down, and the husband whispered to the wife, 'It is pitifully hard to have to wait; the shame will be greater than ever when they find we were only going to plead for *ourselves*.'

Straightway the jollity broke loose again with the reading of the names.

' "You are far from being a bad man – " Signature, "Robert J. Titmarsh".

' "You are far from being a bad man – " Signature, "Eliphalet Weeks".

' "You are far from being a bad man – " Signature, "Oscar B. Wilder".'

At this point the house lit upon the idea of taking the eight words out of the Chairman's hands. He was not unthankful for that. Thenceforward he held up each note in its turn, and waited. The house droned out the eight words in a massed and measured and musical deep volume of sound (with a daringly close resemblance to a well-known church chant) – ' "You are f-a-r from being a b-a-a-a-d man." ' Then the Chair said, 'Signature, "Archibald Wilcox".' And so on, and so on, name after name, and everybody had an increasingly and gloriously good time except the wretched Nineteen. Now and then, when a particularly shining name was called, the house made the Chair wait while it chanted the whole of the test-remark from the beginning to the closing words, 'And go to hell or Hadleyburg – try and make it the for-or-m-e-r!' and in these special cases they added a grand and agonised and imposing 'A-a-a-a-*men*!'

The list dwindled, dwindled, dwindled, poor old Richards keeping tally of the count, wincing when a name resembling his own was pronounced, and waiting in miserable suspense for the time to come when it would be his humiliating privilege to rise with Mary and finish his plea, which he was intending to word thus: '. . . for until now we have never done any wrong thing, but have gone our humble way unreproached. We are very poor, we are old, and have no chick nor child to help us; we were sorely tempted, and we fell. It was my purpose when I got up before to make confession and beg that my name might not be read out in this public place, for it seemed to us that we could not bear it; but I was prevented. It was just; it was our place to suffer with the rest. It has been hard for us. It is the first time we have ever heard our name fall from anyone's lips – sullied. Be merciful – for the sake of the better days; make our shame as light to bear as in your charity you can.' At this point in his reverie Mary nudged him, perceiving that his mind was absent. The house was chanting, 'You are f–a–r,' etc.

'Be ready,' Mary whispered. 'Your name comes now; he has read eighteen.'

The chant ended.

'Next! next! next!' came volleying from all over the house.

Burgess put his hand into his pocket. The old couple, trembling, began to rise. Burgess fumbled a moment, then said,

'I find I have read them all.'

Faint with joy and surprise, the couple sank into their seats, and Mary whispered,

'Oh, bless God, we are saved! – he has lost ours – I wouldn't give this for a hundred of those sacks!'

The house burst out with its *Mikado* travesty, and sang it three times with ever-increasing enthusiasm, rising to its feet when it reached for the third time the closing line –

> 'But the Symbols are here, you bet!'

and finishing up with cheers and a tiger for 'Hadleyburg purity and our eighteen immortal representatives of it.'

Then Wingate, the saddler, got up and proposed cheers 'for the cleanest man in town, the one solitary important citizen in it who didn't try to steal that money – Edward Richards.'

They were given with great and moving heartiness; then somebody proposed that Richards be elected sole guardian and Symbol of the now Sacred Hadleyburg Tradition, with power and right to stand up and look the whole sarcastic world in the face.

Passed, by acclamation; then they sang the *Mikado* again, and ended it with,

> 'And there's *one* Symbol left, you bet!'

There was a pause; then –

A voice: 'Now, then, who's to get the sack?'

The tanner (with bitter sarcasm): 'That's easy. The money has to be divided among the eighteen Incorruptibles. They gave the suffering stranger twenty dollars apiece – and that remark – each in his turn – it took twenty-two minutes for the procession to move past. Staked the stranger – total contribution, $360. All they want is just the loan back – and interest – forty thousand dollars altogether.'

Many voices (derisively): 'That's it! Divvy! divvy! Be kind to the poor – don't keep them waiting!'

The Chair: 'Order! I now offer the stranger's remaining document. It says: "If no claimant shall appear [grand chorus of groans], I desire that you open the sack and count out the money to the principal citizens of your town, they to take it in trust [cries of 'Oh! Oh! Oh!'], and use it in such ways as to them shall seem best for the propagation and preservation of your community's noble reputation for incorruptible honesty [more cries] – a reputation to which their names and their efforts will add a new and far-reaching lustre." [Enthusiastic outburst of sarcastic applause.] That seems to be all. No – here is a postscript:

' "PS – CITIZENS OF HADLEYBURG: There *is* no test-remark – nobody made one. [Great sensation.] There wasn't any pauper stranger, nor any twenty-dollar contribution, nor any accompanying benediction and compliment – these are all inventions. [General buzz and hum of astonishment and delight.] Allow me to tell my story – it will take but a word or two. I passed through your town at a certain time, and received a deep offence which I had not earned. Any other man would have been content to kill one or two of you and call it square, but to me that would have been a trivial revenge, and inadequate; for the dead do not *suffer*. Besides, I could not kill you all – and, anyway, made as I am, even that would not have satisfied me. I wanted to damage every man in the place, and every woman – and not in their bodies or in their estate, but in their vanity – the place where feeble and foolish people are most vulnerable. So I disguised myself and came back and studied you. You were easy game. You had an old and lofty reputation for honesty, and naturally you were proud of it – it was your treasure of treasures, the very apple of your eye. As soon as I found out that you carefully and vigilantly kept yourselves and your children *out of temptation*, I knew how to proceed. Why, you simple creatures, the weakest of all weak things is a virtue which has not been tested in the fire. I laid a plan, and gathered a list of names. My project was to corrupt Hadleyburg the Incorruptible. My idea was to make liars and thieves of nearly half a hundred smirchless men and women who had never in their lives uttered a lie or stolen a penny. I was afraid of Goodson. He was neither born nor reared in Hadleyburg. I was afraid that if I started to operate my scheme by getting my letter laid before you, you would say to yourselves, 'Goodson is the only man among us who would give away twenty dollars to a poor devil' – and then you might not bite at my bait. But Heaven took Goodson; then I knew I was safe, and I set my trap and baited it. It may be that I shall not catch all the men to whom I mailed the pretended test secret, but I shall catch the most of them, if I know Hadleyburg nature. [Voices: 'Right – he got every last one of them.'] I believe they will even steal ostensible *gamble*-money, rather than miss, poor, tempted, and mistrained fellows. I am hoping to eternally and everlastingly squelch your vanity and give Hadleyburg a new renown – one that will *stick* – and spread far. If I have succeeded, open the sack and summon the Committee on Propagation and Preservation of the Hadleyburg Reputation." '

A cyclone of voices: 'Open it! Open it! The Eighteen to the front! Committee on Propagation of the Tradition! Forward – the Incorruptibles!'

The Chair ripped the sack wide, and gathered up a handful of bright, broad, yellow coins, shook them together, then examined them –

'Friends, they are only gilded disks of lead!'

There was a crashing outbreak of delight over this news, and when the noise had subsided, the tanner called out:

'By right of apparent seniority in this business, Mr Wilson is Chairman of the Committee on Propagation of the Tradition. I suggest that he step forward on behalf of his pals, and receive in trust the money.'

A hundred voices: 'Wilson! Wilson! Wilson! Speech! Speech!'

Wilson (in a voice trembling with anger): 'You will allow me to say, and without apologies for my language, *damn* the money!'

A voice: 'Oh, and him a Baptist!'

A voice: 'Seventeen Symbols left! Step up, gentlemen, and assume your trust!'

There was a pause – no response.

The saddler: 'Mr Chairman, we've got *one* clean man left, anyway, out of the late aristocracy; and he needs money, and deserves it. I move that you appoint Jack Halliday to get up there and auction off that sack of gilt twenty-dollar pieces, and give the result to the right man – the man whom Hadleyburg delights to honour – Edward Richards.'

This was received with great enthusiasm, the dog taking a hand again; the saddler started the bids at a dollar, the Brixton folk and Barnum's representative fought hard for it, the people cheered every jump that the bids made, the excitement climbed moment by moment higher and higher, the bidders got on their mettle and grew steadily more and more daring, more and more determined, the jumps went from a dollar up to five, then to ten, then to twenty, then fifty, then to a hundred, then –

At the beginning of the auction Richards whispered in distress to his wife: 'O Mary, can we allow it? It – it – you see, it is an honour-reward, a testimonial to purity of character, and – and – can we allow it? Hadn't I better get up and – O Mary, what ought we to do? – what do you think we – [Halliday's voice: 'Fifteen I'm bid! – fifteen for the sack! – twenty! – ah, thanks! – thirty – thanks again! Thirty, thirty, thirty! – do I hear forty? – forty it is! Keep the ball rolling, gentlemen, keep it rolling! – fifty! – thanks, noble Roman! going at fifty, fifty, fifty! – seventy! – ninety! – splendid! – a hundred! – pile it up, pile it up! – hundred and twenty – forty! – just in time! – hundred and fifty! – *two* hundred! – superb! Do I hear two h – thanks! – two hundred and fifty! – ']

'It is another temptation, Edward – I'm all in a tremble – but, oh, we've escaped one temptation, and that ought to warn us to – ['Six did I hear? – thanks! – six fifty, six f – *seven* hundred!'] And yet, Edward, when you think – nobody susp – ['Eight hundred dollars! – hurrah! – make it nine! – Mr Parsons, did I hear you say – thanks – nine! – this noble sack of virgin lead going at only nine hundred dollars, gilding and all – come! do I hear – a thousand! – gratefully yours! – did someone say eleven? – a sack which is going to be the most celebrated in the whole Uni – '] O Edward' (beginning to sob), 'we are *so* poor! – but – but – do as you think best – do as you think best.'

Edward fell – that is, he sat still; sat with a conscience which was not satisfied, but which was overpowered by circumstances.

Meantime a stranger, who looked like an amateur detective gotten up as an impossible English earl, had been watching the evening's proceedings with manifest interest, and with a contented expression in his face; and he had been privately commenting to himself. He was now soliloquising somewhat like this: 'None of the Eighteen are bidding; that is not satisfactory; I must change that – the dramatic unities require it; they must buy the sack they tried to steal; they must pay a heavy price, too – some of them are rich. And another thing, when I make a mistake in Hadleyburg nature the man that puts that error upon me is entitled to a high honorarium, and someone must pay it. This poor old Richards has brought my judgment to shame; he is an honest man – I don't understand it, but I acknowledge it. Yes, he saw my deuces *and* with a straight flush, and by rights the pot is his. And it shall be a jackpot, too, if I can manage it. He disappointed me, but let that pass.'

He was watching the bidding. At a thousand, the market broke; the prices tumbled swiftly. He waited – and still watched. One competitor dropped out; then another, and another. He put in a bid or two, now. When the bids had sunk to ten dollars, he added a five; someone raised him a three; he waited a moment, then flung in a fifty-dollar jump, and the sack was his – at $1,282. The house broke out in cheers – then stopped; for he was on his feet, and had lifted his hand. He began to speak.

'I desire to say a word, and ask a favour. I am a speculator in rarities, and I have dealings with persons interested in numismatics all over the world. I can make a profit on this purchase, just as it stands; but there is a way, if I can get your approval, whereby I can make every one of these leaden twenty-dollar pieces worth its face in gold, and perhaps more. Grant me that approval, and I will give part of my gains to your Mr Richards, whose invulnerable probity you have so justly and so cordially recognised tonight; his share shall be ten thousand dollars, and I will hand him the money tomorrow. [Great applause from the house. But the 'invulnerable probity' made the Richardses blush prettily; however, it went for modesty, and did no harm.] If you will pass my proposition by a good majority – I would like a two-thirds vote – I will regard that as the town's consent, and that is all I ask. Rarities are always helped by any device which will rouse curiosity and compel remark. Now if I may have your permission to stamp upon the faces of each of these ostensible coins the names of the eighteen gentlemen who – '

Nine-tenths of the audience were on their feet in a moment – dog and all – and the proposition was carried with a whirlwind of approving applause and laughter.

They sat down, and all the Symbols except 'Dr' Clay Harkness got up, violently protesting against the proposed outrage, and threatening to –

'I beg you not to threaten me,' said the stranger, calmly. 'I know my legal rights, and am not accustomed to being frightened at bluster.' (Applause.) He sat down. 'Dr' Harkness saw an opportunity here. He was one of the two very rich men of the place, and Pinkerton was the other. Harkness was proprietor of a mint; that is to say, a popular patent medicine. He was running for the Legislature on one ticket, and Pinkerton on the other. It was a close race and a hot one, and getting hotter every day. Both had strong appetites for money; each had bought a great tract of land, with a purpose; there was going to be a new railway, and each wanted to be in the Legislature and help locate the route to his own advantage; a single vote might make the decision, and with it two or three fortunes. The stake was large, and Harkness was a daring speculator. He was sitting close to the stranger. He leaned over while one or another of the other Symbols was entertaining the house with protests and appeals, and asked, in a whisper,

'What is your price for the sack?'

'Forty thousand dollars.'

'I'll give you twenty.'

'No.'

'Twenty-five.'

'No.'

'Say thirty.'

'The price is forty thousand dollars; not a penny less.'

'All right, I'll give it. I will come to the hotel at ten in the morning. I don't want it known; will see you privately.'

'Very good.' Then the stranger got up and said to the house:

'I find it late. The speeches of these gentlemen are not without merit, not without interest, not without grace; yet if I may be excused I will take my leave. I thank you for the great favour which you have shown me in granting my petition. I ask the Chair to keep the sack for me until tomorrow, and to hand these three five-hundred-dollar notes to Mr Richards.' They were passed up to the Chair. 'At nine I will call for the sack, and at eleven will deliver the rest of the ten thousand to Mr Richards in person, at his home. Good-night.'

Then he slipped out, and left the audience making a vast noise, which was composed of a mixture of cheers, the *Mikado* song, dog-disapproval, and the chant, 'You are f–a–r from being a b–a–a–d man – a–a–a a–men!'

❧ 4 ☙

At home the Richardses had to endure congratulations and compliments until midnight. Then they were left to themselves. They looked a little sad, and they sat silent and thinking. Finally Mary sighed and said:

'Do you think we are to blame, Edward – *much* to blame?' and her eyes wandered to the accusing triplet of big bank notes lying on the table, where the congratulators had been gloating over them and reverently fingering them. Edward did not answer at once; then he brought out a sigh and said, hesitatingly:

'We – we couldn't help it, Mary. It – well, it was ordered. *All* things are.'

Mary glanced up and looked at him steadily, but he didn't return the look. Presently she said:

'I thought congratulations and praises always tasted good. But – it seems to me, now – Edward?'

'Well?'

'Are you going to stay in the bank?'

'N–no.'

'Resign?'

'In the morning – by note.'

'It does seem best.'

Richards bowed his head in his hands and muttered:

'Before, I was not afraid to let oceans of people's money pour through my hands, but – Mary, I am so tired, so tired – '

'We will go to bed.'

At nine in the morning the stranger called for the sack and took it to the hotel in a cab. At ten Harkness had a talk with him privately.

The stranger asked for and got five cheques on a metropolitan bank – drawn to 'Bearer' – four for $1,500 each, and one for $34,000. He put one of the former in his pocketbook, and the remainder, representing $38,500, he put in an envelope, and with these he added a note, which he wrote after Harkness was gone. At eleven he called at the Richards house and knocked. Mrs Richards peeped through the shutters, then went and received the envelope, and the stranger disappeared without a word. She came back flushed and a little unsteady on her legs, and gasped out:

'I am sure I recognised him! Last night it seemed to me that maybe I had seen him somewhere before.'

'He is the man that brought the sack here?'

'I am almost sure of it.'

'Then he is the ostensible Stephenson, too, and sold every important citizen in this town with his bogus secret. Now if he has sent cheques instead of money, we are sold, too, after we thought we had escaped. I was beginning to feel fairly comfortable once more, after my night's rest, but the look of that envelope makes me sick. It isn't fat enough; $8,500 in even the largest bank notes makes more bulk than that.'

'Edward, why do you object to cheques?'

'Cheques signed by Stephenson! I am resigned to take the $8,500 if it could come in bank notes – for it does seem that it was so ordered, Mary – but I have never had much courage, and I have not the pluck to try to market a cheque signed with that disastrous name. It would be a trap. That man tried to catch me; we escaped somehow or other; and now he is trying a new way. If it is cheques – '

'Oh, Edward, it is *too* bad!' and she held up the cheques and began to cry.

'Put them in the fire! quick! we mustn't be tempted. It is a trick to make the world laugh at *us*, along with the rest, and – Give them to *me*, since you can't do it!' He snatched them and tried to hold his grip till he could get to the stove; but he was human, he was a cashier, and he stopped a moment to make sure of the signature. Then he came near to fainting.

'Fan me, Mary, fan me! They are the same as gold!'

'Oh, how lovely, Edward! Why?'

'Signed by Harkness. What can the mystery of that be, Mary?'

'Edward, do you think – '

'Look here – look at this! Fifteen – fifteen – fifteen – thirty-four. Thirty-eight thousand five hundred! Mary, the sack isn't worth twelve dollars, and Harkness – apparently – has paid about par for it.'

'And does it all come to us, do you think – instead of the ten thousand?'

'Why, it looks like it. And the cheques are made to "Bearer", too.'

'Is that good, Edward? What is it for?'

'A hint to collect them at some distant bank, I reckon. Perhaps Harkness doesn't want the matter known. What is that – a note?'

'Yes. It was with the cheques.'

It was in the 'Stephenson' handwriting, but there was no signature. It said:

> I am a disappointed man. Your honesty is beyond the reach of temptation. I had a different idea about it, but I wronged you in that, and I beg pardon, and do it sincerely. I honour you – and that is sincere too. This town is not worthy to kiss the hem of your garment. Dear sir, I made a square bet with myself that there were nineteen debauchable men in your self-righteous community. I have lost. Take the whole pot, you are entitled to it.

Richards drew a deep sigh, and said:

'It seems written with fire – it burns so. Mary – I am miserable again.'

'I, too. Ah, dear, I wish – '

'To think, Mary – he *believes* in me.'

'Oh, don't, Edward – I can't bear it.'

'If those beautiful words were deserved, Mary – and God knows I believed I deserved them once – I think I could give the forty thousand dollars for them. And I would put that paper away, as representing more than gold and jewels, and keep it always. But now – We could not live in the shadow of its accusing presence, Mary.'

He put it in the fire.

A messenger arrived and delivered an envelope. Richards took from it a note and read it; it was from Burgess.

> You saved me, in a difficult time. I saved you last night. It was at cost of a lie, but I made the sacrifice freely, and out of a grateful heart. None in this village knows so well as I know how brave and good and noble you are. At bottom you cannot respect me, knowing as you do of that matter of which I am accused, and by the general voice condemned; but I beg, that you will at least believe that I am a grateful man; it will help me to bear my burden.
>
> [*Signed*] BURGESS

'Saved, once more. And on such terms!' He put the note in the fire.

'I – I wish I were dead, Mary, I wish I were out of it all.'

'Oh, these are bitter, bitter days, Edward. The stabs, through their very generosity, are so deep – and they come so fast!'

Three days before the election each of two thousand voters suddenly found himself in possession of a prized memento – one of the renowned bogus double-eagles. Around one of its faces was stamped these words: 'THE REMARK I MADE TO THE POOR STRANGER WAS – ' Around the other face was stamped these: 'Go AND REFORM. [*signed*] PINKERTON.' Thus the entire remaining refuse of the renowned joke was emptied upon a single head, and with calamitous effect. It revived the recent vast laugh and concentrated it upon Pinkerton; and Harkness's election was a walkover.

Within twenty-four hours after the Richardses had received their cheques their consciences were quieting down, discouraged; the old couple were learning to reconcile themselves to the sin which they had committed. But they were to learn, now, that a sin takes on new and real terrors when there seems a chance that it is going to be found out. This gives it a fresh and most substantial and important aspect. At church the morning sermon was of the usual pattern; it was the same old things said in the same old way; they had heard them a thousand times and found them innocuous, next to meaningless, and easy to sleep under; but now it was different: the sermon seemed to bristle with accusations; it seemed aimed straight and specially at people who were concealing deadly sins. After church they got away from the mob of congratulators as soon as they could, and hurried homeward, chilled to the bone at they did not know what – vague, shadowy, indefinite fears. And by chance they caught a glimpse of Mr Burgess as he turned a corner. He paid no attention to their nod of recognition! He hadn't seen it; but they did not know that. What could his conduct mean? It might mean – it might mean – oh, a dozen dreadful things. Was it possible that he knew that Richards could have cleared him of guilt in that bygone time, and had been silently waiting for a chance to even up accounts? At home, in their distress they got to imagining that their servant might have been in the next room listening when Richards revealed the secret to his wife that he knew of Burgess's innocence; next, Richards began to imagine that he had heard the swish of a gown in there at that time; next, he was sure he *had* heard it. They would call Sarah in, on a pretext, and watch her face: if she had been betraying them to Mr Burgess, it would show in her manner. They asked her some questions – questions which were so random and incoherent and seemingly purposeless that the girl felt sure that the old people's minds had been affected by their sudden good fortune; the sharp and watchful gaze which they bent upon her frightened her, and that completed the business. She blushed, she became nervous and confused, and to the old people these were plain signs of guilt – guilt of some fearful sort or other – without doubt she was a spy and a traitor. When they were alone again they began to piece many unrelated things together and get horrible results out of the combination. When things had got about to the worst, Richards was delivered of a sudden gasp, and his wife asked,

'Oh, what is it? – what is it?'

'The note – Burgess's note! Its language was sarcastic, I see it now.' He quoted: ' "At bottom you cannot respect me, *knowing*, as you do, of *that matter* of which I am accused" – oh, it is perfectly plain, now, God help me! He knows that I know! You see the ingenuity of the phrasing. It was a trap – and like a fool, I walked into it. And Mary – ?'

'Oh, it is dreadful – I know what you are going to say – he didn't return your transcript of the pretended test-remark.'

'No – kept it to destroy us with. Mary, he has exposed us to some already. I know it – I know it well. I saw it in a dozen faces after church. Ah, he wouldn't answer our nod of recognition – *he* knew what he had been doing!'

In the night the doctor was called. The news went around in the morning that the old couple were rather seriously ill – prostrated by the exhausting excitement growing out of their great windfall, the congratulations, and the late hours, the doctor said. The town was sincerely distressed; for these old people were about all it had left to be proud of, now.

Two days later the news was worse. The old couple were delirious, and were doing strange things. By witness of the nurses, Richards had exhibited cheques – for $8,500? No – for an amazing sum – $38,500! What could be the explanation of this gigantic piece of luck?

The following day the nurses had more news – and wonderful. They had concluded to hide the cheques, lest harm come to them; but when they searched they were gone from under the patient's pillow – vanished away. The patient said:

'Let the pillow alone; what do you want?'

'We thought it best that the cheques – '

'You will never see them again – they are destroyed. They came from Satan. I saw the hellbrand on them, and I knew they were sent to betray me to sin.' Then he fell to gabbling strange and dreadful things which were not clearly understandable, and which the doctor admonished them to keep to themselves.

Richards was right; the cheques were never seen again.

A nurse must have talked in her sleep, for within two days the forbidden gabblings were the property of the town; and they were of a surprising sort. They seemed to indicate that Richards had been a claimant for the sack himself, and that Burgess had concealed that fact and then maliciously betrayed it.

Burgess was taxed with this and stoutly denied it. And he said it was not fair to attach weight to the chatter of a sick old man who was out of his mind. Still, suspicion was in the air, and there was much talk.

After a day or two it was reported that Mrs Richards's delirious deliveries were getting to be duplicates of her husband's. Suspicion flamed up into conviction, now, and the town's pride in the purity of its one undiscredited important citizen began to dim down and flicker toward extinction.

Six days passed, then came more news. The old couple were dying. Richards's mind cleared in his latest hour, and he sent for Burgess. Burgess said:

'Let the room be cleared. I think he wishes to say something in privacy.'

'No!' said Richards: 'I want witnesses. I want you all to hear my confession, so that I may die a man, and not a dog. I was clean – artificially – like the rest; and like the rest I fell when temptation came. I signed a lie, and claimed the miserable sack. Mr Burgess remembered that I had done him a service, and in gratitude (and ignorance) he suppressed my claim and saved me. You know the thing that was charged against Burgess years ago. My testimony, and mine alone, could have cleared him, and I was a coward, and left him to suffer disgrace – '

'No – no – Mr Richards, you – '

'My servant betrayed my secret to him – '

'No one has betrayed anything to me – '

' – and then he did a natural and justifiable thing, he repented of the saving kindness which he had done me, and he *exposed* me – as I deserved – '

'Never! – I make oath – '

'Out of my heart I forgive him.'

Burgess's impassioned protestations fell upon deaf ears; the dying man passed away without knowing that once more he had done poor Burgess a wrong. The old wife died that night.

The last of the sacred Nineteen had fallen a prey to the fiendish sack; the town was stripped of the last rag of its ancient glory. Its mourning was not showy, but it was deep.

By act of the Legislature – upon prayer and petition – Hadleyburg was allowed to change its name to (never mind what – I will not give it away), and leave one word out of the motto that for many generations had graced the town's official seal.

It is an honest town once more, and the man will have to rise early that catches it napping again.

My Début as a Literary Person

In those early days I had already published one little thing ('The Jumping Frog') in an Eastern paper, but I did not consider that that counted. In my view, a person who published things in a mere newspaper could not properly claim recognition as a Literary Person: he must rise away above that; he must appear in a magazine. He would then be a Literary Person; also, he would be famous – right away. These two ambitions were strong upon me. This was in 1866. I prepared my contribution, and then looked around for the best magazine to go up to glory in. I selected the most important one in New York. The contribution was accepted. I signed it 'Mark Twain'; for that name had some currency on the Pacific coast, and it was my idea to spread it all over the world, now, at this one jump. The article appeared in the December number, and I sat up a month waiting for the January number; for that one would contain the year's list of contributors, my name would be in it, and I should be famous and could give the banquet I was meditating.

I did not give the banquet. I had not written the 'Mark Twain' distinctly; it was a fresh name to Eastern printers, and they put it 'Mike Swain' or 'MacSwain', I do not remember which. At any rate, I was not celebrated, and I did not give the banquet. I was a Literary Person, but that was all – a buried one; buried alive.

My article was about the burning of the clipper-ship *Hornet* on the line, 3rd of May 1866. There were thirty-one men on board at the time, and I was in Honolulu when the fifteen lean and ghostly survivors arrived there after a voyage of forty-three days in an open boat, through the blazing tropics, on *ten days' rations* of food. A very remarkable trip; but it was conducted by a captain who was a remarkable man, otherwise there would have been no survivors. He was a New-Englander of the best sea-going stock of the old capable times – Captain Josiah Mitchell.

I was in the islands to write letters for the weekly edition of the

Sacramento *Union*, a rich and influential daily journal which hadn't any use for them, but could afford to spend twenty dollars a week for nothing. The proprietors were lovable and well-beloved men: long ago dead, no doubt, but in me there is at least one person who still holds them in grateful remembrance; for I dearly wanted to see the islands, and they listened to me and gave me the opportunity when there was but slender likelihood that it could profit them in any way.

I had been in the islands several months when the survivors arrived. I was laid up in my room at the time, and unable to walk. Here was a great occasion to serve my journal, and I not able to take advantage of it. Necessarily I was in deep trouble. But by good luck his Excellency Anson Burlingame was there at the time, on his way to take up his post in China, where he did such good work for the United States. He came and put me on a stretcher and had me carried to the hospital where the shipwrecked men were, and I never needed to ask a question. He attended to all of that himself, and I had nothing to do but make the notes. It was like him to take that trouble. He was a great man and a great American, and it was in his fine nature to come down from his high office and do a friendly turn whenever he could.

We got through with this work at six in the evening. I took no dinner, for there was no time to spare if I would beat the other correspondents. I spent four hours arranging the notes in their proper order, then wrote all night and beyond it; with this result: that I had a very long and detailed account of the *Hornet* episode ready at nine in the morning, while the correspondents of the San Francisco journals had nothing but a brief outline report – for they didn't sit up. The now-and-then schooner was to sail for San Francisco about nine; when I reached the dock she was free forward and was just casting off her stern-line. My fat envelope was thrown by a strong hand, and fell on board all right, and my victory was a safe thing. All in due time the ship reached San Francisco, but it was my complete report which made the stir and was telegraphed to the New York papers, by Mr Cash; he was in charge of the Pacific bureau of the New York *Herald* at the time.

When I returned to California by and by, I went up to Sacramento and presented a bill for general correspondence at twenty dollars a week. It was paid. Then I presented a bill for 'special' service on the *Hornet* matter of three columns of solid nonpareil at *a hundred dollars a column*. The cashier didn't faint, but he came rather near it. He sent for the proprietors, and they came and never uttered a protest. They only laughed in their jolly fashion, and said it was robbery, but no matter; it was a grand 'scoop' (the bill or my *Hornet* report, I didn't know which);

'Pay it. It's all right.' The best men that ever owned a newspaper.

The *Hornet* survivors reached the Sandwich Islands the 15th of June. They were mere skinny skeletons; their clothes hung limp about them and fitted them no better than a flag fits the flagstaff in a calm. But they were well nursed in the hospital; the people of Honolulu kept them supplied with all the dainties they could need; they gathered strength fast, and were presently nearly as good as new. Within a fortnight the most of them took ship for San Francisco; that is, if my dates have not gone astray in my memory. I went in the same ship, a sailing-vessel. Captain Mitchell of the *Hornet* was along; also the only passengers the *Hornet* had carried. These were two young gentlemen from Stamford, Connecticut – brothers: Samuel Ferguson, aged twenty-eight, a graduate of Trinity College, Hartford, and Henry Ferguson, aged eighteen, a student of the same college. The elder brother had had some trouble with his lungs, which induced his physician to prescribe a long sea-voyage. This terrible disaster, however, developed the disease which later ended fatally. The younger brother is still living, and is fifty years old this year (1898). The *Hornet* was a clipper of the first class and a fast sailer; the young men's quarters were roomy and comfortable, and were well stocked with books, and also with canned meats and fruits to help out the ship-fare with; and when the ship cleared from New York harbour in the first week of January, there was promise that she would make quick and pleasant work of the fourteen or fifteen thousand miles in front of her. As soon as the cold latitudes were left behind and the vessel entered summer weather, the voyage became a holiday picnic. The ship flew southward under a cloud of sail which needed no attention, no modifying or change of any kind, for days together. The young men read, strolled the ample deck, rested and drowsed in the shade of the canvas, took their meals with the captain, and when the day was done they played dummy whist with him till bedtime. After the snow and ice and tempests of the Horn, the ship bowled northward into summer weather again, and the trip was a picnic once more.

Until the early morning of the 3rd of May. Computed position of the ship 112° 10' west longitude; latitude 2° above the equator; no wind, no sea – dead calm; temperature of the atmosphere, tropical, blistering, unimaginable by one who has not been roasted in it. There was a cry of fire. An unfaithful sailor had disobeyed the rules and gone into the booby-hatch with an open light to draw some varnish from a cask. The proper result followed, and the vessel's hours were numbered.

There was not much time to spare, but the captain made the most of it. The three boats were launched – long-boat and two quarter-boats.

That the time was very short and the hurry and excitement considerable is indicated by the fact that in launching the boats a hole was stove in the side of one of them by some sort of collision, and an oar driven through the side of another. The captain's first care was to have four sick sailors brought up and placed on deck out of harm's way – among them a 'Portyghee'. This man had not done a day's work on the voyage, but had lain in his hammock four months nursing an abscess. When we were taking notes in the Honolulu hospital and a sailor told this to Mr Burlingame, the third mate, who was lying near, raised his head with an effort, and in a weak voice made this correction – with solemnity and feeling:

'*Raising* abscesses! He had a family of them. He done it to keep from standing his watch.'

Any provisions that lay handy were gathered up by the men and the two passengers and brought and dumped on the deck where the 'Portyghee' lay; then they ran for more. The sailor who was telling this to Mr Burlingame added:

'We pulled together thirty-two days' rations for the thirty-one men that way.'

The third mate lifted his head again and made another correction – with bitterness:

'The Portyghee et twenty-two of them while he was soldiering there and nobody noticing. A damned hound.'

The fire spread with great rapidity. The smoke and flame drove the men back, and they had to stop their incomplete work of fetching provisions, and take to the boats with only ten days' rations secured .

Each boat had a compass, a quadrant, a copy of Bowditch's *Navigator*, and a nautical almanac, and the captain's and chief mate's boats had chronometers. There were thirty-one men all told. The captain took an account of stock, with the following result: four hams, nearly thirty pounds of salt pork, half-box of raisins, one hundred pounds of bread, twelve two-pound cans of oysters, clams, and assorted meats, a keg containing four pounds of butter, twelve gallons of water in a forty-gallon 'scuttle-butt', four one-gallon demijohns full of water, three bottles of brandy (the property of passengers), some pipes, matches, and a hundred pounds of tobacco. No medicines. Of course the whole party had to go on short rations at once.

The captain and the two passengers kept diaries. On our voyage to San Francisco we ran into a calm in the middle of the Pacific, and did not move a rod during fourteen days; this gave me a chance to copy the diaries. Samuel Ferguson's is the fullest; I will draw upon it now. When the following paragraph was written the ship was about one hundred and twenty days out from port, and all hands were putting in the lazy time about as usual, as no one was forecasting disaster.

May 2. Latitude 1° 28' N., longitude 111° 38' W. Another hot and sluggish day; at one time, however, the clouds promised wind, and there came a slight breeze – just enough to keep us going. The only thing to chronicle today is the quantities of fish about; nine bonitos were caught this forenoon, and some large albacores seen. After dinner the first mate hooked a fellow which he could not hold, so he let the line go to the captain, who was on the bow. He, holding on, brought the fish to with a jerk, and snap went the line, hook and all. We also saw astern, swimming lazily after us, an enormous shark, which must have been nine or ten feet long. We tried him with all sorts of lines and a piece of pork, but he declined to take hold. I suppose he had appeased his appetite on the heads and other remains of the bonitos we had thrown overboard.

Next day's entry records the disaster. The three boats got away, retired to a short distance, and stopped. The two injured ones were leaking badly; some of the men were kept busy bailing, others patched the holes as well as they could. The captain, the two passengers, and eleven men were in the long-boat, with a share of the provisions and water, and with no room to spare, for the boat was only twenty-one feet long, six wide, and three deep. The chief mate and eight men were in one of the small boats, the second mate and seven men in the other. The passengers had saved no clothing but what they had on, excepting their overcoats. The ship, clothed in flame and sending up a vast column of black smoke into the sky, made a grand picture in the solitudes of the sea, and hour after hour the outcasts sat and watched it. Meantime the captain ciphered on the immensity of the distance that stretched between him and the nearest available land, and then scaled the rations down to meet the emergency: half a biscuit for breakfast; one biscuit and some canned meat for dinner; half a biscuit for tea; a few swallows of water for each meal. And so hunger began to gnaw while the ship was still burning.

May 4. The ship burned all night very brightly, and hopes are that some ship has seen the light and is bearing down upon us. None seen, however, this forenoon, so we have determined to go together north and a little west to some islands in 18° or 19° north latitude and 114° to 115° west longitude, hoping in the meantime to be picked up by some ship. The ship sank suddenly at about 5 a.m. We find the sun very hot and scorching, but all try to keep out of it as much as we can.

They did a quite natural thing now: waited several hours for that possible ship that might have seen the light to work her slow way to them through the nearly dead calm. Then they gave it up and set about their plans. If you will look at the map you will say that their course could be easily decided. Albemarle Island (Galapagos group) lies straight eastward nearly a thousand miles; the islands referred to in the diary indefinitely as 'some islands' (Revillagigedo Islands) lie, as they think, in some widely uncertain region northward about one thousand miles and westward one hundred or one hundred and fifty miles. Acapulco, on the Mexican coast, lies about northeast something short of one thousand miles. You will say random rocks in the ocean are not what is wanted; let them strike for Acapulco and the solid continent. That does look like the rational course, but one presently guesses from the diaries that the thing would have been wholly irrational – indeed, suicidal. If the boats struck for Albemarle they would be in the doldrums all the way; and that means a watery perdition, with winds which are wholly crazy, and blow from all points of the compass at once and also perpendicularly. If the boats tried for Acapulco they would get out of the doldrums when half-way there – in case they ever got half-way – and then they would be in a lamentable case, for there they would meet the northeast trades coming down in their teeth, and these boats were so rigged that they could not sail within eight points of the wind. So they wisely started northward, with a slight slant to the west. They had but ten days' short allowance of food; the long-boat was towing the others; they could not depend on making any sort of definite progress in the doldrums, and they had four or five hundred miles of doldrums in front of them yet. *They* are the real equator, a tossing, roaring, rainy belt, ten or twelve hundred miles broad, which girdles the globe.

It rained hard the first night, and all got drenched, but they filled up their water-butt. The brothers were in the stern with the captain, who steered. The quarters were cramped; no one got much sleep. 'Kept on our course till squalls headed us off.'

Stormy and squally the next morning, with drenching rains. A heavy and dangerous 'cobbling' sea. One marvels how such boats could live in it. It is called a feat of desperate daring when one man and a dog cross the Atlantic in a boat the size of a long-boat, and indeed it is; but this long-boat was overloaded with men and other plunder, and was only three feet deep. 'We naturally thought often of all at home, and were glad to remember that it was Sacrament Sunday, and that prayers would go up from our friends for us, although they know not our peril.'

The captain got not even a catnap during the first three days and nights, but he got a few winks of sleep the fourth night. 'The worst sea yet.' About ten at night the captain changed his course and headed east-northeast, hoping to make Clipperton Rock. If he failed, no matter; he would be in a better position to make those other islands. I will mention here that he did not find that rock.

On the 8th of May no wind all day; sun blistering hot; they take to the oars. Plenty of dolphins, but they couldn't catch any. 'I think we are all beginning to realise more and more the awful situation we are in.' 'It often takes a ship a week to get through the doldrums; how much longer, then, such a craft as ours.' 'We are so crowded that we cannot stretch ourselves out for a good sleep, but have to take it any way we can get it.'

Of course this feature will grow more and more trying, but it will be human nature to cease to set it down; there will be five weeks of it yet – we must try to remember that for the diarist; it will make our beds the softer.

The 9th of May the sun gives him a warning: 'Looking with both eyes, the horizon crossed thus + .' 'Henry keeps well, but broods over our troubles more than I wish he did.' They caught two dolphins; they tasted well. 'The captain believed the compass out of the way, but the long-invisible north star came out – a welcome sight – and indorsed the compass.'

May 10, 'latitude 7° o' 3" N., longitude 111° 32' W.' So they have made about three hundred miles of northing in the six days since they left the region of the lost ship. 'Drifting in calms all day.' And baking hot, of course; I have been down there, and I remember that detail. 'Even as the captain says, all romance has long since vanished, and I think the most of us are beginning to look the fact of our awful situation full in the face.'

'We are making but little headway on our course.' Bad news from the rearmost boat: the men are improvident; 'they have eaten up all of the canned meats brought from the ship, and are now growing discontented.' Not so with the chief mate's people – they are evidently under the eye of a *man*.

Under date of May 11: 'Standing still! or worse; we lost more last night than we made yesterday.' In fact, they have lost three miles of the three hundred of northing they had so laboriously made. 'The cock that was rescued and pitched into the boat while the ship was on fire still lives, and crows with the breaking of dawn, cheering us a good deal.' What has he been living on for a week? Did the starving men feed him from their dire poverty? 'The second mate's boat out of water again, showing that they overdrink their allowance. The captain spoke pretty sharply to them.' It is true: I have the remark in my old notebook; I got it of the third mate in the hospital at Honolulu. But there is not room for it here, and it is too combustible, anyway. Besides, the third mate admired it, and what he admired he was likely to enhance.

They were still watching hopefully for ships. The captain was a thoughtful man, and probably did not disclose to them that that was substantially a waste of time. 'In this latitude the horizon is filled with little upright clouds that look very much like ships.' Mr Ferguson saved three bottles of brandy from his private stores when he left the ship, and the liquor came good in these days. 'The captain serves out two tablespoonfuls of brandy and water – half and half – to our crew.' He means the watch that is on duty; they stood regular watches – four hours on and four off. The chief mate was an excellent officer – a self-possessed, resolute, fine, all-round man. The diarist makes the following note – there is character in it: 'I offered one bottle of brandy to the chief mate, but he declined, saying he could keep the after-boat quiet, and we had not enough for all.'

Henry Ferguson's diary to date, given in full:

May 4, 5, 6, doldrums. May 7, 8, 9, doldrums. May 10, 11, 12, doldrums. Tells it all. Never saw, never felt, never heard, never experienced such heat, such darkness, such lightning and thunder, and wind and rain, in my life before.

That boy's diary is of the economical sort that a person might properly be expected to keep in such circumstances – and be forgiven for the economy, too. His brother, perishing of consumption, hunger, thirst, blazing heat, drowning rains, loss of sleep, lack of exercise, was persistently faithful and circumstantial with his diary from the first day to the last – an instance of noteworthy fidelity and resolution. In spite of the tossing and plunging boat he wrote it close and fine, in a hand as easy to read as print. They can't seem to get north of 7° N.; they are still there the next day:

May 12. A good rain last night, and we caught a good deal, though not enough to fill up our tank, pails, etc. Our object is to get out of these doldrums, but it seems as if we cannot do it. Today we have had it very variable, and hope we are on the northern edge, though we are not much above 7°. This morning we all thought we had made out a sail; but it was one of those deceiving clouds. Rained a good deal today, making all hands wet and uncomfortable; we filled up pretty nearly all our water-pots, however. I hope we may have a fine night, for the captain certainly wants rest, and while there is any danger of squalls, or danger of any kind, he is always on hand. I never would have believed that open boats such as ours, with their loads, could live in some of the seas we have had.

During the night, 12th-13th, 'the cry of *"A ship!"* brought us to our feet.' It seemed to be the glimmer of a vessel's signal-lantern rising out of the curve of the sea. There was a season of breathless hope while they stood watching, with their hands shading their eyes, and their hearts in their throats; then the promise failed: the light was a rising star. It is a long time ago – thirty-two years – and it doesn't matter now, yet one is sorry for their disappointment. 'Thought often of those at home today, and of the disappointment they will feel next Sunday at not hearing from us by telegraph from San Francisco.' It will be many weeks yet before the telegram is received, and it will come as a thunderclap of joy then, and with the seeming of a miracle, for it will raise from the grave men mourned as dead. 'Today our rations were reduced to a quarter of a biscuit a meal, with about half a pint of water.' This is on the 13th of May, with more than a month of voyaging in front of them yet! However, as they do not know that, 'we are all feeling pretty cheerful'.

In the afternoon of the 14th there was a thunderstorm, 'which toward night seemed to close in around us on every side, making it very dark and squally'. 'Our situation is becoming more and more desperate', for they were making very little northing, 'and every day diminishes our small stock of provisions'. They realise that the boats must soon separate, and each fight for its own life. Towing the quarter-boats is a hindering business.

That night and next day, light and baffling winds and but little progress. Hard to bear, that persistent standing still, and the food wasting away. 'Everything in a perfect sop; and all so cramped, and no change of clothes.' Soon the sun comes out and roasts them. 'Joe caught another dolphin today; in his maw we found a flying-fish and two skip-jacks.' There is an event, now, which rouses an enthusiasm of hope: a land-bird arrives! It rests on the yard for awhile, and they can look at it all they like, and envy it, and thank it for its message. As a subject of talk it is beyond price – a fresh, new topic for tongues tired to death of talking upon a single theme: Shall we ever see the land again; and when? Is the bird from Clipperton Rock? They hope so; and they take heart of grace to believe so. As it turned out, the bird had no message; it merely came to mock.

May 16, 'the cock still lives, and daily carols forth His praise'. It will be a rainy night, 'but I do not care if we can fill up our water-butts'.

On the 17th one of those majestic spectres of the deep, a water-spout, stalked by them, and they trembled for their lives. Young Henry set it down in his scanty journal with the judicious comment that 'it might have been a fine sight from a ship'.

From Captain Mitchell's log for this day: 'Only half a bushel of breadcrumbs left.' (And a month to wander the seas yet.)

It rained all night and all day; everybody uncomfortable. Now came a swordfish chasing a bonito; and the poor thing, seeking help and friends, took refuge under the rudder. The big swordfish kept hovering around, scaring everybody badly. The men's mouths watered for him, for he would have made a whole banquet; but no one dared to touch him, of course, for he would sink a boat promptly if molested. Providence protected the poor bonito from the cruel swordfish. This was just and right. Providence next befriended the shipwrecked sailors: they got the bonito. This was also just and right. But in the distribution of mercies the swordfish himself got overlooked. He now went away; to muse over these subtleties, probably. 'The men in all the boats seem pretty well; the feeblest of the sick ones (not able for a long time to stand his watch on board the ship) is wonderfully recovered.' This is the third mate's detested 'Portyghee' that raised the family of abscesses.

> Passed a most awful night. Rained hard nearly all the time, and blew in squalls, accompanied by terrific thunder and lightning, from all points of the compass. – *Henry's Log.*

> Most awful night I ever witnessed. – *Captain's Log.*

Latitude, May 18, 11° 11'. So they have averaged but forty miles of northing a day during the fortnight. Further talk of separating. 'Too bad, but it must be done for the safety of the whole.' 'At first I never dreamed, but now hardly shut my eyes for a catnap without conjuring up something or other – to be accounted for by weakness, I suppose.' But for their disaster they think they would be arriving in San Francisco about this time. 'I should have liked to send B— the telegram for her birthday.' This was a young sister.

On the 19th the captain called up the quarter-boats and said one would have to go off on its own hook. The long-boat could no longer tow both of them. The second mate refused to go, but the chief mate was ready; in fact, he was always ready when there was a man's work to the fore. He took the second mate's boat; six of its crew elected to remain, and two of his own crew came with him (nine in the boat, now, including himself). He sailed away, and toward sunset passed out of sight. The diarist was sorry to see him go. It was natural; one could have better spared the 'Portyghee'. After thirty-two years I find my prejudice against this 'Portyghee' reviving. His very looks have long passed out of my memory; but no matter, I am coming to hate him as religiously as ever. 'Water will now be a scarce article, for as we get out of the doldrums we shall get showers only now and then in the trades. This life is telling severely on my strength. Henry holds out first-rate.' Henry did not start well, but under hardships he improved straight along.

Latitude, Sunday, May 20, 12° 0' 9". They ought to be well out of the doldrums now, but they are not. No breeze – the longed-for trades still missing. They are still anxiously watching for a sail, but they have only 'visions of ships that come to naught – the shadow without the substance'. The second mate catches a booby this afternoon, a bird which consists mainly of feathers; 'but as they have no other meat, it will go well'.

May 21, they strike the trades at last! The second mate catches three more boobies, and gives the long-boat one. Dinner 'half a can of mincemeat divided up and served around, which strengthened us somewhat'. They have to keep a man bailing all the time; the hole knocked in the boat when she was launched from the burning ship was never efficiently mended. 'Heading about northwest now.' They hope they have easting enough to make some of those indefinite isles. Failing that, they think they will be in a better position to be picked up. It was an infinitely slender chance, but the captain probably refrained from mentioning that.

The next day is to be an eventful one.

May 22. Last night wind headed us off, so that part of the time we had to steer east-southeast and then west-northwest, and so on. This morning we were all startled by a cry of '*Sail ho!*' Sure enough we could see it! And for a time we cut adrift from the second mate's boat, and steered so as to attract its attention. This was about half-past five a.m. After sailing in a state of high excitement for almost twenty minutes we made it out to be the chief mate's boat. Of course we were glad to see them and have them report all well; but still it was a bitter disappointment to us all. Now that we are in the trades it seems impossible to make northing enough to strike the isles. We have determined to do the best we can, and get in the route of vessels. Such being the determination, it became necessary to cast off the other boat, which, after a good deal of unpleasant-ness, was done, we again dividing water and stores, and taking Cox into our boat. This makes our number fifteen. The second mate's crew wanted to all get in with us and cast the other boat adrift. It was a very painful separation.

So those isles that they have struggled for so long and so hopefully have to be given up. What with lying birds that come to mock, and isles that are but a dream, and 'visions of ships that come to naught', it is a pathetic time they are having, with much heartbreak in it. It was odd that the vanished boat, three days lost to sight in that vast solitude, should appear again. But it brought Cox – we can't be certain why. But if it hadn't, the diarist would never have seen the land again.

Our chances as we go west increase in regard to being picked up, but each day our scanty fare is so much reduced. Without the fish, turtle, and birds sent us, I do not know how we should have got along. The other day I offered to read prayers morning and evening for the captain, and last night commenced. The men, although of various nationalities and religions, are very attentive, and always uncovered. May God grant my weak endeavour its issue.

Latitude, May 24, 14° 18' N. Five oysters apiece for dinner and three spoonfuls of juice, a gill of water, and a piece of biscuit the size of a silver dollar. 'We are plainly getting weaker – God have mercy upon us all!' That night heavy seas break over the weather side and make everybody wet and uncomfortable, besides requiring constant bailing. Next day 'nothing particular happened'. Perhaps some of us would have regarded it differently. 'Passed a spar, but not near enough to see what it was.' They saw some whales blow; there were flying-fish skimming the seas, but none came aboard. Misty weather, with fine rain, very penetrating.

Latitude, May 26, 15° 50'. They caught a flying-fish and a booby, but had to eat them raw. 'The men grow weaker, and, I think, despondent; they say very little, though.' And so, to all the other imaginable and unimaginable horrors, silence is added – the muteness and brooding of coming despair. 'It seems our best chance to get in the track of ships, with the hope that someone will run near enough to our speck to see it.' He hopes the other boats stood west and have been picked up. (They will never be heard of again in this world.)

Sunday, May 27. Latitude 10° 0' 5"; longitude, by chronometer, 177° 22'. Our fourth Sunday! When we left the ship we reckoned on having about ten days' supplies, and now we hope to be able, by rigid economy, to make them last another week if possible.* Last night the sea was comparatively quiet, but the wind headed us off to about west-northwest, which has been about our course all day today. Another flying-fish came aboard last night, and one more today – both small ones. No birds. A booby is a great catch, and a good large one makes a small dinner for the fifteen of us – that is, of course, as dinners go in the *Hornet's* long-boat. Tried this morning to read the full service to myself, with the communion, but found it too much; am too weak, and get sleepy, and cannot give strict attention; so I put off half till this afternoon. I trust God will hear the prayers gone up for us at home today, and graciously answer them by sending us succour and help in this our season of deep distress.

The next day was 'a good day for seeing a ship'. But none was seen. The diarist 'still feels pretty well', though very weak; his brother Henry 'bears up and keeps his strength the best of any on board'. 'I do not feel despondent at all, for I fully trust that the Almighty will hear our and the home prayers, and He who suffers not a sparrow to fall sees and cares for us, His creatures.'

Considering the situation and circumstances, the record for next day, May 29, is one which has a surprise in it for those dull people who think that nothing but medicines and doctors can cure the sick. A little starvation can really do more for the average sick man than can the best medicines and the best doctors. I do not mean a restricted diet; I mean *total abstention from food for one or two days.* I speak from experience; starvation has been my cold and fever doctor for fifteen years, and has

---

* There are nineteen days of voyaging ahead yet. – M. T.

accomplished a cure in all instances. The third mate told me in Honolulu that the 'Portyghee' had lain in his hammock for months, raising his family of abscesses and feeding like a cannibal. We have seen that in spite of dreadful weather, deprivation of sleep, scorching, drenching, and all manner of miseries, thirteen days of starvation 'wonderfully recovered' him. There were four sailors down sick when the ship was burned. Twenty-five days of pitiless starvation have followed, and now we have this curious record: *'All the men are hearty and strong; even the ones that were down sick are well*, except poor Peter.' When I wrote an article some months ago urging temporary abstention from food as a remedy for an inactive appetite and for disease, I was accused of jesting, but I was in earnest. *'We are all wonderfully well and strong, comparatively speaking.'* On this day the starvation regimen drew its belt a couple of buckle-holes tighter: the bread ration was reduced from the usual piece of cracker the size of a silver dollar *to the half of that, and one meal was abolished from the daily three.* This will weaken the men physically, but if there are any diseases of an ordinary sort left in them they will disappear.

> Two quarts breadcrumbs left, one-third of a ham, three small cans of oysters, and twenty gallons of water. – *Captain's Log.*

The hopeful tone of the diaries is persistent. It is remarkable. Look at the map and see where the boat is: latitude 16° 44', longitude 119° 20'. It is more than two hundred miles west of the Revillagigedo Islands, so they are quite out of the question against the trades, rigged as this boat is. The nearest land available for such a boat is the American group, *six hundred and fifty miles away*, westward; still, there is no note of surrender, none even of discouragement! Yet, May 30, 'we have now left: *one can of oysters; three pounds of raisins, one can of soup; one-third of a ham; three pints of biscuit-crumbs*'. And fifteen starved men to live on it while they creep and crawl six hundred and fifty miles. 'Somehow I feel much encouraged by this change of course (west by north) which we have made today.' Six hundred and fifty miles on a hatful of provisions. Let us be thankful, even after thirty-two years, that they are mercifully ignorant of the fact that it isn't six hundred and fifty that they must creep on the hatful, but *twenty-two hundred!* Isn't the situation romantic enough just as it stands? No. Providence added a startling detail: pulling an oar in that boat, for common seaman's wages, was a *banished duke* – Danish. We hear no more of him; just that mention, that is all, with the simple remark added that 'he is one of our best men' – a high enough compliment for a duke or any other man in those manhood-testing circumstances. With that little glimpse of him at his oar, and that fine word of praise, he vanishes out of our knowledge for all time. For all time, unless he should chance upon this note and reveal himself.

The last day of May is come. And now there is a disaster to report: think of it, reflect upon it, and try to understand how much it means, when you sit down with your family and pass your eye over your breakfast-table. Yesterday there were three pints of breadcrumbs; this morning the little bag is found open and *some of the crumbs missing.* 'We dislike to suspect any one of such a rascally act, but there is no question that this grave crime has been committed. Two days will certainly finish the remaining morsels. God grant us strength to reach the American group!' The third mate told me in Honolulu that in these days the men remembered with bitterness that the 'Portyghee' had devoured twenty-two days' rations while he lay waiting to be transferred from the burning ship, and that now they cursed him and swore an oath that if it came to cannibalism he should be the first to suffer for the rest.

The captain has lost his glasses, and therefore he cannot read our pocket prayer-books as much as I think he would like, though he is not familiar with them.

Further of the captain: 'He is a good man, and has been most kind to us – almost fatherly. He says that if he had been offered the command of the ship sooner he should have brought his two daughters with him.' It makes one shudder yet to think how narrow an escape it was.

The two meals (rations) a day are as follows: fourteen raisins and a piece of cracker the size of a cent, for tea; a gill of water, and a piece of ham and a piece of bread, each the size of a cent, for breakfast. – *Captain's Log.*

He means a cent in *thickness* as well as in circumference. Samuel Ferguson's diary says the ham was shaved 'about as thin as it could be cut'.

June 1. Last night and today sea very high and cobbling, breaking over and making us all wet and cold. Weather squally, and there is no doubt that only careful management – with God's protecting care – preserved us through both the night and the day; and really it is most marvellous how every morsel that passes our lips is blessed to us. It makes me think daily of the miracle of the loaves and fishes. Henry keeps up wonderfully, which is a great consolation to me. I somehow have great confidence, and hope that our afflictions will soon be ended, though we are running rapidly across the track of both outward and inward bound vessels, and away from them; our chief hope is a whaler, man-of-war, or some Australian ship. The isles we are steering for are put down in Bowditch, but on my map are said to be doubtful. God grant they may be there!

Hardest day yet. – *Captain's Log.*

Doubtful! It was worse than that. A week later *they sailed straight over them.*

June 2. Latitude 18° 9'. Squally, cloudy, a heavy sea . . . I cannot help thinking of the cheerful and comfortable time we had aboard the *Hornet.*

Two days' scanty supplies left – ten rations of water apiece and a little morsel of bread. *But the sun shines, and God is merciful.* – *Captain's Log.*

Sunday, June 3. Latitude 17° 54'. Heavy sea all night, and from 4 a.m. very wet, the sea breaking over us in frequent sluices, and soaking everything aft, particularly. All day the sea has been very high, and it is a wonder that we are not swamped. Heaven grant that it may go down this evening! Our suspense and condition are getting terrible. I managed this morning to crawl, more than step, to the forward end of the boat, and was surprised to find that I was so weak, especially in the legs and knees. The sun has been out again, and I have dried some things, and hope for a better night.

June 4. Latitude 17° 6', longitude 131° 30'. Shipped hardly any seas last night, and today the sea has gone down somewhat, although it is still too high for comfort, as we have an occasional reminder that water is wet. The sun has been out all day, and so we have had a good drying. I have been trying for the last ten or twelve days to get a pair of drawers dry enough to put on, and today at last succeeded. I mention this to show the state in which we have lived. If our chronometer is anywhere near right, we ought to see the American Isles tomorrow or next day. If they are not there, we have only the chance for a few days, of a stray ship, for we cannot eke out the provisions more than five or six days longer, and our strength is failing very fast. I was much surprised today to note how my legs have wasted away above my knees: they are hardly thicker than my upper arm used to be. Still, I trust in God's infinite mercy, and feel sure He will do what is best for us. To survive, as we have done, thirty-two days in an open boat, with only about ten days' fair provisions for thirty-one men in the first place, and these divided twice subsequently, is more than mere unassisted *human* art and strength could have accomplished and endured.

Bread and raisins all gone. – *Captain's Log*.

Men growing dreadfully discontented, and awful grumbling and unpleasant talk is arising. God save us from all strife of men; and if we must die now, take us Himself, and not embitter our bitter death still more. – *Henry's Log*.

June 5. Quiet night and pretty comfortable day, though our sail and block show signs of failing, and need taking down – which latter is something of a job, as it requires the climbing of the mast. We also had news from forward, there being discontent and some threatening complaints of unfair allowances, etc., all as unreasonable as foolish; still, these things bid us be on our guard. I am getting miserably weak, but try to keep up the best I can. If we cannot find those isles we can only try to make northwest and get in the track of Sandwich Island bound vessels, living as best we can in the meantime. Today we changed to one meal, and that at about noon, with a small ration of water at 8 or 9 a.m., another at 12 noon, and a third at 5 or 6 p.m.

Nothing left but a little piece of ham and a gill of water, all around. – *Captain's Log*.

They are down to *one* meal a day now – such as it is – *and fifteen hundred miles to crawl yet!* And now the horrors deepen, and though they escaped actual mutiny, the attitude of the men became alarming. Now we seem to see why that curious accident happened, so long ago: I mean Cox's return, after he had been far away and out of sight several days in the chief mate's boat. If he had not come back the captain and the two young passengers would have been slain by these sailors, who were becoming crazed through their sufferings.

Note secretly passed by Henry to his brother. Cox told me last night that there is getting to be a good deal of ugly talk among the men against the captain and us aft. They say that the captain is the cause of all; that he did not try to save the ship at all, nor to get provisions, and even would not let the men put in some they had; and that partiality is shown us in apportioning our rations aft. — asked Cox the other day if he would starve first or eat human flesh. Cox answered he would starve. — then told him he would be only killing himself. If we do not find these islands we would do well to prepare for anything. — is the loudest of all.

Reply. We can depend on —, I think, and —, and Cox, can we not?

Second Note. I guess so, and very likely on —; but there is no telling. — and Cox are certain. There is nothing definite said or hinted as yet, as I understand Cox; but starving men are the same as maniacs. It would be well to keep a watch on your pistol, so as to have it and the cartridges safe from theft.

Henry's Log. June 5. Dreadful forebodings. God spare us from all such horrors! Some of the men getting to talk a good deal. Nothing to write down. Heart very sad.

Henry's Log. June 6. Passed some seaweed, and something that looked like the trunk of an old tree, but no birds; beginning to be afraid islands not there. Today it was said to the captain, in the hearing of all, that some of the men would not shrink, when a man was dead, from using the flesh, though they would not kill. Horrible! God give us all full use of our reason, and spare us from such things! 'From plague, pestilence, and famine, from battle and murder, and from sudden death, good Lord, deliver us!'

June 6. Latitude 16° 30', longitude (chron.) 134°. Dry night and wind steady enough to require no change in sail; but this a.m. an attempt to lower it proved abortive. First the third mate tried and got up to the block, and fastened a temporary arrangement to reeve the halyards through, but had to come down, weak and almost fainting, before finishing; then Joe tried, and after twice ascending, fixed it and brought down the block; but it was very exhausting work, and afterward he was good for nothing all day. The clue-iron which we are trying to make serve for the broken block works, however, very indifferently, and will, I am afraid, soon cut the rope. It is very necessary to get everything connected with the sail in good, easy running order before we get too weak to do anything with it.

Only three meals left. – *Captain's log.*

June 7. Latitude 16° 35' N., longitude 136° 30' W. Night wet and uncomfortable. Today shows us pretty conclusively that the American Isles are not there, though we have had some signs that looked like them. At noon we decided to abandon looking any farther for them, and tonight haul a little more northerly, so as to get in the way of Sandwich Island vessels, which fortunately come down pretty well this way – say to latitude 19° to 20° – to get the benefit of the trade winds. Of course all the westing we have made is gain, and I hope the chronometer is wrong in our favour, for I do not see how any such delicate instrument can keep good time with the constant jarring and thumping we get from the sea. With the strong trade we have, I hope that a week from Sunday will put us in sight of the Sandwich Islands, if we are not safe by that time by being picked up.

It is twelve hundred miles to the Sandwich Islands; the provisions are virtually exhausted, but not the perishing diarist's pluck.

June 8. My cough troubled me a good deal last night, and therefore I got hardly any sleep at all. Still, I make out pretty well, and should not complain. Yesterday the third mate mended the block, and this p.m. the sail, after some difficulty, was got down, and Harry got to the top of the mast and rove the halyards through after some hardship, so that it now works easy and well. This getting up the mast is no easy matter at any time with the sea we have, and is very exhausting in our present state. We could only reward Harry by an extra ration of water. We have made good time and course today. Heading her up, however, makes the boat ship seas and keeps us all wet; however, it cannot be helped. Writing is a rather precarious thing these times. Our meal today for the fifteen consists of half a can of 'soup and boullie'; the other half is reserved for tomorrow. Henry still keeps up grandly, and is a great favourite. God grant he may be spared!

A better feeling prevails among the men. – *Captain's Log.*

June 9. Latitude 17° 53'. Finished today, I may say, our whole stock of provisions.* We have only left a lower end of a ham-bone, with some of the outer rind and skin on. In regard to the water, however,

* Six days to sail yet, nevertheless. – M. T.

I think we have got ten days' supply at our present rate of allowance. This, with what nourishment we can get from boot-legs and such chewable matter, we hope will enable us to weather it out till we get to the Sandwich Islands, or, sailing in the meantime in the track of vessels thither bound, be picked up. My hope is in the latter, for in all human probability I cannot stand the other. Still we have been marvellously protected, and God, I hope, will preserve us all in His own good time and way. The men are getting weaker, but are still quiet and orderly.

Sunday, June 10. Latitude 18° 40', longitude 142° 34'. A pretty good night last night, with some wettings, and again another beautiful Sunday. I cannot but think how we should all enjoy it at home, and what a contrast is here! How terrible their suspense must begin to be! God grant that it may be relieved before very long, and He certainly seems to be with us in everything we do, and has preserved this boat miraculously; for since we left the ship we have sailed considerably over three thousand miles, which, taking into consideration our meagre stock of provisions, is almost unprecedented. As yet I do not feel the stint of food so much as I do that of water. Even Henry, who is naturally a good water-drinker, can save half of his allowance from time to time, when I cannot. My diseased throat may have something to do with that, however.

Nothing is now left which by any flattery can be called food. But they must manage somehow for five days more, for at noon they have still eight hundred miles to go. It is a race for life now.

This is no time for comments or other interruptions from me – every moment is valuable. I will take up the boy brother's diary at this point, and clear the seas before it and let it fly.

Henry Ferguson's Log. Sunday, June 10. Our ham-bone has given us a taste of food today, and we have got left a little meat and the remainder of the bone for tomorrow. Certainly never was there such a sweet knuckle-bone, or one that was so thoroughly appreciated . . . I do not know that I feel any worse than I did last Sunday, notwithstanding the reduction of diet; and I trust that we may all have strength given us to sustain the sufferings and hardships of the coming week. We estimate that we are within seven hundred miles of the Sandwich Islands, and that our average, daily, is somewhat over a hundred miles, so that our hopes have some foundation in reason. Heaven send we may all live to see land!

June 11. Ate the meat and rind of our ham-bone, and have the bone and the greasy cloth from around the ham left to eat tomorrow. God send us birds or fish, and let us not perish of hunger, or be brought to the dreadful alternative of feeding on human flesh! As I feel now, I do not think anything could persuade me; but you cannot tell what you will do when you are reduced by hunger and your mind wandering. I hope and pray we can make out to reach the islands before we get to this strait; but we have one or two desperate men aboard, though they are quiet enough now. *It is my firm trust and belief that we are going to be saved.*

All food gone. – *Captain's Log.**

June 12. Stiff breeze, and we are fairly flying – dead ahead of it – and toward the islands. Good hope, but the prospects of hunger are awful. Ate ham-bone today. It is the captain's birthday; he is fifty-four years old.

June 13. The ham-rags are not quite all gone yet, and the bootlegs, we find, are very palatable after we get the salt out of them. A little smoke, I think, does some little good; but I don't know.

June 14. Hunger does not pain us much, but we are dreadfully weak. Our water is getting frightfully low. God grant we may see land soon! *Nothing to eat*, but feel better than I did yesterday. Toward evening saw a magnificent rainbow – *the first we had seen*. Captain said, 'Cheer up, boys; it's a prophecy – *it's the bow of promise!*'

June 15. God be forever praised for His infinite mercy! LAND IN SIGHT! Rapidly neared it and soon were *sure* of it . . . Two noble Kanakas swam out and took the boat ashore. We were joyfully received by two white men – Mr Jones and his steward Charley – and a crowd of native men, women, and children. They treated us splendidly – aided us, and carried us up the bank, and brought us water, poi, bananas, and green cocoanuts; but the white men took care of us and prevented those who would have eaten too much from doing so. Everybody overjoyed to see us, and all sympathy

---

* It was at this time discovered that the crazed sailors had gotten the delusion that the captain had *a million dollars* in gold concealed aft, and they were conspiring to kill him and the two passengers and seize it. – M. T.

expressed in faces, deeds, and words. We were then helped up to the house; and help we needed. Mr Jones and Charley are the only white men here. Treated us splendidly. Gave us first about a teaspoonful of spirits in water, and then to each a cup of warm tea, with a little bread. Takes *every* care of us. Gave us later another cup of tea, and bread the same, and then let us go to rest. *It is the happiest day of my life* . . . God in His mercy has heard our prayer . . . Everybody is so kind. Words cannot tell.

June 16. Mr Jones gave us a delightful bed, and we surely had a good night's rest; but not sleep – we were too happy to sleep; would keep the reality and not let it turn to a delusion – dreaded that we might wake up and find ourselves in the boat again.

It is an amazing adventure. There is nothing of its sort in history that surpasses it in impossibilities made possible. In one extraordinary detail – the survival of *every person* in the boat – it probably stands alone in the history of adventures of its kind. Usually merely a part of a boat's company survives – officers, mainly, and other educated and tenderly reared men, unused to hardship and heavy labour; the untrained, roughly reared hard workers succumb. But in this case even the rudest and roughest stood the privations and miseries of the voyage almost as well as did the college-bred young brothers and the captain. I mean, physically. The minds of most of the sailors broke down in the fourth week and went to temporary ruin, but physically the endurance exhibited was astonishing. Those men did not survive by any merit of their own, of course, but by merit of the character and intelligence of the captain; they lived by the mastery of his spirit. Without him they would have been children without a nurse; they would have exhausted their provisions in a week, and their pluck would not have lasted even as long as the provisions.

The boat came near to being wrecked at the last. As it approached the shore the sail was let go, and came down with a run; then the captain saw that he was drifting swiftly toward an ugly reef, and an effort was made to hoist the sail again: but it could not be done; the men's strength was wholly exhausted; they could not even pull an oar. They were helpless, and death imminent. It was then that they were discovered by the two Kanakas who achieved the rescue. They swam out and manned the boat and piloted her through a narrow and hardly noticeable break in the reef – the only break in it in a stretch of thirty-five miles! The spot where the landing was made was the only one in that stretch where footing could have been found on the shore; everywhere else precipices came sheer down into forty fathoms of water. Also, in all that stretch this was the only spot where anybody lived.

Within ten days after the landing all the men but one were up and creeping about. Properly, they ought to have killed themselves with the 'food' of the last few days – some of them, at any rate – men who had freighted their stomachs with strips of leather from old boots and with chips from the butter-cask; a freightage which they did not get rid of by digestion, but by other means. The captain and the two passengers did not eat strips and chips, as the sailors did, but *scraped* the boot-leather and the wood, and made a pulp of the scrapings by moistening them with water. The third mate told me that the boots were old and full of holes; then added thoughtfully, 'but the holes digested the best'. Speaking of digestion, here is a remarkable thing, and worth noting: during this strange voyage, and for a while afterward on shore, the bowels of some of the men virtually ceased from their functions; in some cases there was no action for twenty and thirty days, and in one case for forty-four! Sleeping also came to be rare. Yet the men did very well without it. During many days the captain did not sleep at all – twenty-one, I think, on one stretch.

When the landing was made, all the men were successfully protected from overeating except the 'Portyghee'; he escaped the watch and ate an incredible number of bananas: a hundred and fifty-two, the third mate said, but this was undoubtedly an exaggeration; I think it was a hundred and fifty-one. He was already nearly full of leather; it was hanging out of his ears. (I do not state this on the third mate's authority, for we have seen what sort of person he was; I state it on my own.) The 'Portyghee' ought to have died, of course, and even now it seems a pity that he didn't; but he got well, and as early as any of them; and all full of leather, too, the way he was, and butter-timber and handkerchiefs and bananas. Some of the men did eat handkerchiefs in those last days, also socks; and he was one of them.

It is to the credit of the men that they did not kill the rooster that crowed so gallantly mornings. He lived eighteen days, and then stood up and stretched his neck and made a brave, weak effort to do his duty once more, and died in the act. It is a picturesque detail; and so is that rainbow, too – the only one seen in the forty-three days – raising its triumphal arch in the skies for the sturdy fighters to sail under to victory and rescue.

With ten days' provisions Captain Josiah Mitchell performed this memorable voyage of forty-three days and eight hours in an open boat, sailing four thousand miles in reality and thirty-three hundred and sixty by direct courses, and brought every man safe to land. A bright, simple-hearted, unassuming, plucky, and most companionable man. I walked the deck with him twenty-eight days – when I was not copying diaries – and I remember him with reverent honour. If he is alive he is eighty-six years old now.

If I remember rightly, Samuel Ferguson died soon after we reached San Francisco. I do not think he lived to see his home again; his disease had been seriously aggravated by his hardships.

For a time it was hoped that the two quarter-boats would presently be heard of, but this hope suffered disappointment. They went down with all on board, no doubt, not even sparing that knightly chief mate.

The authors of the diaries allowed me to copy them exactly as they were written, and the extracts that I have given are without any smoothing over or revision. These diaries are finely modest and unaffected, and with unconscious and unintentional art they rise toward the climax with graduated and gathering force and swing and dramatic intensity; they sweep you along with a cumulative rush, and when the cry rings out at last, 'Land in sight!' your heart is in your mouth, and for a moment you think it is you that have been saved. The last two paragraphs are not improvable by anybody's art; they are literary gold; and their very pauses and uncompleted sentences have in them an eloquence not reachable by any words.

The interest of this story is unquenchable; it is of the sort that time cannot decay. I have not looked at the diaries for thirty-two years, but I find that they have lost nothing in that time. Lost? They have gained; for by some subtle law all tragic human experiences gain in pathos by the perspective of time. We realise this when in Naples we stand musing over the poor Pompeian mother, lost in the historic storm of volcanic ashes eighteen centuries ago, who lies with her child gripped close to her breast, trying to save it, and whose despair and grief have been preserved for us by the fiery envelope which took her life but eternalised her form and features. She moves us, she haunts us, she stays in our thoughts for many days, we do not know why, for she is nothing to us, she has been nothing to anyone for eighteen centuries; whereas of the like case today we should say, 'Poor thing! it is pitiful,' and forget it in an hour.

The Eskimo Maiden's Romance

'Yes, I will tell you anything about my life that you would like to know, Mr Twain,' she said, in her soft voice, and letting her honest eyes rest placidly upon my face, 'for it is kind and good of you to like me and care to know about me.'

She had been absently scraping blubber-grease from her cheeks with a small bone-knife and transferring it to her fur sleeve, while she watched the Aurora Borealis swing its flaming streamers out of the sky and wash the lonely snow-plain and the templed icebergs with the rich hues of the prism, a spectacle of almost intolerable splendour and beauty; but now she shook off her reverie and prepared to give me the humble little history I had asked for.

She settled herself comfortably on the block of ice which we were using as a sofa, and I made ready to listen.

She was a beautiful creature. I speak from the Eskimo point of view. Others would have thought her a trifle over-plump. She was just twenty years old, and was held to be by far the most bewitching girl in her tribe. Even now, in the open air, with her cumbersome and shapeless fur coat and trousers and boots and vast hood, the beauty of her face at least was apparent; but her figure had to be taken on trust. Among all the guests who came and went, I had seen no girl at her father's hospitable trough who could be called her equal. Yet she was not spoiled. She was sweet and natural and sincere, and if she was aware that she was a belle, there was nothing about her ways to show that she possessed that knowledge.

She had been my daily comrade for a week now, and the better I knew her the better I liked her. She had been tenderly and carefully brought up, in an atmosphere of singularly rare refinement for the polar regions, for her father was the most important man of his tribe and ranked at the top of Eskimo cultivation. I made long dog-sledge trips across the mighty ice floes with Lasca – that was her name – and found her company always pleasant and her conversation agreeable. I went fishing with her, but not in her perilous boat: I merely followed along on the ice and watched her strike her game with her fatally accurate spear. We went sealing together; several times I stood by while she and the family dug blubber from a stranded whale, and once I went part of the way when she was hunting a bear, but turned back before the finish, because at bottom I am afraid of bears.

However, she was ready to begin her story now, and this is what she said:

'Our tribe had always been used to wander about from place to place over the frozen seas, like the other tribes, but my father got tired of that two years ago, and built this great mansion of frozen snow-blocks – look at it; it is seven feet high and three or four times as long as any of the others – and here we have stayed ever since. He was very proud of his house, and that was reasonable; for if you have examined it with care you must have noticed how much finer and completer it is than houses usually are. But if you have not, you must, for you will find it has luxurious appointments that are quite beyond the common. For instance, in that end of it which you have called the "parlour", the raised platform for the accommodation of guests and the family at meals is the largest you have ever seen in any house – is it not so?'

'Yes, you are quite right, Lasca; it is the largest; we have nothing resembling it in even the finest houses in the United States.' This admission made her eyes sparkle with pride and pleasure. I noted that, and took my cue.

'I thought it must have surprised you,' she said. 'And another thing: it is bedded far deeper in furs than is usual; all kinds of furs – seal, sea-otter, silver-grey fox, bear, marten, sable – every kind of fur in profusion; and the same with the ice-block sleeping-benches along the walls, which you call "beds". Are your platforms and sleeping-benches better provided at home?'

'Indeed, they are not, Lasca – they do not begin to be.' That pleased her again. All she was thinking of was the *number* of furs her æsthetic father took the trouble to keep on hand, not their value. I could have told her that those masses of rich furs constituted wealth – or would in my country – but she would not have understood that; those were not the kind of things that ranked as riches with her people. I could have told her that the clothes she had on, or the everyday clothes of the commonest person about her, were worth twelve or fifteen hundred dollars, and that I was not acquainted with anybody at home who wore twelve-hundred-dollar toilets to go fishing in; but she would not have understood it, so I said nothing. She resumed:

'And then the slop-tubs. We have two in the parlour, and two in the rest of the house. It is very seldom that one has two in the parlour. Have you two in the parlour at home?'

The memory of those tubs made me gasp, but I recovered myself before she noticed, and said with effusion:

'Why, Lasca, it is a shame of me to expose my country, and you must not let it go further, for I am speaking to you in confidence; but I give you my word of honour that not even the richest man in the city of New York has two slop-tubs in his drawing-room.'

She clapped her fur-clad hands in innocent delight, and exclaimed:

'Oh, but you cannot mean it, you cannot *mean* it!'

'Indeed, I am in earnest, dear. There is Vanderbilt. Vanderbilt is almost the richest man in the whole world. Now, if I were on my dying bed, I could say to you that not even he has two in his drawing-room. Why, he hasn't even *one* – I wish I may die in my tracks if it isn't true.'

Her lovely eyes stood wide with amazement, and she said, slowly, and with a sort of awe in her voice:

'How strange – how incredible – one is not able to realise it. Is he penurious?'

'No – it isn't that. It isn't the expense he minds, but – er – well, you know, it would look like showing off. Yes, that is it, that is the idea; he is a plain man in his way, and shrinks from display.'

'Why, that humility is right enough,' said Lasca, 'if one does not carry it too far – but what does the place *look* like?'

'Well, necessarily it looks pretty barren and unfinished, but – '

'I should think so! I never heard anything like it. Is it a fine house – that is, otherwise?'

'Pretty fine, yes. It is very well thought of.'

The girl was silent awhile, and sat dreamily gnawing a candle-end, apparently trying to think the thing out. At last she gave her head a little toss and spoke out her opinion with decision:

'Well, to my mind there's a breed of humility which is *itself* a species of showing-off, when you get down to the marrow of it; and when a man is able to afford two slop-tubs in his parlour, and don't do it, it *may* be that he is truly humble-minded, but it's a hundred times more likely that he is just trying to strike the public eye. In my judgment, your Mr Vanderbilt knows what he is about.'

I tried to modify this verdict, feeling that a double slop-tub standard was not a fair one to try everybody by, although a sound enough one in its own habitat; but the girl's head was set, and she was not to be persuaded. Presently she said:

'Do the rich people, with you, have as good sleeping-benches as ours, and made out of as nice broad ice-blocks?'

'Well, they are pretty good – good enough – but they are not made of ice-blocks.'

'I want to know! *Why* aren't they made of ice-blocks?'

I explained the difficulties in the way, and the expensiveness of ice in a country where you have to keep a sharp eye on your ice man or your ice bill will weigh more than your ice. Then she cried out.:

'Dear me, do you *buy* your ice?'

'We most surely do, dear.'

She burst into a gale of guileless laughter, and said:

'Oh, I *never* heard of anything so silly! My, there's plenty of it – it isn't worth anything. Why, there is a hundred miles of it in sight, right now. I wouldn't give a fish bladder for the whole of it.'

'Well, it's because you don't know how to value it, you little provincial muggins. If you had it in New York in midsummer, you could buy all the whales in the market with it.'

She looked at me doubtfully, and said:

'Are you speaking true?'

'Absolutely. I take my oath to it.'

This made her thoughtful. Presently she said, with a little sigh:

'I wish *I* could live there.'

I had merely meant to furnish her a standard of values which she could understand; but my purpose had miscarried. I had only given her the impression that whales were cheap and plenty in New York, and set her mouth to watering for them. It seemed best to try to mitigate the evil which I had done, so I said:

'But you wouldn't care for whale meat if you lived there. Nobody does.'

'What!'

'Indeed they don't.'

'*Why* don't they?'

'Wel–l–l, I hardly know. It's prejudice, I think. Yes, that is it – just prejudice. I reckon somebody that hadn't anything better to do started a prejudice against it, some time or other, and once you get a caprice like that fairly going, you know, it will last no end of time.'

'That is true – *perfectly* true,' said the girl, reflectively. 'Like our prejudice against soap, here – our tribes had a prejudice against soap at first, you know.'

I glanced at her to see if she was in earnest. Evidently she was. I hesitated, then said, cautiously:

'But pardon me. They *had* a prejudice against soap? Had?' – with falling inflection.

'Yes – but that was only at first; nobody would eat it.'

'Oh – I understand. I didn't get your idea before.'

She resumed:

'It was just a prejudice. The first time soap came here from the foreigners, nobody liked it; but as soon as it got to be fashionable, everybody liked it, and now everybody has it that can afford it. Are you fond of it?'

'Yes, indeed! I should die if I couldn't have it – especially here . Do you like it?'

'I just *adore* it! Do you like candles?'

'I regard them as an absolute necessity. Are you fond of them?'

Her eyes fairly danced, and she exclaimed:

'Oh! Don't mention it! Candles! – and soap! – '

'And fish-interiors! – '

'And train-oil! – '

'And slush! – '

'And whale-blubber! – '

'And carrion! and sour-krout! and beeswax! and tar! and turpentine! and molasses! and – '

'Don't – oh, don't – I shall expire with ecstasy! – '

'And then serve it all up in a slush-bucket, and invite the neighbours and sail in!'

But this vision of an ideal feast was too much for her, and she swooned away, poor thing. I rubbed snow in her face and brought her to, and after a while got her excitement cooled down. By and by she drifted into her story again:

'So we began to live here, in the fine house. But I was not happy. The reason was this: I was born for love; for me there could be no true happiness without it. I wanted to be loved for myself alone. I wanted an idol, and I wanted to be my idol's idol; nothing less than mutual idolatry would satisfy my fervent nature. I had suitors in plenty – in over-plenty, indeed – but in each and every case they had a fatal defect; sooner or later I discovered that defect – not one of them failed to betray it – it was not me they wanted, but my wealth.'

'Your wealth?'

'Yes; for my father is much the richest man in this tribe – or in any tribe in these regions.'

I wondered what her father's wealth consisted of. It couldn't be the house – anybody could build its mate. It couldn't be the furs – they were not valued. It couldn't be the sledge, the dogs, the harpoons, the boat, the bone fish-hooks and needles, and such things – no, these were not wealth. Then what could it be that made this man so rich and brought this swarm of sordid suitors to his house? It seemed to me, finally, that the best way to find out would be to ask. So I did it. The girl was so manifestly gratified by the question that I saw she had been aching to have me ask it. She was suffering fully as much to tell as I was to know. She snuggled confidentially up to me and said:

'Guess how much he is worth – you never can!'

I pretended to consider the matter deeply, she watching my anxious and labouring countenance with a devouring and delighted interest; and when, at last, I gave it up and begged her to appease my longing by telling me herself how much this polar Vanderbilt was worth, she put her mouth close to my ear and whispered, impressively:

'*Twenty-two fish-hooks* – not bone, but foreign – *made out of real iron!*'

Then she sprang back dramatically, to observe the effect. I did my level best not to disappoint her.

I turned pale and murmured:

'Great Scott!'

'It's as true as you live, Mr Twain!'

Lasca, you are deceiving me – you cannot mean it.'

She was frightened and troubled. She exclaimed:

'Mr Twain, every word of it is true – every word. You believe me – you *do* believe me, now *don't* you? *Say* you believe me – *do* say you believe me!'

'I – well, yes, I do – I am *trying* to. But it was all so *sudden*. So sudden and prostrating. You shouldn't do such a thing in that sudden way. It – '

'Oh, I'm *so* sorry! If I had only thought – '

'Well, it's all right, and I don't blame you any more, for you are young and thoughtless, and of course you couldn't foresee what an effect – '

'But oh, dear, I ought certainly to have *known* better. Why – '

'You see, Lasca, if you had said five or six hooks, to start with, and then gradually – '

'Oh, I see, I see – then gradually added one, and then two, and then – ah, why couldn't I have thought of that!'

'Never mind, child, it's all right – I am better now – I shall be over it in a little while. *But* – to spring the whole twenty-two on a person unprepared and not very strong anyway – '

'Oh, it *was* a crime! But you forgive me – say you forgive me. Do!'

After harvesting a good deal of very pleasant coaxing and petting and persuading, I forgave her and she was happy again, and by and by she got under way with her narrative once more. I presently discovered that the family treasury contained still another feature – a jewel of some sort, apparently – and that she was trying to get around speaking squarely about it, lest I get paralysed again. But I wanted to know about that thing, too, and urged her to tell me what it was. She was afraid. But I insisted, and said I would brace myself this time and be prepared, then the shock would not hurt me. She was full of misgivings, but the temptation to reveal that marvel to me and enjoy my astonishment and admiration was too strong for her, and she confessed that she had it on her person, and said that if I was *sure* I was prepared – and so on and so on – and with that she reached into her bosom and brought out a battered square of brass, watching my eye anxiously the while. I fell over against her in a quite well-acted faint, which delighted her heart and nearly frightened it out of her, too, at the same time. When I came to and got calm, she was eager to know what I thought of her jewel.

'What do I think of it? I think it is the most exquisite thing I ever saw.'

'Do you really? How nice of you to say that! But it *is* a love, now isn't it?'

'Well, I should say so! I'd rather own it than the equator.'

'I thought you would admire it,' she said. 'I think it is *so* lovely. And there isn't another one in all these latitudes. People have come all the way from the Open Polar Sea to look at it. Did you ever see one before?'

I said no, this was the first one I had ever seen. It cost me a pang to tell that generous lie, for I had seen a million of them in my time, this humble jewel of hers being nothing but a battered old New York Central baggage check.

'Land!' said I, 'you don't go about with it on your person this way, alone and with no protection, not even a dog?'

'Ssh! not so loud,' she said. 'Nobody knows I carry it with me. They think it is in papa's treasury. That is where it generally is.'

'Where is the treasury?'

It was a blunt question, and for a moment she looked startled and a little suspicious, but I said:

'Oh, come, don't you be afraid about me. At home we have seventy millions of people, and although I say it myself that shouldn't, there is not one person among them all but would trust me with untold fish-hooks.'

This reassured her, and she told me where the hooks were hidden in the house. Then she wandered from her course to brag a little about the size of the sheets of transparent ice that formed the windows of the mansion, and asked me if I had ever seen their like at home, and I came right out frankly and confessed that I hadn't, which pleased her more than she could find words to dress her gratification in. It was so easy to please her, and such a pleasure to do it, that I went on and said:

'Ah, Lasca, you *are* a fortunate girl! – this beautiful house, this dainty jewel, that rich treasure, all this elegant snow, and sumptuous icebergs and limitless sterility, and public bears and walruses, and noble freedom and largeness, and everybody's admiring eyes upon you, and everybody's homage and respect at your command without the asking; young, rich, beautiful, sought, courted, envied, not a requirement unsatisfied, not a desire ungratified, nothing to wish for that you cannot have – it is immeasurable good fortune! I have seen myriads of girls, but none of whom these extraordinary things could be truthfully said but you alone. And you are worthy – worthy of it all, Lasca – I believe it in my heart.'

It made her infinitely proud and happy to hear me say this, and she thanked me over and over again for that closing remark, and her voice and eyes showed that she was touched. Presently she said:

'Still, it is not all sunshine – there is a cloudy side. The burden of wealth is a heavy one to bear. Sometimes I have doubted if it were not better to be poor – at least not inordinately rich. It pains me to see neighbouring tribesmen stare as they pass by, and overhear them say, reverently, one to another, "There – that is she – the millionaire's daughter!" And sometimes they say sorrowfully, "She is rolling in fish-hooks, and I – I have nothing." It breaks my heart. When I was a child and we were poor, we slept with the door open, if we chose, but now – now we have to have a night watchman. In those days my father was gentle and courteous to all; but now he is austere and haughty, and cannot abide familiarity. Once his family were his sole thought, but now he goes about thinking of his fish-hooks all the time. And his wealth makes everybody cringing and obsequious to him. Formerly nobody laughed at his jokes, they being always stale and far-fetched and poor, and destitute of the one element that can really justify a joke – the element of humour; but now everybody laughs and cackles at those dismal things, and if any fails to do it my father is deeply displeased, and shows it. Formerly his opinion was not sought upon any matter and was not valuable when he volunteered it; it has that infirmity yet, but nevertheless it is sought by all and applauded by all – and he helps do the applauding himself, having no true delicacy and a plentiful want of tact. He has lowered the tone of all our tribe. Once they were a frank and manly race, now they are measly hypocrites, and sodden with servility. In my heart of hearts I hate all the ways of millionaires! Our tribe was once plain, simple folk, and content with the bone fish-hooks of their fathers; now they are eaten up with avarice and would sacrifice every sentiment of honour and honesty to possess themselves of the debasing iron fish-hooks of the foreigner. However, I must not dwell on these sad things. As I have said, it was my dream to be loved for myself alone.

'At last, this dream seemed about to be fulfilled. A stranger came by, one day, who said his name was Kalula. I told him my name, and he said he loved me. My heart gave a great bound of gratitude and pleasure, for I had loved him at sight, and now I said so. He took me to his breast and said he would not wish to be happier than he was now. We went strolling together far over the ice floes, telling all about each other, and planning, oh, the loveliest future! When we were tired at last we sat down and ate, for he had soap and candles and I had brought along some blubber. We were hungry, and nothing was ever so good.

'He belonged to a tribe whose haunts were far to the north, and I found that he had never heard of my father, which rejoiced me exceedingly. I mean he had heard of the millionaire, but had never heard his name – so, you see, he could not know that I was the heiress. You may be sure that I did not tell him. I was loved for myself at last, and was satisfied. I was so happy – oh, happier than you can think!

'By and by it was toward supper time, and I led him home. As we approached our house he was amazed, and cried out:

' "How splendid! Is *that* your father's?"

'It gave me a pang to hear that tone and see that admiring light in his eye, but the feeling quickly passed away, for I loved him so, and he looked so handsome and noble. All my family of aunts and uncles and cousins were pleased with him, and many guests were called in, and the house was shut up tight and the rag-lamps lighted, and when every-thing was hot and comfortable and suffocating, we began a joyous feast in celebration of my betrothal.

'When the feast was over, my father's vanity overcame him, and he could not resist the temptation to show off his riches and let Kalula see what grand good fortune he had stumbled into – and mainly, of course, he wanted to enjoy the poor man's amazement. I could have cried – but it would have done no good to try to dissuade my father, so I said nothing, but merely sat there and suffered.

'My father went straight to the hiding place, in full sight of everybody, and got out the fish-hooks and brought them and flung them scatteringly over my head, so that they fell in glittering confusion on the platform at my lover's knee.

'Of course, the astounding spectacle took the poor lad's breath away. He could only stare in stupid astonishment, and wonder how a single individual could possess such incredible riches. Then presently he glanced brilliantly up and exclaimed:

' "Ah, it is *you* who are the renowned millionaire!"

'My father and all the rest burst into shouts of happy laughter, and when my father gathered the treasure carelessly up as if it might be mere rubbish and of no consequence, and carried it back to its place, poor Kalula's surprise was a study. He said:

' "Is it possible that you put such things away without counting them?"

'My father delivered a vainglorious horse-laugh, and said:

' "Well, truly, a body may know *you* have never been rich, since a mere matter of a fish-hook or two is such a mighty matter in your eyes."

'Kalula was confused, and hung his head, but said:

' "Ah, indeed, sir, I was never worth the value of the barb of one of those precious things, and I have never seen any man before who was so rich in them as to render the counting of his hoard worthwhile, since the wealthiest man I have ever known, till now, was possessed of but three."

'My foolish father roared again with jejune delight, and allowed the impression to remain that he was not accustomed to count his hooks and keep sharp watch over them. He was showing off, you see. Count them? Why, he counted them every day!

'I had met and got acquainted with my darling just at dawn; I had brought him home just at dark, three hours afterward – for the days were shortening toward the six-months night at that time. We kept up the festivities many hours; then, at last, the guests departed and the rest of us distributed ourselves along the walls on sleeping-benches, and soon all were steeped in dreams but me. I was too happy, too excited, to sleep. After I had lain quiet a long, long time, a dim form passed by me and was swallowed up in the gloom that pervaded the farther end of the house. I could not make out who it was, or whether it was man or woman. Presently that figure or another one passed me going the other way. I wondered what it all meant, but wondering did no good; and while I was still wondering, I fell asleep.

'I do not know how long I slept, but at last I came suddenly broad awake and heard my father say in a terrible voice, "By the great Snow God, there's a fish-hook gone!" Something told me that that meant sorrow for me, and the blood in my veins turned cold. The presentiment was confirmed in the same instant: my father shouted, "Up, everybody, and seize the stranger!" Then there was an outburst of cries and curses from all sides, and a wild rush of dim forms through the obscurity. I flew to my beloved's help, but what could I do but wait and wring my hands? – he was already fenced away from me by a living wall, he was being bound hand and foot. Not until he was secured would they let me get to him. I flung myself upon his poor insulted form and cried my grief out upon his breast, while my father and all my family scoffed at me and heaped threats and shameful epithets upon him. He bore his ill usage with a tranquil dignity which endeared him to me more than ever, and made me proud and happy to suffer with him and for him. I heard my father order that the elders of the tribe be called together to try my Kalula for his life.

' "What?" I said, "before any search has been made for the lost hook?"'

' "Lost hook!" they all shouted, in derision; and my father added, mockingly, "Stand back, everybody, and be properly serious – she is going to hunt up that *lost* hook; oh, without doubt she will find it!" – whereat they all laughed again.

'I was not disturbed – I had no fears, no doubts. I said:

' "It is for you to laugh now; it is your turn. But ours is coming; wait and see."

'I got a rag-lamp. I thought I should find that miserable thing in one little moment; and I set about the matter with such confidence that those people grew grave, beginning to suspect that perhaps they had been too hasty. But, alas and alas! – oh, the bitterness of that search! There was deep silence while one might count his fingers ten or twelve times, then my heart began to sink, and around me the mockings began again, and grew steadily louder and more assured, until at last, when I gave up, they burst into volley after volley of cruel laughter.

'None will ever know what I suffered then. But my love was my support and my strength, and I took my rightful place at my Kalula's side, and put my arm about his neck, and whispered in his ear, saying:

' "You are innocent, my own – that I know; but say it to me yourself, for my comfort, then I can bear whatever is in store for us.'

'He answered:

' "As surely as I stand upon the brink of death at this moment, I am innocent. Be comforted, then, O bruised heart; be at peace, O thou breath of my nostrils, life of my life!"

' "Now, then, let the elders come!" – and as I said the words there was a gathering sound of crunching snow outside, and then a vision of stooping forms filing in at the door – the elders.

'My father formally accused the prisoner, and detailed the happenings of the night. He said that the watchman was outside the door, and that in the house were none but the family and the stranger. "Would the family steal their own property?"

'He paused. The elders sat silent many minutes; at last, one after another said to his neighbour, "This looks bad for the stranger' – sorrowful words for me to hear. Then my father sat down. O miserable, miserable me! at that very moment I could have proved my darling innocent, but I did not know it!

'The chief of the court asked:

' "Is there any here to defend the prisoner?"

'I rose and said:

' "Why should *he* steal that hook, or any or all of them? In another day he would have been heir to the whole!"

'I stood waiting. There was a long silence, the steam from the many breaths rising about me like a fog. At last, one elder after another nodded his head slowly several times, and muttered, "There is force in what the child has said". Oh, the heartlift that was in those words! – so transient, but oh, so precious! I sat down.

' "If any would say further, let him speak now, or after hold his peace," said the chief of the court.

'My father rose and said:

' "In the night a form passed by me in the gloom, going toward the treasury, and presently returned. I think, now, it was the stranger."

'Oh, I was like to swoon! I had supposed that that was my secret; not the grip of the great Ice God himself could have dragged it out of my heart.

The chief of the court said sternly to my poor Kalula:

' "Speak!"

'Kalula hesitated, then answered:

' "It was I. I could not sleep for thinking of the beautiful hooks. I went there and kissed them and fondled them, to appease my spirit and drown it in a harmless joy, then I put them back. I may have dropped one, but I stole none."

'Oh, a fatal admission to make in such a place! There was an awful hush. I knew he had pronounced his own doom, and that all was over. On every face you could see the words hieroglyphed: "It is a confession! – and paltry, lame, and thin."

'I sat drawing in my breath in faint gasps – and waiting. Presently, I heard the solemn words I knew were coming; and each word, as it came, was a knife in my heart:

' "It is the command of the court that the accused be subjected to the *trial by water*."

'Oh, curses be upon the head of him who brought "trial by water" to our land! It came, generations ago, from some far country, that lies none knows where. Before that, our fathers used augury and other unsure methods of trial, and doubtless some poor, guilty creatures escaped with their lives sometimes; but it is not so with trial by water, which is an invention by wiser men than we poor, ignorant savages are. By it the innocent are proved innocent, without doubt or question, for they drown; and the guilty are proven guilty with the same certainty, for they do not drown. My heart was breaking in my bosom, for I said, "He is innocent, and he will go down under the waves and I shall never see him more."

'I never left his side after that. I mourned in his arms all the precious hours, and he poured out the deep stream of his love upon me, and oh, I was so miserable and so happy! At last, they tore him from me, and I followed sobbing after them, and saw them fling him into the sea – then I covered my face with my hands. Agony? Oh, I know the deepest deeps of that word!

'The next moment the people burst into a shout of malicious joy, and I took away my hands, startled. Oh, bitter sight – he was *swimming!*

'My heart turned instantly to stone, to ice. I said, "He was guilty, and he lied to me!"

'I turned my back in scorn and went my way homeward.

'They took him far out to sea and set him on an iceberg that was drifting southward in the great waters. Then my family came home, and my father said to me:

' "Your thief sent his dying message to you, saying, 'Tell her I am innocent, and that all the days and all the hours and all the minutes while I starve and perish I shall love her and think of her and bless the day that gave me sight of her sweet face.' Quite pretty, even poetical!"

'I said, "He is dirt – let me never hear mention of him again." And oh, to think – he *was* innocent all the time!

'Nine months – nine dull, sad months – went by, and at last came the day of the Great Annual Sacrifice, when all the maidens of the tribe wash their faces and comb their hair. With the first sweep of my comb, out came the fatal fish-hook from where it had been all those months nestling, and I fell fainting into the arms of my remorseful father! Groaning, he said, "We murdered him, and I shall never smile again!" He has kept his word. Listen: from that day to this not a month goes by that I do not comb my hair. But oh, where is the good of it all now!'

So ended the poor maid's humble little tale – whereby we learn that, since a hundred million dollars in New York and twenty-two fish-hooks on the border of the Arctic Circle represent the same financial supremacy, a man in straitened circumstances is a fool to stay in New York when he can buy ten cents' worth of fish-hooks and emigrate.

My First Lie, and How I Got Out of It

As I understand it, what you desire is information about 'my first lie, and how I got out of it'. I was born in 1835; I am well along, and my memory is not as good as it was. If you had asked about my first truth it would have been easier for me and kinder of you, for I remember that fairly well; I remember it as if it were last week. The family think it was the week before, but that is flattery and probably has a selfish project back of it. When a person has become seasoned by experience and has reached the age of sixty-four, which is the age of discretion, he likes a family compliment as well as ever, but he does not lose his head over it as in the old innocent days.

I do not remember my first lie, it is too far back; but I remember my second one very well. I was nine days old at the time, and had noticed that if a pin was sticking in me and I advertised it in the usual fashion, I was lovingly petted and coddled and pitied in a most agreeable way and got a ration between meals besides. It was human nature to want to get these riches, and I fell. I lied about the pin – advertising one when there wasn't any. You would have done it; George Washington did it; anybody would have done it. During the first half of my life I never knew a child that was able to rise above that temptation and keep from telling that lie. Up to 1867 all the civilised children that were ever born into the world were liars – including George. Then the safety-pin came in and blocked the game. But is that reform worth anything? No; for it is reform by force and has no virtue in it; it merely stops that form of lying; it doesn't impair the disposition to lie, by a shade. It is the cradle application of conversion by fire and sword, or of the temperance principle through prohibition.

To return to that early lie. They found no pin, and they realised that another liar had been added to the world's supply. For by grace of a rare inspiration, a quite commonplace but seldom noticed fact was borne in upon their understandings – that almost all lies are acts, and speech has no part in them. Then, if they examined a little further they recognised that all people are liars from the cradle onward, without exception, and that they begin to lie as soon as they wake in the morning, and keep it up, without rest or refreshment, until they go to sleep at night. If they arrived at that truth it probably grieved them – did, if they had been heedlessly and ignorantly educated by their books and teachers; for why should a person grieve over a thing which by the eternal law of his make he cannot help? He didn't invent the law; it is merely his business to obey it and keep still; join the universal conspiracy and keep so still that he shall deceive his fellow-conspirators into imagining that he doesn't know that the law exists. It is what we all do – we that know. I am speaking of the lie of silent assertion; we can tell it without saying a word, and we all do it – we that know. In the magnitude of its territorial spread it is one of the most majestic lies that the civilisations make it their sacred and anxious care to guard and watch and propagate.

For instance: It would not be possible for a humane and intelligent person to invent a rational excuse for slavery; yet you will remember that in the early days of the emancipation agitation in the North, the agitators got but small help or countenance from anyone. Argue and plead and pray as they might, they could not break the universal stillness that reigned, from pulpit and press all the way down to the bottom of society – the clammy stillness created and maintained by the lie of silent assertion – the silent assertion that there wasn't anything going on in which humane and intelligent people were interested.

From the beginning of the Dreyfus case to the end of it, all France, except a couple of dozen moral paladins, lay under the smother of the silent-assertion lie that no wrong was being done to a persecuted and unoffending man. The like smother was over England lately, a good half of the population silently letting on that they were not aware that Mr Chamberlain was trying to manufacture a war in South Africa and was willing to pay fancy prices for the materials.

Now there we have instances of three prominent ostensible civilisations working the silent-assertion lie. Could one find other instances in the three countries? I think so. Not so very many, perhaps, but say a billion – just so as to keep within bounds. Are those countries working that kind of lie, day in and day out, in thousands and thousands of varieties, without ever resting? Yes, we know that to be true. The universal conspiracy of the silent assertion lie is hard at work always and everywhere, and always in the interest of a stupidity or a sham, never in the interest of a thing fine or respectable. Is it the most timid and shabby of all lies? It seems to have the look of it. For ages and ages it has mutely laboured in the interest of despotisms and aristocracies and chattel slaveries, and military slaveries, and religious slaveries, and has kept them alive; keeps them alive yet, here and there and yonder, all about the globe; and will go on keeping them alive until the silent-assertion lie retires from business – the silent assertion that nothing is going on which fair and intelligent men are aware of and are engaged by their duty to try to stop.

What I am arriving at is this: When whole races and peoples conspire to propagate gigantic mute lies in the interest of tyrannies and shams, why should we care anything about the trifling lies told by individuals? Why should we try to make it appear that abstention from lying is a virtue? Why should we want to beguile ourselves in that way? Why should we without shame help the nation lie, and then be ashamed to do a little lying on our own account? Why shouldn't we be honest and honourable, and lie every time we get a chance? That is to say, why shouldn't we be consistent, and either lie all the time or not at all? Why should we help the nation lie the whole day long and then object to telling one little individual private lie in our own interest to go to bed on? Just for the refreshment of it, I mean, and to take the rancid taste out of our mouth.

Here in England they have the oddest ways. They won't tell a spoken lie – nothing can persuade them. Except in a large moral interest, like politics or religion, I mean. To tell a spoken lie to get even the poorest little personal advantage out of it is a thing which is impossible to them. They make me ashamed of myself sometimes, they are so bigoted. They will not even tell a lie for the fun of it; they will not tell it when it hasn't even a suggestion of damage or advantage in it for anyone. This has a restraining influence upon me in spite of reason, and I am always getting out of practice.

Of course, they tell all sorts of little unspoken lies, just like anybody; but they don't notice it until their attention is called to it. They have got me so that sometimes I never tell a verbal lie now except in a modified form; and even in the modified form they don't approve of it. Still, that is as far as I can go in the interest of the growing friendly relations between the two countries; I must keep some of my self-respect – and my health. I can live on a low diet, but I can't get along on no sustenance at all.

Of course, there are times when these people have to come out with a spoken lie, for that is a thing which happens to everybody once in a while, and would happen to the angels if they came down here much. Particularly to the angels, in fact, for the lies I speak of are self-sacrificing ones told for a generous object, not a mean one; but even when these people tell a lie of that sort it seems to scare them and unsettle their minds. It is a wonderful thing to see, and shows that they are all insane. In fact, it is a country full of the most interesting superstitions.

I have an English friend of twenty-five years' standing, and yesterday when we were coming downtown on top of the bus I happened to tell him a lie – a modified one, of course; a half-breed, a mulatto: I can't seem to tell any other kind now, the market is so flat. I was explaining to him how I got out of an embarrassment in Austria last year. I do not know what might have become of me if I hadn't happened to remember to tell the police that I belonged to the same family as the Prince of Wales. That made everything pleasant and they let me go; and apologised, too, and were ever so kind and obliging and polite, and couldn't do too much for me, and explained how the mistake came to be made, and promised to hang the officer that did it, and hoped I would let bygones be bygones and not say anything about it; and I said they could depend on me. My friend said, austerely:

'You call it a modified lie? Where is the modification?'

I explained that it lay in the form of my statement to the police.

'I didn't say I belonged to the royal family: I only said I belonged to the same family as the Prince – meaning the human family, of course; and if those people had had any penetration they would have known it. I can't go around furnishing brains to the police; it is not to be expected.'

'How did you feel after that performance?'

'Well, of course I was distressed to find that the police had misunderstood me, but as long as I had not told any lie I knew there was no occasion to sit up nights and worry about it.'

My friend struggled with the case several minutes, turning it over and examining it in his mind; then he said that so far as he could see the modification was itself a lie, being a misleading reservation of an explanatory fact; so I had told two lies instead of one.

'I wouldn't have done it,' said he: 'I have never told a lie, and I should be very sorry to do such a thing.'

Just then he lifted his hat and smiled a basketful of surprised and delighted smiles down at a gentleman who was passing in a hansom.

'Who was that, G——?'

'I don't know.'

'Then why did you do that?'

'Because I saw he thought he knew me and was expecting it of me. If I hadn't done it he would have been hurt. I didn't want to embarrass him before the whole street.'

'Well, your heart was right, G—, and your act was right. What you did was kindly and courteous and beautiful; I would have done it myself: but it was a lie.'

'A lie? I didn't say a word. How do you make it out?'

'I know you didn't speak, still you said to him very plainly and enthusiastically in dumb show, "Hello! you in town? Awful glad to see you, old fellow; when did you get back?" Concealed in your actions was what you have called "a misleading reservation of an explanatory fact" – the fact that you had never seen him before. You expressed joy in encountering him – a lie; and you made that reservation – another lie. It was my pair over again. But don't be troubled – we all do it.'

Two hours later, at dinner, when quite other matters were being discussed, he told how he happened along once just in the nick of time to do a great service for a family who were old friends of his. The head of it had suddenly died in circumstances and surroundings of a ruinously disgraceful character. If known, the facts would break the hearts of the innocent family and put upon them a load of unendurable shame. There was no help but in a giant lie, and he girded up his loins and told it.

'The family never found out, G—?'

'Never. In all these years they have never suspected. They were proud of him, and always had reason to be; they are proud of him yet, and to them his memory is sacred and stainless and beautiful.'

'They had a narrow escape, G—.'

'Indeed they had.'

'For the very next man that came along might have been one of these heartless and shameless truthmongers. You have told the truth a million times in your life, G—, but that one golden lie atones for it all. Persevere.'

Some may think me not strict enough in my morals, but that position is hardly tenable. There are many kinds of lying which I do not approve. I do not like an injurious lie, except when it injures somebody else; and I do not like the lie of bravado, nor the lie of virtuous ecstasy: the latter was affected by Bryant, the former by Carlyle.

Mr Bryant said, 'Truth crushed to earth will rise again.'

I have taken medals at thirteen world's fairs, and may claim to be not without capacity, but I never told as big a one as that which Mr Bryant was playing to the gallery; we all do it. Carlyle said, in substance, this – I do not remember the exact words: 'This gospel is eternal – that a lie shall not live.'

I have a reverent affection for Carlyle's books, and have read his *Revolution* eight times; and so I prefer to think he was not entirely at himself when he told that one. To me it is plain that he said it in a moment of excitement, when chasing Americans out of his backyard with brickbats. They used to go there and worship. At bottom he was probably fond of them, but he was always able to conceal it. He kept bricks for them, but he was not a good shot, and it is a matter of history that when he fired they dodged, and carried off the brick; for as a nation we like relics, and so long as we get them we do not much care what the reliquary thinks about it. I am quite sure that when he told that large one about a lie not being able to live, he had just missed an American and was over-excited. He told it above thirty years ago, but it is alive yet; alive, and very healthy and hearty, and likely to outlive any fact in history. Carlyle was truthful when calm, but give him Americans enough and bricks enough and he could have taken medals himself.

As regards that time that George Washington told the truth, a word must be said, of course. It is the principal jewel in the crown of America, and it is but natural that we should work it for all it is worth, as Milton says in his *Lay of the Last Minstrel*. It was a timely and judicious truth, and I should have told it myself in the circumstances. But I should have stopped there. It was a stately truth, a lofty truth – a Tower; and I think it was a mistake to go on and distract attention from its sublimity by building another Tower alongside of it fourteen times as high. I refer to his remark that he 'could not lie'. I should have fed that to the marines: or left it to Carlyle; it is just in his style. It would have taken a medal at any European fair, and would have got an Honourable Mention even at Chicago if it had been saved up. But let it pass: the Father of his Country was excited. I have been in those circumstances, and I recollect.

With the truth he told I have no objection to offer, as already indicated. I think it was not premeditated, but an inspiration. With his fine military mind, he had probably arranged to let his brother Edward in for the cherry-tree results, but by an inspiration he saw his opportunity in time and took advantage of it. By telling the truth he could astonish his father; his father would tell the neighbours; the neighbours would spread it; would travel to all firesides; in the end it would make him President, and not only that, but First President. He was a far-seeing boy and would be likely to think of these things. Therefore, to my mind, he stands justified for what he did. But not for the other Tower: it was a mistake. Still, I don't know about that; upon reflection I think perhaps it wasn't. For indeed it is that Tower that makes the other one live. If he hadn't said 'I cannot tell a lie,' there would have been no convulsion. That was the earthquake that rocked the planet. That is the kind of statement that lives forever, and a fact barnacled to it has a good chance to share its immortality.

To sum up, on the whole I am satisfied with things the way they are. There is a prejudice against the spoken lie, but none against any other, and by examination and mathematical computation I find that the proportion of the spoken lie to the other varieties is as 1 to 22,894. Therefore the spoken lie is of no consequence, and it is not worth while to go around fussing about it and trying to make believe that it is an important matter. The silent colossal National Lie that is the support and confederate of all the tyrannies and shams and inequalities and unfairnesses that afflict the peoples – that is the one to throw bricks and sermons at. But let us be judicious and let somebody else begin.

And then – But I have wandered from my text. How did I get out of my second lie? I think I got out with honour, but I cannot be sure, for it was a long time ago and some of the details have faded out of my memory. I recollect that I was reversed and stretched across someone's knee, and that something happened, but I cannot now remember what it was. I think there was music; but it is all dim now and blurred by the lapse of time, and this may be only a senile fancy.

The Belated Russian Passport

One Fly makes a Summer – *Pudd'nhead Wilson's Calendar*

❦ I ❦

A great beer-saloon in the Friedrichstrasse, Berlin, toward mid-afternoon. At a hundred round tables gentlemen sat smoking and drinking; flitting here and there and everywhere were white-aproned waiters bearing foaming mugs to the thirsty. At a table near the main entrance were grouped half a dozen lively young fellows – American students – drinking goodbye to a visiting Yale youth on his travels, who had been spending a few days in the German capital.

'But why do you cut your tour short in the middle, Parrish?' asked one of the students. 'I wish I had your chance. What do you want to go home for?'

'Yes,' said another, 'what is the idea? You want to explain, you know, because it looks like insanity. Homesick?'

A girlish blush rose in Parrish's fresh young face, and after a little hesitation he confessed that that was his trouble.

'I was never away from home before,' he said, 'and every day I get more and more lonesome. I have not seen a friend for weeks, and it's been horrible. I meant to stick the trip through, for pride's sake, but seeing you boys has finished me. It's been heaven to me, and I can't take up that companionless dreariness again. If I had company – but I haven't, you know, so it's no use. They used to call me Miss Nancy when I was a small chap, and I reckon I'm that yet – girlish and timorous; and all that. I ought to have *been* a girl! I can't stand it; I'm going home.'

The boys rallied him good-naturedly, and said he was making the mistake of his life; and one of them added that he ought at least to see St Petersburg before turning back.

'Don't!' said Parrish, appealingly. 'It was my dearest dream, and I'm throwing it away. Don't say a word more on that head, for I'm made of water, and can't stand out against anybody's persuasion. I *can't* go alone; I think I should die.' He slapped his breast pocket, and added: 'Here is my protection against a change of mind; I've bought ticket and sleeper for Paris, and I leave tonight. Drink, now – this is on me – bumpers – this is for home!'

The goodbyes were said, and Alfred Parrish was left to his thoughts and his loneliness. But for a moment only. A sturdy middle-aged man with a brisk and businesslike bearing, and an air of decision and confidence suggestive of military training, came bustling from the next table, and seated himself at Parrish's side, and began to speak, with concentrated interest and earnestness. His eyes, his face, his person, his whole system, seemed to exude energy. He was full of steam – racing pressure – one could almost hear his gauge-cocks sing. He extended a frank hand, shook Parrish's cordially, and said, with a most convincing air of strenuous conviction:

'Ah, but you *mustn't*; really you mustn't; it would be the greatest mistake; you would always regret it. Be persuaded, I beg you; don't do it – don't!'

There was such a friendly note in it, and such a seeming of genuineness, that it brought a sort of uplift to the youth's despondent spirits, and a telltale moisture betrayed itself in his eyes, an unintentional confession that he was touched and grateful. The alert stranger noted that sign, was quite content with that response, and followed up his advantage without waiting for a spoken one:

'No, don't do it; it would be a mistake. I have heard everything that was said – you will pardon that – I was so close by that I couldn't help it. And it troubled me to think that you would cut your travels short when you really *want* to see St Petersburg, and are right here almost in sight of it! Reconsider it – ah, you *must* reconsider it. It is such a short distance – it is very soon done and very soon over – and think what a memory it will be!'

Then he went on and made a picture of the Russian capital and its wonders, which made Alfred Parrish's mouth water and his roused spirits cry out with longing. Then –

'Of course you must see St Petersburg – you *must!* Why, it will be a joy to you – a joy! I know, because I know the place as familiarly as I know my own birthplace in America. Ten years – I've known it ten years. Ask anybody there; they'll tell you; they all know me – Major Jackson. The very dogs know me. Do go; oh, you must go; you must, indeed.'

Alfred Parrish was quivering with eagerness now. He would go. His face said it as plainly as his tongue could have done it. Then – the old shadow fell, and he said, sorrowfully:

'Oh no – no, it's no use; I can't. I should die of the loneliness.'

The Major said, with astonishment: 'The loneliness! Why, I'm going *with* you!'

It was startlingly unexpected. And not quite pleasant. Things were moving too rapidly. Was this a trap? Was this stranger a sharper? Whence all this gratuitous interest in a wandering and unknown lad? Then he glanced at the Major's frank and winning and beaming face, and was ashamed; and wished he knew how to get out of this scrape without hurting the feelings of its contriver. But he was not handy in matters of diplomacy, and went at the difficulty with conscious awkwardness and small confidence. He said, with a quite overdone show of unselfishness:

'Oh no, no, you are too kind; I couldn't – I couldn't allow you to put yourself to such an inconvenience on my – '

'Inconvenience? None in the world, my boy; I was going tonight, anyway; I leave in the express at nine. Come! we'll go together. You shan't be lonely a single minute. Come along – say the word!'

So that excuse had failed. What to do now? Parrish was disheartened; it seemed to him that no subterfuge which his poor invention could contrive would ever rescue him from these toils. Still, he must make another effort, and he did; and before he had finished his new excuse he thought he recognised that it was unanswerable:

'Ah, but most unfortunately luck is against me, and it is impossible. Look at these' – and he took out his tickets and laid them on the table. 'I am booked through to Paris, and I couldn't get these tickets and baggage coupons changed for St Petersburg, of course, and would have to lose the money; and if I could afford to lose the money I should be rather short after I bought the new tickets – for there is all the cash I've got about me' – and he laid a five-hundred-mark banknote on the table.

In a moment the Major had the tickets and coupons and was on his feet, and saying, with enthusiasm:

'Good! It's all right, and everything safe. They'll change the tickets and baggage pasters for *me*; they all know me – everybody knows me. Sit right where you are; I'll be back right away.' Then he reached for the banknote, and added, 'I'll take this along, for there will be a little extra pay on the new tickets, maybe' – and the next moment he was flying out at the door.

❧ 2 ❧

Alfred Parrish was paralysed. It was all so sudden. So sudden, so daring, so incredible, so impossible. His mouth was open, but his tongue wouldn't work; he tried to shout 'Stop him', but his lungs were empty; he wanted to pursue, but his legs refused to do anything but tremble; then they gave way under him and let him down into his chair. His throat was dry, he was gasping and swallowing with dismay, his head was in a whirl. What must he do? He did not know. One thing seemed plain, however – he must pull himself together, and try to overtake that man. Of course the man could not get back the ticket-money, but would he throw the tickets away on that account? No; he would certainly go to the station and sell them to someone at half-price; and today, too, for they would be worthless tomorrow, by German custom. These reflections gave him hope and strength, and he rose and started. But he took only a couple of steps, then he felt a sudden sickness, and tottered back to his chair again, weak with a dread that his movement had been noticed – for the last round of beer was at his expense; it had not been paid for, and he hadn't a pfennig. He was a prisoner – Heaven only could know what might happen if he tried to leave the place. He was timid, scared, crushed; and he had not German enough to state his case and beg for help and indulgence.

Then his thoughts began to persecute him. How could he have been such a fool? What possessed him to listen to such a manifest adventurer? *And here comes the waiter!* He buried himself in the newspaper – trembling. The waiter passed by. It filled him with thankfulness. The hands of the clock seemed to stand still, yet he could not keep his eyes from them.

Ten minutes dragged by. The waiter again! Again he hid behind the paper. The waiter paused – apparently a week – then passed on.

Another ten minutes of misery – once more the waiter; this time he wiped off the table, and seemed to be a month at it; then paused two months, and went away.

Parrish felt that he could not endure another visit; he must take the chances: he must run the gauntlet; he must escape. But the waiter stayed around about the neighbourhood for five minutes – months and months seemingly, Parrish watching him with a despairing eye, and feeling the infirmities of age creeping upon him and his hair gradually turning grey.

At last the waiter wandered away – stopped at a table, collected a bill, wandered farther, collected another bill, wandered farther – Parrish's praying eye riveted on him all the time, his heart thumping, his breath coming and going in quick little gasps of anxiety mixed with hope.

The waiter stopped again to collect, and Parrish said to himself, it is now or never! and started for the door. One step – two steps – three – four – he was nearing the door – five – his legs shaking under him – was that a swift step behind him? – the thought shrivelled his heart – six steps – seven, and he was out! – eight – nine – ten – eleven – twelve – there *is* a pursuing step! – he turned the corner, and picked up his heels to fly – a heavy hand fell on his shoulder, and the strength went out of his body!

It was the Major. He asked not a question, he showed no surprise. He said, in his breezy and exhilarating fashion:

'Confound those people, they delayed me; that's why I was gone so long. New man in the ticket-office, and he didn't know me, and wouldn't make the exchange because it was irregular; so I had to hunt up my old friend, the great mogul – the stationmaster, you know – hi, there, cab! cab! – jump in, Parrish! – Russian consulate, cabby, and let them fly! – so, as I say, that all cost time. But it's all right now, and everything straight; your luggage reweighed, rechecked, fare-ticket and sleeper changed, and I've got the documents for it in my pocket; also the change – I'll keep it for you. Whoop along, cabby, whoop along; don't let them go to sleep!'

Poor Parrish was trying his best to get in a word edgeways, as the cab flew farther and farther from the bilked beer-hall, and now at last he succeeded, and wanted to return at once and pay his little bill.

'Oh, never mind about that,' said the Major, placidly; 'that's all right, they know me, everybody knows me – I'll square it next time I'm in Berlin – push along, cabby, push along – no great lot of time to spare, now.'

They arrived at the Russian consulate, a moment after-hours, and hurried in. No one there but a clerk. The Major laid his card on the desk, and said, in the Russian tongue, 'Now, then, if you'll visa this young man's passport for Petersburg as quickly as – '

'But, dear sir, I'm not authorised, and the consul has just gone.'

'Gone where?'

'Out in the country, where he lives.'

'And he'll be back – '

'Not till morning.'

'Thunder! Oh, well, look here, I'm Major Jackson – he knows me, everybody knows me. You visa it yourself; tell him Major Jackson asked you; it'll be all right.'

But it would be desperately and fatally irregular; the clerk could not be persuaded; he almost fainted at the idea.

'Well, then, I'll tell you what you do,' said the Major. 'Here's stamps and the fee – visa it in the morning, and start it along by mail.'

The clerk said, dubiously, 'He – well, he may perhaps do it, and so – '

'May? He *will!* He knows me – everybody knows me.'

'Very well,' said the clerk, 'I will tell him what you say.' He looked bewildered, and in a measure subjugated; and added, timidly: 'But – but – you know you will beat it to the frontier by twenty-four hours. There are no accommodations there for so long a wait.'

'Who's going to *wait*? Not I, if the court knows herself.'

The clerk was temporarily paralysed, and said, 'Surely, sir, you don't wish it sent to Petersburg!'

'And why not?'

'And the owner of it tarrying at the frontier, twenty-five miles away? It couldn't do him any good, in those circumstances.'

'Tarry – the mischief! Who said he was going to do any tarrying?'

'Why, you know, of course, they'll stop him at the frontier if he has no passport.'

'Indeed they won't! The Chief Inspector knows me – everybody does. I'll be responsible for the young man. You send it straight through to Petersburg – Hôtel de l'Europe, care of Major Jackson: tell the consul not to worry, I'm taking all the risks myself.'

The clerk hesitated, then chanced one more appeal:

'You must bear in mind, sir, that the risks are peculiarly serious, just now. The new edict is in force.'

'What is it?'

'Ten years in Siberia for being in Russia without a passport.'

'Mm – damnation!' He said it in English, for the Russian tongue is but a poor stand-by in spiritual emergencies. He mused a moment, then brisked up and resumed in Russian: 'Oh, it's all right – label her St Petersburg and let her sail! I'll fix it. They all know me there – all the authorities – everybody.'

❦ 3 ❦

The Major turned out to be an adorable travelling companion, and young Parrish was charmed with him. His talk was sunshine and rainbows, and lit up the whole region around, and kept it gay and happy and cheerful; and he was full of accommodating ways, and knew all about how to do things, and when to do them, and the best way. So the long journey was a fairy dream for that young lad who had been so lonely and forlorn and friendless so many homesick weeks. At last, when the two travellers were approaching the frontier, Parrish said something about passports; then started, as if recollecting something, and added:

'Why, come to think, I don't remember your bringing my passport away from the consulate. But you did, didn't you?'

'No; it's coming by mail,' said the Major, comfortably.

'C—coming – by – mail!' gasped the lad; and all the dreadful things he had heard about the terrors and disasters of passportless visitors to Russia rose in his frightened mind and turned him white to the lips. 'Oh, Major – oh, my goodness, what will become of me! How *could* you do such a thing?'

The Major laid a soothing hand upon the youth's shoulder and said:

'Now don't you worry, my boy, don't you worry a bit. I'm taking care of you, and I'm not going to let any harm come to you. The Chief Inspector knows me, and I'll explain to him, and it'll be all right – you'll see. Now don't you give yourself the least discomfort – I'll fix it all up, easy as nothing.'

Alfred trembled, and felt a great sinking inside, but he did what he could to conceal his misery, and to respond with some show of heart to the Major's kindly pettings and reassurings.

At the frontier he got out and stood on the edge of the great crowd, and waited in deep anxiety while the Major plowed his way through the mass to 'explain to the Chief Inspector'. It seemed a cruelly long wait, but at last the Major reappeared. He said, cheerfully, 'Damnation, it's a new inspector, and I don't know him!'

Alfred fell up against a pile of trunks, with a despairing 'Oh, dear, dear, I might have known it!' and was slumping limp and helpless to the ground, but the Major gathered him up and seated him on a box, and sat down by him, with a supporting arm around him, and whispered in his ear:

'Don't worry, laddie, don't – it's going to be all right; you just trust to me. The sub-inspector's as near-sighted as a shad. I watched him, and I know it's so. Now I'll tell you how to do. I'll go and get my passport chalked, then I'll stop right yonder inside the grille where you see those peasants with their packs. You be there, and I'll back up against the grille, and slip my passport to you through the bars, then you tag along after the crowd and hand it in, and trust to Providence and that shad. Mainly the shad. You'll pull through all right – now don't you be afraid.'

'But, oh dear, dear, *your* description and *mine* don't tally any more than – '

'Oh, that's all light – difference between fifty-one and nineteen – just entirely imperceptible to that shad – don't you fret, it's going to come out as right as nails.'

Ten minutes later Alfred was tottering toward the train, pale, and in a collapse, but he had played the shad successfully, and was as grateful as an untaxed dog that has evaded the police.

'I told you so,' said the Major, in splendid spirits. 'I knew it would come out all right if you trusted in Providence like a little trusting child and didn't try to improve on His ideas – it always does.'

Between the frontier and Petersburg the Major laid himself out to restore his young comrade's life, and work up his circulation, and pull him out of his despondency, and make him feel again that life was a joy and worth living. And so, as a consequence, the young fellow entered the city in high feather and marched into the hotel in fine form, and registered his name. But instead of naming a room, the clerk glanced at him inquiringly, and waited. The Major came promptly to the rescue, and said, cordially:

'It's all right – you know me – set him down, I'm responsible.' The clerk looked grave, and shook his head. The Major added: 'It's all right, it'll be here in twenty-four hours – it's coming by mail. Here's mine, and his is coming, right along.'

The clerk was full of politeness, full of deference, but he was firm. He said, in English:

'Indeed, I wish I could accommodate you, Major, and certainly I would if I could; but I have no choice, I must ask him to go; I cannot allow him to remain in the house a moment.'

Parrish began to totter, and emitted a moan; the Major caught him and stayed him with an arm, and said to the clerk, appealingly:

'Come, you know me – everybody does – just let him stay here the one night, and I give you my word – '

The clerk shook his head, and said:

'But, Major, you are endangering me, you are endangering the house. I – I hate to do such a thing, but I – I *must* call the police.'

'Hold on, don't do that. Come along, my boy, and don't you fret – it's going to come out all right. Hi, there, cabby! Jump in, Parrish. Palace of the General of the Secret Police – turn them loose, cabby! Let them go! Make them whiz! Now we're off, and don't you give yourself any uneasiness. Prince Bossloffsky knows me, knows me like a book; he'll soon fix things all right for us.'

They tore through the gay streets and arrived at the palace, which was brilliantly lighted. But it was half-past eight; the Prince was about going in to dinner, the sentinel said, and couldn't receive anyone.

'But he'll receive *me*,' said the Major, robustly, and handed his card. 'I'm Major Jackson. Send it in; it'll be all right.'

The card was sent in, under protest, and the Major and his waif waited in a reception room for some time. At length they were sent for, and conducted to a sumptuous private office and confronted with the Prince, who stood there gorgeously arrayed and frowning like a thundercloud. The Major stated his case, and begged for a twenty-four-hour stay of proceedings until the passport should be forthcoming.

'Oh, impossible!' said the Prince, in faultless English. 'I marvel that you should have done so insane a thing as to bring the lad into the country without a passport, Major, I marvel at it; why, it's ten years in Siberia, and no help for it – catch him! support him!' for poor Parrish was making another trip to the floor. 'Here – quick, give him this. There – take another draught; brandy's the thing, don't you find it so, lad? Now you feel better, poor fellow. Lie down on the sofa. How stupid it was of you, Major, to get him into such a horrible scrape.'

The Major eased the boy down with his strong arms, put a cushion under his head, and whispered in his ear:

'Look as damned sick as you can! Play it for all it's worth; he's touched, you see; got a tender heart under there somewhere; fetch a groan, and say, "Oh, mamma, mamma"; it'll knock him out, sure as guns.'

Parrish was going to do these things anyway, from native impulse, so they came from him promptly, with great and moving sincerity, and the Major whispered: 'Splendid! Do it again; Bernhardt couldn't beat it.'

What with the Major's eloquence and the boy's misery, the point was gained at last; the Prince struck his colours, and said:

'Have it your way; though you deserve a sharp lesson and you ought to get it. I give you exactly twenty-four hours. If the passport is not here then, don't come near me; it's Siberia without hope of pardon.'

While the Major and the lad poured out their thanks, the Prince rang in a couple of soldiers, and in their own language he ordered them to go with these two people, and not lose sight of the younger one a moment for the next twenty-four hours; and if, at the end of that term, the boy could not show a passport, impound him in the dungeons of St Peter and St Paul, and report.

The unfortunates arrived at the hotel with their guards, dined under their eyes, remained in Parrish's room until the Major went off to bed, after cheering up the said Parrish, then one of the soldiers locked himself and Parrish in, and the other one stretched himself across the door outside and soon went off to sleep.

So also did not Alfred Parrish. The moment he was alone with the solemn soldier and the voiceless silence his machine-made cheerfulness began to waste away, his medicated courage began to give off its supporting gases and shrink toward normal, and his poor little heart to shrivel like a raisin. Within thirty minutes he struck bottom; grief, misery, fright, despair, could go no lower. Bed? Bed was not for such as he; bed was not for the doomed, the lost! Sleep? He was not the Hebrew children, he could not sleep in the fire! He could only walk the floor. And not only could, but must. And did, by the hour. And mourned, and wept, and shuddered, and prayed.

Then all-sorrowfully he made his last dispositions, and prepared himself, as well as in him lay, to meet his fate. As a final act, he wrote a letter:

MY DARLING MOTHER – When these sad lines shall have reached you your poor Alfred will be no more. No; worse than that, far worse! Through my own fault and foolishness I have fallen into the hands of a sharper or a lunatic; I do not know which, but in either case I feel that I am lost. Sometimes I think he is a sharper, but most of the time I think he is only mad, for he has a kind, good heart, I know, and he certainly seems to try the hardest that ever a person tried to get me out of the fatal difficulties he has gotten me into.

In a few hours I shall be one of a nameless horde plodding the snowy solitudes of Russia, under the lash, and bound for that land of mystery and misery and termless oblivion, Siberia! I shall not live to see it; my heart is broken and I shall die. Give my picture to *her*, and ask her to keep it in memory of me, and to so live that in the appointed time she may join me in that better world where there is no marriage nor giving in marriage, and where there are no more separations, and troubles never come. Give my yellow dog to Archy Hale, and the other one to Henry Taylor; my blazer I give to brother Will, and my fishing things and Bible.

There is no hope for me. I cannot escape; the soldier stands therewith his gun and never takes his eyes off me, just blinks; there is no other movement, any more than if he was dead. I cannot bribe him, the maniac has my money. My letter of credit is in my trunk, and may never come – *will* never come, I know. Oh, what is to become of me! Pray for me, darling mother, pray for your poor Alfred. But it will do no good.

☞ 4 ☜

In the morning Alfred came out looking scraggy and worn when the Major summoned him to an early breakfast. They fed their guards, they lit cigars, the Major loosened his tongue and set it going, and under its magic influence Alfred gradually and gratefully became hopeful, measurably cheerful, and almost happy once more.

But he would not leave the house. Siberia hung over him black and threatening, his appetite for sights was all gone, he could not have borne the shame of inspecting streets and galleries and churches with a soldier at each elbow and all the world stopping and staring and commenting – no, he would stay within and wait for the Berlin mail and his fate. So, all day long the Major stood gallantly by him in his room, with one soldier standing stiff and motionless against the door with his musket at his shoulder, and the other one drowsing in a chair outside; and all day long the faithful veteran spun campaign yarns, described battles, reeled off explosive anecdotes, with unconquerable energy and sparkle and resolution, and kept the scared student alive and his pulses functioning. The long day wore to a close, and the pair, followed by their guards, went down to the great dining-room and took their seats.

'The suspense will be over before long, now,' sighed poor Alfred.

Just then a pair of Englishmen passed by, and one of them said, 'So we'll get no letters from Berlin tonight.'

Parrish's breath began to fail him. The Englishmen seated themselves at a nearby table, and the other one said:

'No, it isn't as bad as that.' Parrish's breathing improved. 'There is later telegraphic news. The accident did detain the train formidably, but that is all. It will arrive here three hours late tonight.'

Parrish did not get to the floor this time, for the Major jumped for him in time. He had been listening, and foresaw what would happen. He patted Parrish on the back, hoisted him out of his chair, and said, cheerfully:

'Come along, my boy, cheer up, there's absolutely nothing to worry about. I know a way out. Bother the passport; let it lag a week if it wants to, we can do without it.'

Parrish was too sick to hear him; hope was gone, Siberia present; he moved off on legs of lead, upheld by the Major, who walked him to the American legation, heartening him on the way with assurances that on his recommendation the minister wouldn't hesitate a moment to grant him a new passport.

'I had that card up my sleeve all the time,' he said. 'The minister knows me – knows me familiarly – chummed together hours and hours under a pile of other wounded at Cold Harbour; been chummies ever since, in spirit, though we haven't met much in the body. Cheer up, laddie, everything's looking splendid! By gracious! I feel as cocky as a buck angel. Here we are, and our troubles are at an end! If we ever really had any.'

There, alongside the door, was the trademark of the richest and freest and mightiest republic of all the ages: the pine disk, with the planked eagle spread upon it, his head and shoulders among the stars, and his claws full of out-of-date war material; and at that sight the tears came into Alfred's eyes, the pride of country rose in his heart, Hail Columbia boomed up in his breast, and all his fears and sorrows vanished away; for here he was safe, safe! not all the powers of the earth would venture to cross that threshold to lay a hand upon him!

For economy's sake the mightiest republic's legations in Europe consist of a room and a half on the ninth floor, when the tenth is occupied, and the legation furniture consists of a minister or an ambassador with a brakeman's salary, a secretary of legation who sells matches and mends crockery for a living, a hired girl for interpreter and general utility, pictures of the American liners, a chromo of the reigning President, a desk, three chairs, kerosene-lamp, a cat, a clock, and a cuspidor with motto, 'In God We Trust.'

The party climbed up there, followed by the escort. A man sat at the desk writing official things on wrapping paper with a nail. He rose and faced about; the cat climbed down and got under the desk; the hired girl squeezed herself up into the corner by the vodka-jug to make room; the soldiers squeezed themselves up against the wall alongside of her, with muskets at shoulder arms. Alfred was radiant with happiness and the sense of rescue. The Major cordially shook hands with the official, rattled off his case in easy and fluent style, and asked for the desired passport.

The official seated his guests, then said: 'Well, I am only the secretary of legation, you know, and I wouldn't like to grant a passport while the minister is on Russian soil. There is far too much responsibility.'

'All right, send for him.'

The secretary smiled, and said: 'That's easier said than done. He's away up in the wilds, somewhere, on his vacation.'

'Ger-reat Scott!' ejaculated the Major.

Alfred groaned; the colour went out of his face, and he began to slowly collapse in his clothes. The secretary said, wonderingly:

'Why, what are you Great-Scotting about, Major? The Prince gave you twenty-four hours. Look at the clock; you're all right; you've half an hour left; the train is just due; the passport will arrive in time.'

'Man, there's news! The train is three hours behind time! This boy's life and liberty are wasting away by minutes, and only thirty of them left! In half an hour he's the same as dead and damned to all eternity! By God, we *must* have the passport!'

'Oh, I am dying, I know it!' wailed the lad, and buried his face in his arms on the desk. A quick change came over the secretary, his placidity vanished away, excitement flamed up in his face and eyes, and he exclaimed:

'I see the whole ghastliness of the situation, but, Lord help us, what can I do? What can you suggest?'

'Why, hang it, give him the passport!'

'Impossible! totally impossible! You know nothing about him; three days ago you had never heard of him; there's no way in the world to identify him. He is lost, lost – there's no possibility of saving him!'

The boy groaned again, and sobbed out, 'Lord, Lord, it's the last of earth for Alfred Parrish!'

Another change came over the secretary.

In the midst of a passionate outburst of pity, vexation, and hopelessness, he stopped short, his manner calmed down, and he asked, in the indifferent voice which one uses in introducing the subject of the weather when there is nothing to talk about, 'Is that your name?'

The youth sobbed out a yes.

'Where are you from?'

'Bridgeport.'

The secretary shook his head – shook it again – and muttered to himself. After a moment:

'Born there?'

'No; New Haven.'

'Ah-h.' The secretary glanced at the Major, who was listening intently, with blank and unenlightened face, and indicated rather than said, 'There is vodka there, in case the soldiers are thirsty.' The Major sprang up, poured for them, and received their gratitude. The questioning went on.

'How long did you live in New Haven?'

'Till I was fourteen. Came back two years ago to enter Yale.'

'When you lived there, what street did you live on?'

'Parker Street.'

With a vague half-light of comprehension dawning in his eye, the Major glanced an inquiry at the secretary. The secretary nodded, the Major poured vodka again.

'What number?'

'It hadn't any.'

The boy sat up and gave the secretary a pathetic look which said, 'Why do you want to torture me with these foolish things, when I am miserable enough without it?'

The secretary went on, unheeding: 'What kind of a house was it?'

'Brick – two storey.'

'Flush with the sidewalk?'

'No, small yard in front.'

'Iron fence?'

'No, palings.'

The Major poured vodka again – without instructions – poured brimmers this time; and his face had cleared and was alive now.

'What do you see when you enter the door?'

'A narrow hall; door at the end of it, and a door at your right.'

'Anything else?'

'Hat-rack.'

'Room at the right?'

'Parlour.'

'Carpet?'

'Yes.'

'Kind of carpet?'

'Old-fashioned Wilton.'

'Figures?'

'Yes – hawking-party, horseback.'

The Major cast an eye at the clock – only six minutes left! He faced about with the jug, and as he poured he glanced at the secretary, then at the clock – inquiringly. The secretary nodded; the Major covered the clock from view with his body a moment, and set the hands back half an hour; then he refreshed the men – double rations.

'Room beyond the hall and hat-rack?'

'Dining-room.'

'Stove?'

'Grate.'

'Did your people own the house?'

'Yes.'

'Do they own it yet?'

'No; sold it when we moved to Bridgeport.'

The secretary paused a little, then said, 'Did you have a nickname among your playmates?'

The colour slowly rose in the youth's pale cheeks, and he dropped his eyes. He seemed to struggle with himself a moment or two, then he said, plaintively, 'They called me Miss Nancy.'

The secretary mused awhile, then he dug up another question:

'Any ornaments in the dining-room?'

'Well, y – no.'

'*None?* None at *all?*'

'No.'

'The mischief! Isn't that a little odd? Think!'

The youth thought and thought; the secretary waited, slightly panting. At last the imperilled waif looked up sadly and shook his head.

'Think – *think!*' cried the Major, in anxious solicitude; and poured again.

'Come!' said the secretary, 'not even a *picture?*'

'Oh, certainly! but you said ornament.'

'Ah! What did your father think of it?'

The colour rose again. The boy was silent.

'Speak,' said the secretary.

'Speak,' cried the Major, and his trembling hand poured more vodka outside the glasses than inside.

'I – I can't tell you what he said,' murmured the boy.

'Quick! quick!' said the secretary; 'out with it; there's no time to lose –

home and liberty or Siberia and death depend upon the answer.'

'Oh, have pity! he is a clergyman, and – '

'No matter; out with it, or – '

'He said it was the hellfiredest nightmare he ever struck!'

'Saved!' shouted the secretary, and seized his nail and a blank passport. '*I* identify you; I've lived in the house, and I painted the picture myself!'

'Oh, come to my arms, my poor rescued boy!' cried the Major. 'We will always be grateful to God that He made this artist! – if He did.'

Two Little Tales

The Man with a Message for the Director-General

Some days ago, in this second month of 1900, a friend made an afternoon call upon me here in London. We are of that age when men who are smoking away their time in chat do not talk quite so much about the pleasantnesses of life as about its exasperations. By and by this friend began to abuse the War Office. It appeared that he had a friend who had been inventing something which could be made very useful to the soldiers in South Africa. It was a light and very cheap and durable boot, which would remain dry in wet weather, and keep its shape and firmness. The inventor wanted to get the government's attention called to it, but he was an unknown man and knew the great officials would pay no heed to a message from him.

'This shows that he was an ass – like the rest of us,' I said, interrupting. 'Go on.'

'But why have you said that? The man spoke the truth.'

'The man spoke a lie. Go on.'

'I will *prove* that he – '

'You can't prove anything of the kind. I am very old and very wise. You must not argue with me: it is irreverent and offensive. Go on.'

'Very well. But you will presently see. I am not unknown, yet even *I* was not able to get the man's message to the Director-General of the Shoe-Leather Department.'

'This is another lie. Pray go on.'

'But I assure you on my honour that I failed.'

'Oh, certainly. I knew *that.* You didn't need to tell me.'

'Then where is the lie?'

'It is in your intimation that you were *not able* to get the Director-General's immediate attention to the man's message. It is a lie, because you *could* have gotten his immediate attention to it.'

'I tell you I couldn't. In three months I haven't accomplished it.'

'Certainly. Of course. I could know that without your telling me. You *could* have gotten his immediate attention if you had gone at it in a sane way; and so could the other man.'

'I *did* go at it in a sane way.'

'You didn't.'

'How do *you* know? What do you know about the circumstances?'

'Nothing at all. But you didn't go at it in a sane way. That much I know to a certainty.'

'How can you know it, when you don't know what method I used?'

'I know by the result. The result is perfect proof. You went at it in an insane way. I am very old and very w – '

'Oh, yes, I know. But will you let me tell you *how* I proceeded? I think that will settle whether it was insanity or not.'

'No; that has already been settled. But go on, since you so desire to expose yourself. I am very o – '

'Certainly, certainly. I sat down and wrote a courteous letter to the Director-General of the Shoe-Leather Department, explai – '

'Do you know him personally?'

'No.'

'You have scored one for my side. You began insanely. Go on.'

'In the letter I made the great value and inexpensiveness of the invention clear, and offered to – '

'Call and see him? Of course you did. Score two against yourself. I am v – '

'He didn't answer for three days.'

'Necessarily. Proceed.'

'Sent me three gruff lines thanking me for my trouble, and proposing – '

'Nothing.'

'That's it – proposing nothing. Then I wrote him more elaborately and – '

'Score three – '

' – and got no answer. At the end of a week I wrote and asked, with some touch of asperity, for an answer to that letter.'

'Four. Go on.'

'An answer came back saying the letter had not been received, and asking for a copy. I traced the letter through the post-office, and found that it *had* been received; but I sent a copy and said nothing. Two weeks passed without further notice of me. In the meantime I gradually got myself cooled down to a polite-letter temperature. Then I wrote and proposed an interview for next day, and said that if I did not hear from him in the meantime I should take his silence for assent.'

'Score five.'

'I arrived at twelve sharp, and was given a chair in the anteroom and told to wait. I waited until half-past one; then I left, ashamed and angry. I waited another week, to cool down; then I wrote and made another appointment with him for next day noon.'

'Score six.'

'He answered, assenting. I arrived promptly, and kept a chair warm until half-past two. I left then, and shook the dust of that place from my shoes for good and all. For rudeness, inefficiency, incapacity, indifference to the army's interests, the Director-General of the Shoe-Leather Department of the War Office is, in my o – '

'Peace! I am very old and very wise, and have seen many seemingly intelligent people who hadn't common sense enough to go at a simple and easy thing like this in a common-sense way. You are not a curiosity to me; I have personally known millions and billions like you. You have lost three months quite unnecessarily; the inventor has lost three months; the soldiers have lost three – nine months altogether. I will now read you a little tale which I wrote last night. Then you will call on the Director-General at noon tomorrow and transact your business.'

'Splendid! Do you know him?'

'No; but listen to the tale.'

SECOND STORY

How the Chimney-Sweep got the Ear of the Emperor

◈ I ◈

Summer was come, and all the strong were bowed by the burden of the awful heat, and many of the weak were prostrate and dying. For weeks the army had been wasting away with a plague of dysentery, that scourge of the soldier, and there was but little help. The doctors were in despair; such efficacy as their drugs and their science had once had – and it was not much at its best – was a thing of the past, and promised to remain so.

The Emperor commanded the physicians of greatest renown to appear before him for a consultation, for he was profoundly disturbed.

He was very severe with them, and called them to account for letting his soldiers die: and asked them if they knew their trade, or didn't; and were they properly healers, or merely assassins? Then the principal assassin, who was also the oldest doctor in the land and the most venerable in appearance, answered and said:

'We have done what we could, your Majesty, and for a good reason it has been little. No medicine and no physician can cure that disease; only nature and a good constitution can do it. I am old, and I know. No doctor and no medicine can cure it – I repeat it and I emphasise it. Sometimes they seem to help nature a little – a very little – but as a rule, they merely do damage.'

The Emperor was a profane and passionate man, and he deluged the doctors with rugged and unfamiliar names, and drove them from his presence.

Within a day he was attacked by that fell disease himself. The news flew from mouth to mouth, and carried consternation with it over all the land.

All the talk was about this awful disaster, and there was general depression, for few had hope. The Emperor himself was very melancholy, and sighed and said:

'The will of God be done. Send for the assassins again, and let us get over with it.'

They came, and felt his pulse and looked at his tongue, and fetched the drug store and emptied it into him, and sat down patiently to wait – for they were not paid by the job, but by the year.

❧ 2 ❧

Tommy was sixteen and a bright lad, but he was not in society. His rank was too humble for that, and his employment too base. In fact, it was the lowest of all employments, for he was second in command to his father, who emptied cesspools and drove a night-cart. Tommy's closest friend was Jimmy the chimney-sweep, a slim little fellow of fourteen, who was honest and industrious, and had a good heart, and supported a bedridden mother by his dangerous and unpleasant trade.

About a month after the Emperor fell ill, these two lads met one evening about nine. Tommy was on his way to his night-work, and of course was not in his Sundays, but in his dreadful work-clothes, and not smelling very well. Jimmy was on his way home from his day's labour, and was blacker than any other object imaginable, and he had his brushes on his shoulder and his soot-bag at his waist, and no feature of his sable face was distinguishable except his lively eyes.

They sat down on the kerbstone to talk; and of course it was upon the one subject – the nation's calamity, the Emperor's disorder. Jimmy was full of a great project, and burning to unfold it. He said:

'Tommy, I can cure his Majesty. I know how to do it.'

Tommy was surprised.

'What! You?'

'Yes, I.'

'Why, you little fool, the best doctors can't.'

'I don't care: I can do it. I can cure him in fifteen minutes.'

'Oh, come off! What are you giving me?'

'The facts – that's all.'

Jimmy's manner was so serious that it sobered Tommy, who said:

'I believe you are in earnest, Jimmy. Are you in earnest?'

'I give you my word.'

'What is the plan? How'll you cure him?'

'Tell him to eat a slice of ripe watermelon.'

It caught Tommy rather suddenly, and he was shouting with laughter at the absurdity of the idea before he could put on a stopper. But he sobered down when he saw that Jimmy was wounded. He patted Jimmy's knee affectionately, not minding the soot, and said:

'I take the laugh all back. I didn't mean any harm, Jimmy, and I won't do it again. You see, it seemed so funny, because wherever there's a soldier-camp and dysentery, the doctors always put up a sign saying anybody caught bringing watermelons there will be flogged with the cat till he can't stand.'

'I know it – the idiots!' said Jimmy, with both tears and anger in his voice. 'There's plenty of watermelons, and not one of all those soldiers ought to have died.'

'But, Jimmy, what put the notion into your head?'

'It isn't a notion; it's a fact. Do you know that old grey-headed Zulu? Well, this long time back he has been curing a lot of our friends, and my mother has seen him do it, and so have I. It takes only one or two slices of melon, and it don't make any difference whether the disease is new or old; it cures it.'

'It's very odd. But, Jimmy, if it is so, the Emperor ought to be told of it.'

'Of course; and my mother has told people, hoping they could get the word to him; but they are poor working-folks and ignorant, and don't know how to manage it.'

'Of course they don't, the blunderheads,' said Tommy, scornfully. '*I'll* get it to him!'

'You? You night-cart polecat!' And it was Jimmy's turn to laugh. But Tommy retorted sturdily:

'Oh, laugh if you like; but I'll *do* it!'

It had such an assured and confident sound that it made an impression, and Jimmy asked gravely:

'Do you know the Emperor?'

'Do *I* know him? Why, how you talk! Of course I don't.'

'Then how'll you do it?'

'It's very simple and very easy. Guess. How would *you* do it, Jimmy?'

'Send him a letter. I never thought of it till this minute. But I'll bet that's your way.'

'I'll bet it ain't. Tell me, how would you send it?'

'Why, through the mail, of course.'

Tommy overwhelmed him with scoffings, and said:

'Now, don't you suppose every crank in the empire is doing the same thing? Do you mean to say you haven't thought of that?'

'Well – no,' said Jimmy, abashed.

'You *might* have thought of it, if you weren't so young and inexperienced. Why, Jimmy, when even a common *general*, or a poet, or an actor, or anybody that's a little famous gets sick, all the cranks in the kingdom load up the mails with certain-sure quack cures for him. And so, what's bound to happen when it's the Emperor?'

'I suppose it's worse,' said Jimmy, sheepishly.

'Well, I should think so! Look here, Jimmy: every single night we cart off as many as six loads of that kind of letters from the back yard of the palace, where they're thrown. Eighty thousand letters in one night! Do you reckon anybody reads them? Sho! not a single one. It's what would happen to your letter if you wrote it – which you won't, I reckon?'

'No,' sighed Jimmy, crushed.

'But it's all right, Jimmy. Don't you fret: there's more than one way to skin a cat. *I'll* get the word to him.'

'Oh, if you only *could*, Tommy, I should love you forever!'

'I'll do it, I tell you. Don't you worry; you depend on me.'

'Indeed I will, Tommy, for you do know so much. You're not like other boys: they never know anything. How'll you manage, Tommy?'

Tommy was greatly pleased. He settled himself for reposeful talk, and said:

'Do you know that ragged poor thing that thinks he's a butcher because he goes around with a basket and sells cat's meat and rotten livers? Well, to begin with, I'll tell *him*.'

Jimmy was deeply disappointed and chagrined, and said:

'Now, Tommy, it's a shame to talk so. You know my heart's in it, and it's not right.'

Tommy gave him a love-pat, and said:

'Don't you be troubled, Jimmy. *I* know what I'm about. Pretty soon you'll see. That half-breed butcher will tell the old woman that sells chestnuts at the corner of the lane – she's his closest friend, and I'll ask him to; then, by request, she'll tell her rich aunt that keeps the little fruit shop on the corner two blocks above; and that one will tell her particular friend, the man that keeps the game shop; and he will tell his friend the sergeant of police; and the sergeant will tell his captain, and the captain will tell the magistrate, and the magistrate will tell his brother-in-law the county judge, and the county judge will tell the sheriff, and the sheriff will tell the Lord Mayor, and the Lord Mayor will tell the President of the Council, and the President of the Council will tell the – '

'By George, but it's a wonderful scheme, Tommy! How ever *did* you – '

' – Rear-Admiral, and the Rear will tell the Vice, and the Vice will tell the Admiral of the Blue, and the Blue will tell the Red, and the Red will tell the White, and the White will tell the First Lord of the Admiralty, and the First Lord will tell the Speaker of the House, and the Speaker – '

'Go it, Tommy; you're 'most there!'

' – will tell the Master of the Hounds, and the Master will tell the Head Groom of the Stables, and the Head Groom will tell the Chief Equerry, and the Chief Equerry will tell the First Lord in Waiting, and the First Lord will tell the Lord High Chamberlain, and the Lord High Chamberlain will tell the Master of the Household, and the Master of the Household will tell the little pet page that fans the flies off the Emperor, and the page will get down on his knees and whisper it to his Majesty – and the game's made!'

'I've *got* to get up and hurrah a couple of times, Tommy. It's the grandest idea that ever was. Whatever put it into your head?'

'Sit down and listen, and I'll give you some wisdom – and don't you ever forget it as long as you live. Now, then, who is the closest friend you've got, and the one you couldn't and wouldn't ever refuse anything in the world to?'

'Why, it's you, Tommy. You know that.'

'Suppose you wanted to ask a pretty large favour of the cat's-meat man. Well, you don't know him, and he would tell you to go to thunder, for he is that kind of a person; but he is my next best friend after you, and would run his legs off to do me a kindness – *any* kindness, he don't care what it is. Now, I'll ask you: which is the most common-sensible – for you to go and ask him to tell the chestnut-woman about your watermelon cure, or for you to get me to do it for you?'

'To get you to do it for me, of course. I wouldn't ever have thought of that, Tommy; it's splendid!'

'It's *a philosophy*, you see. Mighty good word – and large. It goes on this idea: everybody in the world, little and big, has one *special* friend, a friend that he's *glad* to do favours to – not sour about it, but *glad* – glad clear to the marrow. And so, I don't care where you start, you can get at anybody's ear that you want to – I don't care how low you are, nor how high he is. And it's so simple: you've only to find the *first* friend, that is all; that ends your part of the work. He finds the next friend himself, and that one finds the third, and so on, friend after friend, link after link, like a chain; and you can go up it or down it, as high as you like or as low as you like.'

' It's just beautiful, Tommy.'

'It's as simple and easy as a–b–c; but did you ever hear of anybody trying it? No; everybody is a fool. He goes to a stranger without any introduction, or writes him a letter, and of course he strikes a cold wave – and serves him gorgeously right. Now, the Emperor don't know me, but that's no matter – he'll eat his watermelon tomorrow. You'll see. Hi-hi – stop! It's the cat's-meat man. Goodbye, Jimmy; I'll overtake him.'

He did overtake him, and said:

'Say, will you do me a favour?'

'*Will I*? Well, I should *say*! I'm your man. Name it, and see me fly!'

'Go tell the chestnut-woman to put down everything and carry this message to her first-best friend, and tell the friend to pass it along.' He worded the message, and said, 'Now, then, rush!'

The next moment the chimney-sweep's word to the Emperor was on its way.

❧ 3 ❧

The next evening, toward midnight, the doctors sat whispering to-gether in the imperial sickroom, and they were in deep trouble, for the Emperor was in very bad case. They could not hide it from themselves that every time they emptied a fresh drugstore into him he got worse. It saddened them, for they were expecting that result. The poor emaciated Emperor lay motionless, with his eyes closed, and the page that was his darling was fanning the flies away and crying softly. Presently the boy heard the silken rustle of a portière, and turned and saw the Lord High Great Master of the Household peering in at the door and excitedly motioning to him to come. Lightly and swiftly the page tiptoed his way to his dear and worshipped friend the Master, who said:

'Only you can persuade him, my child, and oh, don't fail to do it! Take this, make him eat it, and he is saved.'

'On my head be it. He shall eat it!'

It was a couple of great slices of ruddy, fresh watermelon.

The next morning the news flew everywhere that the Emperor was sound and well again, and had hanged the doctors. A wave of joy swept the land, and frantic preparations were made to illuminate.

After breakfast his Majesty sat meditating. His gratitude was un-speakable, and he was trying to devise a reward rich enough to properly testify it to his benefactor. He got it arranged in his mind, and called the page, and asked him if he had invented that cure. The boy said no – he got it from the Master of the Household.

He was sent away, and the Emperor went to devising again. The Master was an earl; he would make him a duke, and give him a vast estate which belonged to a member of the Opposition. He had him called, and asked him if he was the inventor of the remedy. But the Master was an honest man, and said he got it of the Grand Chamber-lain. He was sent away, and the Emperor thought some more. The Chamberlain was a viscount; he would make him an earl, and give him a large income. But the Chamberlain referred him to the First Lord in Waiting, and there was some more thinking; his Majesty thought out a smaller reward. But the First Lord in Waiting referred him back further, and he had to sit down and think out a further and becomingly and suitably smaller reward.

Then, to break the tediousness of the inquiry and hurry the business, he sent for the Grand High Chief Detective, and commanded him to trace the cure to the bottom, so that he could properly reward his benefactor.

At nine in the evening the High Chief Detective brought the word. He had traced the cure down to a lad named Jimmy, a chimney-sweep. The Emperor said, with deep feeling:

'Brave boy, he saved my life, and shall not regret it!'

And sent him a pair of his own boots; and the next best ones he had, too. They were too large for Jimmy, but they fitted the Zulu, so it was all right, and everything as it should be.

CONCLUSION TO THE FIRST STORY

'There – do you get the idea?'

'I am obliged to admit that I do. And it will be as you have said. I will transact the business tomorrow. I intimately know the Director-General's nearest friend. He will give me a note of introduction, with a word to say my matter is of real importance to the government. I will take it along, without an appointment, and send it in, with my card, and I shan't have to wait so much as half a minute.'

That turned out true to the letter, and the government adopted the boots.

About Play-Acting

I have a project to suggest. But first I will write a chapter of introduction.

I have just been witnessing a remarkable play, here at the Burg Theatre in Vienna. I do not know of any play that much resembles it. In fact, it is such a departure from the common laws of the drama that the name 'play' doesn't seem to fit it quite snugly. However, whatever else it may be, it is in any case a great and stately metaphysical poem, and deeply fascinating. 'Deeply fascinating' is the right term, for the audience sat four hours and five minutes without thrice breaking into applause, except at the close of each act; sat rapt and silent – fascinated. This piece is 'The Master of Palmyra'. It is twenty years old; yet I doubt if you have ever heard of it. It is by Wilbrandt, and is his masterpiece and the work which is to make his name permanent in German literature. It has never been played anywhere except in Berlin and in the great Burg Theatre in Vienna. Yet whenever it is put on the stage it packs the house, and the free list is suspended. I know people who have seen it ten times; they know the most of it by heart; they do not tire of it; and they say they shall still be quite willing to go and sit under its spell whenever they get the opportunity.

There is a dash of metempsychosis in it – and it is the strength of the piece. The play gave me the sense of the passage of a dimly connected procession of dream-pictures. The scene of it is Palmyra in Roman times. It covers a wide stretch of time – I don't know how many years – and in the course of it the chief actress is reincarnated several times: four times she is a more or less young woman, and once she is a lad. In the first act she is *Zoë* – a Christian girl who has wandered across the desert from Damascus to try to Christianise the Zeus-worshipping pagans of Palmyra. In this character she is wholly spiritual, a religious enthusiast, a devotee who covets martyrdom – and gets it.

After many years she appears in the second act as *Phœbe*, a graceful and beautiful young light-o'-love from Rome, whose soul is all for the shows and luxuries and delights of this life – a dainty and capricious featherhead, a creature of shower and sunshine, a spoiled child, but a charming one.

In the third act, after an interval of many years, she reappears as *Persida*, mother of a daughter in the fresh bloom of youth. She is now a sort of combination of her two earlier selves: in religious loyalty and subjection she is *Zoë*; in triviality of character and shallowness of judgment – together with a touch of vanity in dress – she is *Phœbe*.

After a lapse of years she appears in the fourth act as *Nymphas*, a beautiful boy, in whose character the previous incarnations are engagingly mixed.

And after another stretch of years all these heredities are joined in the *Zenobia* of the fifth act – a person of gravity, dignity, sweetness, with a heart filled with compassion for all who suffer, and a hand prompt to put into practical form the heart's benignant impulses.

You will easily concede that the actress who proposes to discriminate nicely these five characters, and play them to the satisfaction of a cultivated and exacting audience, has her work cut out for her. Mme Hohenfels has made these parts her peculiar property; and she is well able to meet all the requirements. You perceive, now, where the chief part of the absorbing fascination of this piece lies; it is in watching this extraordinary artist melt these five characters into each other – grow, shade by shade, out of one and into another through a stretch of four hours and five minutes.

There are a number of curious and interesting features in this piece. For instance, its hero, *Apelles*, young, handsome, vigorous, in the first act, remains so all through the long flight of years covered by the five acts. Other men, young in the first act, are touched with grey in the second, are old and racked with infirmities in the third; in the fourth, all but one are gone to their long home, and he is a blind and helpless hulk of ninety or a hundred years. It indicates that the stretch of time covered by the piece is seventy years or more. The scenery undergoes decay, too – the decay of age, assisted and perfected by a conflagration. The fine new temples and palaces of the second act are by and by a wreck of crumbled walls and prostrate columns, mouldy, grass-grown, and desolate; but their former selves are still recognisable in their ruins. The aging men and the aging scenery together convey a profound illusion of that long lapse of time: they make you live it yourself! You leave the theatre with the weight of a century upon you.

Another strong effect: Death, in person, walks about the stage in every act. So far as I could make out, he was supposedly not visible to any excepting two persons – the one he came for and *Apelles*. He used various costumes: but there was always more black about them than any other tint; and so they were always sombre. Also they were always deeply impressive, and indeed awe-inspiring. The face was not subjected to changes, but remained the same, first and last – a ghastly white. To me he was always welcome, he seemed so real – the actual Death, not a play-acting artificiality. He was of a solemn and stately carriage; he had a deep voice, and used it with a noble dignity. Wherever there was a turmoil of merrymaking or fighting or feasting or chaffing or quarrelling, or a gilded pageant, or other manifestation of our trivial and fleeting life, into it drifted that black figure with the corpse-face, and looked its fateful look and passed on; leaving its victim shuddering and smitten. And always its coming made the fussy human pack seem infinitely pitiful and shabby and hardly worth the attention of either saving or damning.

In the beginning of the first act the young girl *Zoë* appears by some great rocks in the desert, and sits down, exhausted, to rest. Presently arrive a pauper couple, stricken with age and infirmities; and they begin to mumble and pray to the Spirit of Life, who is said to inhabit that spot. The Spirit of Life appears; also Death – uninvited. They are (supposably) invisible. Death, tall, black-robed, corpse-faced, stands motionless and waits. The aged couple pray to the Spirit of Life for a means to prop up their existence and continue it. Their prayer fails. The Spirit of Life prophesies *Zoë's* martyrdom: it will take place before night. Soon *Apelles* arrives, young and vigorous and full of enthusiasm; he has led a host against the Persians and won the battle; he is the pet of fortune, rich, honoured, beloved, 'Master of Palmyra'. He has heard that whoever stretches himself out on one of those rocks there, and asks for a deathless life, can have his wish. He laughs at the tradition, but wants to make the trial anyway. The invisible Spirit of Life warns him: 'Life without end can be regret without end.' But he persists: let him keep his youth, his strength, and his mental faculties unimpaired, and he will take all the risks. He has his desire.

From this time forth, act after act, the troubles and sorrows and misfortunes and humiliations of life beat upon him without pity or respite; but he will not give up, he will not confess his mistake. Whenever he meets Death he still furiously defies him – but Death patiently waits. He, the healer of sorrows, is man's best friend: the recognition of this will come. As the years drag on, and on, and on, the friends of the *Master's* youth grow old; and one by one they totter to the grave: he goes on with his proud fight, and will not yield. At length he is wholly alone in the world; all his friends are dead; last of all, his darling of darlings, his son, the lad *Nymphas*, who dies in his arms. His pride is broken now; and he would welcome Death, if Death would come, if Death would hear his prayers and give him peace. The closing act is fine and pathetic. *Apelles* meets *Zenobia*, the helper of all who suffer, and tells her his story, which moves her pity. By common report she is endowed with more than earthly powers; and, since he cannot have the boon of death, he appeals to her to drown his memory in forgetfulness of his griefs – forgetfulness, 'which is death's equivalent'. She says (roughly translated), in an exaltation of compassion:

> 'Come to me!
> Kneel; and may the power be granted me
> To cool the fires of this poor tortured brain,
> And bring it peace and healing.'

He kneels. From her hand, which she lays upon his head, a mysterious influence steals through him; and he sinks into a dreamy tranquillity.

> 'Oh, if I could but so drift
> Through this soft twilight into the night of peace,
> Never to wake again!
> (*Raising his hand, as if in benediction.*)
> O mother earth, farewell!
> Gracious thou wert to me. Farewell!
> Apelles goes to rest.'

Death appears behind him and encloses the uplifted hand in his. *Apelles* shudders, wearily and slowly turns, and recognises his life-long adversary. He smiles and puts all his gratitude into one simple and touching sentence, 'Ich danke dir,' and dies.

Nothing, I think, could be more moving, more beautiful, than this close. This piece is just one long, soulful, sardonic laugh at human life. Its title might properly be 'Is Life a Failure?' and leave the five acts to play with the answer. I am not at all sure that the author meant to laugh at life. I only notice that he has done it. Without putting into words any ungracious or discourteous things about life, the episodes in the piece seem to be saying all the time, inarticulately: 'Note what a silly, poor thing human life is; how childish its ambitions, how ridiculous its pomps, how trivial its dignities, how cheap its heroisms, how capricious its course, how brief its flight, how stingy in happiness, how opulent in miseries, how few its prides, how multitudinous its humiliations, how comic its tragedies, how tragic its comedies, how wearisome and monotonous its repetition of its stupid history through the ages, with never the introduction of a new detail, how hard it has tried, from the Creation down, to play itself upon its possessor as a boon, and has never proved its case in a single instance!'

Take note of some of the details of the piece. Each of the five acts contains an independent tragedy of its own. In each act somebody's edifice of hope, or of ambition, or of happiness, goes down in ruins. Even *Apelles'* perennial youth is only a long tragedy, and his life a failure. There are two martyrdoms in the piece; and they are curiously and sarcastically contrasted. In the first act the pagans persecute *Zoë*, the Christian girl, and a pagan mob slaughters her. In the fourth act those same pagans – now very old and zealous – are become Christians, and they persecute the pagans: a mob of them slaughters the pagan youth, *Nymphas*, who is standing up for the old gods of his fathers. No remark is made about this picturesque failure of civilisation; but there it stands, as an unworded suggestion that civilisation, even when Christianised, was not able wholly to subdue the natural man in that old day – just as in our day, the spectacle of a shipwrecked French crew clubbing women and children who tried to climb into the lifeboats suggests that civilisation has not succeeded in entirely obliterating the natural man even yet. Common sailors! A year ago, in Paris, at a fire, the aristocracy of the same nation clubbed girls and women out of the way to save themselves. Civilisation tested at top and bottom both, you see. And in still another panic of fright we have this same 'tough' civilisation saving its honour by condemning an innocent man to multiform death, and hugging and whitewashing the guilty one.

In the second act a grand Roman official is not above trying to blast *Apelles'* reputation by falsely charging him with misappropriating public moneys. *Apelles*, who is too proud to endure even the suspicion of irregularity, strips himself to naked poverty to square the unfair account; and *his* troubles begin: the blight which is to continue and spread strikes his life; for the frivolous, pretty creature whom he has brought from Rome has no taste for poverty, and agrees to elope with a more competent candidate. Her presence in the house has previously brought down the pride and broken the heart of *Apelles'* poor old mother; and *her* life is a failure. Death comes for her, but is willing to trade her for the Roman girl; so the bargain is struck with *Apelles*, and the mother spared for the present.

No one's life escapes the blight. *Timoleus*, the gay satirist of the first two acts, who scoffed at the pious hypocrisies and money-grubbing ways of the great Roman lords, is grown old and fat and bleary-eyed and racked with disease in the third, has lost his stately purities, and watered the acid of his wit. *His* life has suffered defeat. Unthinkingly he swears by Zeus – from ancient habit – and then quakes with fright; for a fellow-communicant is passing by. Reproached by a pagan friend of his youth for his apostasy, he confesses that principle, when unsupported by an assenting stomach, has to climb down. One must have bread; and 'the bread is Christian now'. Then the poor old wreck, once so proud of iron rectitude, hobbles away, coughing and barking.

In the same act *Apelles* gives his sweet young Christian daughter and her fine young pagan lover his consent and blessing, and makes them utterly happy – for five minutes. Then the priest and the mob come, to tear them apart and put the girl in a nunnery; for marriage between the sects is forbidden. *Apelles'* wife could dissolve the rule; and she wants to do it: but under priestly pressure she wavers; then, fearing that in providing happiness for her child she would be committing a sin dangerous to herself, she goes over to the opposition, throwing the casting vote for the nunnery. The blight has fallen upon the young couple; *their* life is a failure.

In the fourth act, *Longinus*, who made such a prosperous and enviable start in the first act, is left alone in the desert, sick, blind, helpless, incredibly old, to die: not a friend left in the world – another ruined life. And in that act, also, *Apelles'* worshipped boy, *Nymphas*, done to death by the mob, breathes out his last sigh in his father's arms – one more failure. In the fifth act, *Apelles* himself dies, and is glad to do it; he who so ignorantly rejoiced, only four acts before, over the splendid present of an earthly immortality – the very worst failure of the lot!

❦ 2 ❦

Now I approach my project. Opposite is the theatre list for Saturday, 7th May 1898 – cut from the advertising columns of a New York paper.

Now I arrive at my project, and make my suggestion. From the look of this lightsome feast, I conclude that what you need is a tonic. Send for *The Master of Palmyra*. You are trying to make yourself believe that life is a comedy, that its sole business is fun, that there is nothing serious in it. You are ignoring the skeleton in your closet. Send for *The Master*

of Palmyra. You are neglecting a valuable side of your life; presently it will be atrophied. You are eating too much mental sugar; you will bring on Bright's disease of the intellect. You need a tonic; you need it very much. Send for *The Master of Palmyra*. You will not need to translate it: its story is as plain as a procession of pictures.

I have made my suggestion. Now I wish to put an annex to it. And that is this: It is right and wholesome to have those light comedies and entertaining shows; and I shouldn't wish to see them diminished. But none of us is *always* in the comedy spirit: we have our graver moods; they come to us all; the lightest of us cannot escape them. These moods have their appetites – healthy and legitimate appetites – and there ought to be some way of satisfying them. It seems to me that New York ought to have one theatre devoted to tragedy. With her three millions of population, and seventy outside millions to draw upon, she can afford it, she can support it. America devotes more time, labour, money, and attention to distributing literary and musical culture among the general public than does any other nation, perhaps; yet here you find her neglecting what is possibly the most effective of all the breeders and nurses and disseminators of high literary taste and lofty emotion – the tragic stage. To leave that powerful agency out is to haul the culture-wagon with a crippled team. Nowadays, when a mood comes which only Shakespeare can set to music, what must we do? Read Shakespeare ourselves! Isn't it pitiful? It is playing an organ solo on a Jew's harp. *We* can't read. None but the Booths can do it.

Thirty years ago Edwin Booth played *Hamlet* a hundred nights in New York. With three times the population, how often is *Hamlet* played now in a year? If Booth were back now in his prime, how often could he play it in New York? Some will say twenty-five nights. I will say three hundred, and say it with confidence. The tragedians are dead; but I think that the taste and intelligence which made their market are not.

What *has* come over us English-speaking people? During the first half of this century tragedies and great tragedians were as common with us as farce and comedy; and it was the same in England. Now we have not a tragedian, I believe; and London, with her fifty shows and theatres, has but three, I think. It is an astonishing thing, when you come to consider it. Vienna remains upon the ancient basis: there has been no change. She sticks to the former proportions: a number of rollicking comedies, admirably played, every night; and also every night at the Burg Theatre – that wonder of the world for grace and beauty and richness and splendour and costliness – a majestic drama of depth and seriousness, or a standard old tragedy. It is only within the last dozen years that men have learned to do miracles on the stage in the way of grand and enchanting scenic effects; and it is at such a time as this that we have reduced our scenery mainly to different breeds of parlours and varying aspects of furniture and rugs. I think we must have a Burg in New York, and Burg scenery, and a great company like the Burg company. Then, with a tragedy-tonic once or twice a month, we shall enjoy the comedies all the better. Comedy keeps the heart sweet; but we all know that there is wholesome refreshment for both mind and heart in an occasional climb among the pomps of the intellectual snow-summits built by Shakespeare and those others. Do I seem to be preaching? It is out of my line: I only do it because the rest of the clergy seem to be on vacation.

Diplomatic Pay and Clothes

Vienna, *January* 5 – I find in this morning's papers the statement that the Government of the United States has paid to the two members of the Peace Commission entitled to receive money for their services $100,000 each for their six weeks' work in Paris.

I hope that this is true. I will allow myself the satisfaction of considering that it *is* true, and of treating it as a thing finished and settled.

It is a precedent; and ought to be a welcome one to our country. A precedent always has a chance to be valuable (as well as the other way); and its best chance to be valuable (or the other way) is when it takes such a striking form as to fix a whole nation's attention upon it. If it come justified out of the discussion which will follow, it will find a career ready and waiting for it.

We realise that the edifice of public justice is built of precedents, from the ground upward; but we do not always realise that all the other details of our civilisation are likewise built of precedents. The changes also which they undergo are due to the intrusion of new precedents, which hold their ground against opposition, and keep their place. A precedent may die at birth, or it may live – it is mainly a matter of luck. If it be imitated once, it has a chance; if twice a better chance; if three times it is reaching a point where account must be taken of it; if four, five, or six times, it has probably come to stay – for a whole century, possibly. If a town start a new bow, or a new dance, or a new temperance project, or a new kind of hat, and can get the precedent adopted in the next town, the career of that precedent is begun; and it will be unsafe to bet as to where the end of its journey is going to be. It may not get this start at all, and may have no career; but if a crown prince introduce the precedent, it will attract vast attention, and its chances for a career are so great as to amount almost to a certainty.

For a long time we have been reaping damage from a couple of disastrous precedents. One is the precedent of shabby pay to public servants standing for the power and dignity of the Republic in foreign lands; the other is a precedent condemning them to exhibit themselves officially in clothes which are not only without grace or dignity, but are a pretty loud and pious rebuke to the vain and frivolous costumes worn by the other officials. To our day an American ambassador's official costume remains under the reproach of these defects. At a public function in a European court all foreign representatives except ours wear clothes which in some way distinguish them from the unofficial throng, and mark them as standing for their *countries*. But our representative appears in a plain black swallow-tail, which stands for neither country nor people. It has no nationality. It is found in all countries; it is as international as a nightshirt. It has no particular meaning: but our Government tries to give it one; it tries to make it stand for Republican Simplicity, modesty and unpretentiousness. Tries, and without doubt fails, for it is not conceivable that this loud ostentation of simplicity deceives anyone. The statue that advertises its modesty with a fig-leaf really brings its modesty under suspicion. Worn officially, our nonconforming swallow-tail is a declaration of ungracious independence in the matter of manners, and is uncourteous. It says to all around: 'In Rome we do not choose to do as Rome does; we refuse to respect your tastes and your traditions; we make no sacrifices to anyone's customs and prejudices; we yield no jot to the courtesies of life; we prefer our manners, and intrude them here.'

That is not the true American spirit, and those clothes misrepresent us. When a foreigner comes among us and trespasses against our customs and our code of manners, we are offended, and justly so: but our Government commands our ambassadors to wear abroad an official dress which is an offence against foreign manners and customs; and the discredit of it falls upon the nation.

We did not dress our public functionaries in undistinguished raiment before Franklin's time; and the change would not have come if he had been an obscurity. But he was such a colossal figure in the world that whatever he did of an unusual nature attracted the world's attention, and became a precedent. In the case of clothes, the next representative after him, and the next, had to imitate it. After that, the thing was custom: and custom is a petrifaction; nothing but dynamite can dislodge it for a century. We imagine that our queer official costumery was deliberately devised to symbolise our Republican Simplicity – a quality which we have never possessed, and are too old to acquire now, if we had any use for it or any leaning toward it. But it is not so; there was nothing deliberate about it: it grew naturally and heedlessly out of the precedent set by Franklin.

If it had been an intentional thing, and based upon a principle, it would not have stopped where it did: we should have applied it further. Instead of clothing our admirals and generals, for courts-martial and other public functions, in superb dress uniforms blazing with colour and gold, the Government would put them in swallow-tails and white cravats, and make them look like ambassadors and lackeys. If I am wrong in making Franklin the father of our curious official clothes, it is no matter – he will be able to stand it.

It is my opinion – and I make no charge for the suggestion – that, whenever we appoint an ambassador or a minister, we ought to confer upon him the temporary rank of admiral or general, and allow him to wear the corresponding uniform at public functions in foreign countries. I would recommend this for the reason that it is not consonant with the dignity of the United States of America that her representative should appear upon occasions of state in a dress which makes him glaringly conspicuous; and that is what his present undertaker-outfit does when it appears, with its dismal smudge, in the midst of the butterfly splendours of a Continental court. It is a most trying position for a shy man, a modest man, a man accustomed to being like other people. He is .he most striking figure present; there is no hiding from the multitudinous eyes. It would be funny, if it were not such a cruel spectacle, to see the hunted creature in his solemn sables scuffling around in that sea of vivid colour, like a mislaid Presbyterian in perdition. We are all aware that our representative's dress should not compel too much attention; for anybody but an Indian chief knows that that is a vulgarity. I am saying these things in the interest of our national pride and dignity. Our representative is the flag. He is the Republic. He is the United States of America. And when these embodiments pass by, we do not want them scoffed at; we desire that people shall be obliged to concede that they are worthily clothed, and politely.

Our Government is oddly inconsistent in this matter of official dress. When its representative is a civilian who has not been a soldier, it restricts him to the black swallow-tail and white tie; but if he is a civilian who has been a soldier, it allows him to wear the uniform of his former rank as an official dress. When General Sickles was minister to Spain, he always wore, when on official duty, the dress uniform of a major-general. When General Grant visited foreign courts, he went handsomely and properly ablaze in the uniform of a full general, and was introduced by diplomatic survivals of his own Presidential Administration. The latter, by official necessity, went in the meek and lowly swallow-tail – a deliciously sarcastic contrast: the one dress representing the honest and honourable dignity of the nation; the other, the cheap hypocrisy of the Republican Simplicity tradition. In Paris our present representative can perform his official functions reputably clothed; for he was an officer in the Civil War. In London our late ambassador was similarly situated; for he also was an officer in the Civil War. But Mr Choate must represent the Great Republic – even at official breakfast at seven in the morning – in that same old funny swallow-tail.

Our Government's notions about proprieties of costume are indeed very, very odd – as suggested by that last fact. The swallow-tail is recognised the world over as not wearable in the daytime; it is a night-dress, and a night-dress only – a nightshirt is not more so. Yet, when our representative makes an official visit in the morning, he is obliged by his Government to go in that night-dress. It makes the very cab-horses laugh.

The truth is, that for a while during the present century, and up to something short of forty years ago, we had a lucid interval, and dropped the Republican Simplicity sham, and dressed our foreign representatives in a handsome and becoming official costume. This was discarded by and by, and the swallow-tail substituted. I believe it is not now known which statesman brought about this change; but we all know that, stupid as he was as to diplomatic proprieties in dress, he would not have sent his daughter to a state ball in a corn-shucking costume, nor to a corn-shucking in a state ball costume, to be harshly criticised as an ill-mannered offender against the proprieties of custom in both places. And we know another thing, viz.: that he himself would not have wounded the tastes and feelings of a family of mourners by attending a funeral in their house in a costume which was an offence against the dignities and decorum prescribed by tradition and sancti-fied by custom. Yet that man was so heedless as not to reflect that *all* the social customs of civilised peoples are entitled to respectful observance, and that no man with a right spirit of courtesy in him ever has any disposition to transgress these customs.

There is still another argument for a rational diplomatic dress – a business argument. We are a trading nation; and our representative is our business agent. If he is respected, esteemed, and liked where he is stationed, he can exercise an influence which can extend our trade and forward our prosperity. A considerable number of his business activities have their field in his social relations; and clothes which do not offend against local manners and customs and prejudices are a valuable part of his equipment in this matter – would be, if Franklin had died earlier.

I have not done with gratis suggestions yet. We made a great and valuable advance when we instituted the office of ambassador. That lofty rank endows its possessor with several times as much influence, consideration, and effectiveness as the rank of minister bestows. For the sake of the country's dignity and for the sake of her advantage commercially, we should have ambassadors, not ministers, at the great courts of the world.

But not at present salaries! No; if we are to maintain present salaries, let us make no more ambassadors; and let us unmake those we have already made. The great position, without the means of respectably maintaining it – there could be no wisdom in that. A foreign representative, to be valuable to his country, must be on good terms with the officials of the capital and with the rest of the influential folk. He must mingle with this society; he cannot sit at home – it is not business, it butters no commercial parsnips. He must attend the dinners, banquets, suppers, balls, receptions, and must *return* these hospitalities. He should return as good as he gets, too, for the sake of the dignity of his country, and for the sake of Business. Have we ever had a minister or an ambassador who could do this on his salary? No – not once, from Franklin's time to ours. Other countries understand the commercial value of properly lining the pockets of their representatives; but apparently our Government has not learned it. England is the most successful trader of the several trading nations; and she takes good care of the watchmen who keep guard in her commercial towers. It has been a long time, now, since we needed to blush for our representatives abroad. It has become custom to send our fittest. We send men of distinction, cultivation, character – our ablest, our choicest, our best. Then we cripple their efficiency through the meagreness of their pay. Here is a list of salaries for English and American ministers and ambassadors:

CITY	SALARIES	
	AMERICAN	ENGLISH
Paris	$17,500	$45,000
Berlin	17,500	40,000
Vienna	12,000	40,000
Constantinople	10,000	40,000
St Petersburg	17,500	39,000
Rome	12,000	35,000
Washington	—	32,500

Sir Julian Pauncefote, the English ambassador at Washington, has a very fine house besides – at no damage to his salary.

English ambassadors pay no house-rent; they live in palaces owned by England. Our representatives pay house-rent out of their salaries. You can judge by the above figures what kind of houses the United States of America has been used to living in abroad, and what sort of return-entertaining she has done. There is not a salary in our list which would properly house the representative receiving it, and, in addition, pay $3,000 toward his family's bacon and doughnuts – the strange but economical and customary fare of the American ambassador's household, except on Sundays, when petrified Boston crackers are added.

The ambassadors and ministers of foreign nations not only have generous salaries, but their Governments provide them with money wherewith to pay a considerable part of their hospitality bills. I believe our Government pays no hospitality bills except those incurred by the navy. Through this concession to the navy, that arm is able to do us credit in foreign parts; and certainly that is well and politic. But why the Government does not think it well and politic that our diplomats should be able to do us like credit abroad is one of those mysterious inconsistencies which have been puzzling me ever since I stopped trying to understand baseball and took up statesmanship as a pastime.

To return to the matter of house-rent. Good houses, properly furnished, in European capitals, are not to be had at small figures. Consequently, our foreign representatives have been accustomed to live in garrets – sometimes on the roof. Being poor men, it has been the best they could do on the salary which the Government has paid them. How could they adequately return the hospitalities shown them? It was impossible. It would have exhausted the salary in three months. Still, it was their official duty to entertain the influentials after some sort of fashion; and they did the best they could with their limited purse. In return for champagne they furnished lemonade; in return for game they furnished ham; in return for whale they furnished sardines; in return for liquors they furnished condensed milk; in return for the battalion of liveried and powdered flunkeys they furnished the hired girl; in return for the fairy wilderness of sumptuous decorations they draped the stove with the American flag; in return for the orchestra they furnished zither and ballads by the family; in return for the ball – but they didn't return the ball, except in cases where the United States lived on the roof and had room.

Is this an exaggeration? It can hardly be called that. I saw nearly the equivalent of it once, a good many years ago. A minister was trying to create influential friends for a project which might be worth ten millions a year to the agriculturists of the Republic; and our Government had furnished him ham and lemonade to persuade the opposition with. The minister did not succeed. He might not have succeeded if his salary had been what it ought to have been – $50,000 or $60,000 a year – but his chances would have been very greatly improved. And in any case, he and his dinners and his country would not have been joked about by the hard-hearted and pitied by the compassionate.

Any experienced 'drummer' will testify that, when you want to do business, there is no economy in ham and lemonade. The drummer takes his country customer to the theatre, the opera, the circus; dines him, wines him, entertains him all the day and all the night in luxurious style; and plays upon his human nature in all seductive ways. For he knows, by old experience, that this is the best way to get a profitable order out of him. He has his reward. All Governments except our own play the same policy, with the same end in view; and they also have their reward. But ours refuses to do business by business ways, and sticks to ham and lemonade. This is the most expensive diet known to the diplomatic services of the world.

Ours is the only country of first importance that pays its foreign representatives trifling salaries. If we were poor, we could not find great fault with these economies, perhaps – at least one could find a sort of plausible excuse for them. But we are not poor; and the excuse fails. As shown above, some of our important diplomatic representatives receive $12,000; others $17,500. These salaries are all ham and lemonade, and unworthy of the flag. When we have a rich ambassador in London or Paris, he lives as the ambassador of a country like ours ought to live, and it costs him $100,000 a year to do it. But why should we allow him to pay that out of his private pocket? There is nothing fair about it; and the Republic is no proper subject for anyone's charity. In several cases our salaries of $12,000 should be $50,000; and all of the salaries of $17,500 ought to be $75,000 or $100,000, since we pay no representative's house-rent. Our State Department realises the mistake which we are making, and would like to rectify it, but it has not the power.

When a young girl reaches eighteen she is recognised as being a woman. She adds six inches to her skirt, she unplaits her dangling braids and balls her hair on top of her head, she stops sleeping with her little sister and has a room to herself, and becomes in many ways a thundering expense. But she is in society now; and papa has to stand it. There is no avoiding it. Very well. The Great Republic lengthened her skirts last year, balled up her hair, and entered the world's society. This means that, if she would prosper and stand fair with society, she must put aside some of her dearest and darlingest young ways and superstitions, and do as society does. Of course, she can decline if she wants to; but this would be unwise. She ought to realise, now that she has 'come out', that this is a right and proper time to change a part of her style. She is in Rome; and it has long been granted that when one is in Rome it is good policy to do as Rome does. To advantage Rome? No – to advantage herself.

If our Government has really paid representatives of ours on the Paris Commission $100,000 apiece for six weeks' work, I feel sure that it is the best cash investment the nation has made in many years. For it seems quite impossible that, with that precedent on the books, the Government will be able to find excuses for continuing its diplomatic salaries at the present mean figure.

PS – Vienna, *January 10* – I see, by this morning's telegraphic news, that I am not to be the new ambassador here, after all. This – well, I hardly know what to say. I – well, of course, I do not care anything about it; but it is at least a surprise. I have for many months been using my influence at Washington to get this diplomatic see expanded into an ambassadorship, with the idea, of course, th – But never mind. Let it go. It is of no consequence. I say it calmly; for I am calm. But at the same time – However, the subject has no interest for me, and never had. I never really intended to take the place, anyway – I made up my mind to it months and months ago, nearly a year. But now, while I am calm, I would like to say this – that so long as I shall continue to possess an American's proper pride in the honour and dignity of his country, I will not take any ambassadorship in the gift of the flag at a salary short of $75,000 a year. If I shall be charged with wanting to live beyond my country's means, I cannot help it. A country which cannot afford ambassador's wages should be ashamed to have ambassadors.

Think of a Seventeen-thousand-five-hundred-dollar ambassador! Particularly for *America*. Why, it is the most ludicrous spectacle, the most inconsistent and incongruous spectacle, contrivable by even the most diseased imagination. It is a billionaire in a paper collar, a king in a breechclout, an archangel in a tin halo. And, for pure sham and hypocrisy, the salary is just the match of the ambassador's official clothes – that boastful advertisement of a Republican Simplicity which manifests itself at home in Fifty-thousand-dollar salaries to insurance presidents and railway lawyers, and in domestic palaces whose fittings and furnishings often transcend in costly display and splendour and richness the fittings and furnishings of the palaces of the sceptred masters of Europe; and which has invented and exported to the Old World the palace-car, the sleeping-car, the tram-car, the electric trolley, the best bicycles, the best motor cars, the steam-heater, the best and smartest systems of electric calls and telephonic aids to laziness and comfort, the elevator, the private bathroom (hot and cold water on tap), the palace-hotel, with its multifarious conveniences, comforts, shows, and luxuries, the – oh, the list is interminable! In a word, Republican Simplicity found Europe with one shirt on her back, so to speak, as far as *real* luxuries, conveniences, and the comforts of life go, and has clothed her to the chin with the latter. We are the lavishest and showiest and most luxury-loving people on the earth; and at our masthead we fly one true and honest symbol, the gaudiest flag the world has ever seen. Oh, Republican Simplicity, there are many, many humbugs in the world, but none to which you need take off *your* hat!

Is He Living or is He Dead?

I was spending the month of March, 1892, at Mentone, in the Riviera. At this retired spot one has all the advantages, privately, which are to be had at Monte Carlo and Nice, a few miles farther along, publicly. That is to say, one has the flooding sunshine, the balmy air, and the brilliant blue sea, without the marring additions of human pow-wow and fuss and feathers and display. Mentone is quiet, simple, restful, unpretentious; the rich and the gaudy do not come there. As a rule, I mean, the rich do not come there. Now and then a rich man comes, and I presently got acquainted with one of these. Partially to disguise him I will call him Smith. One day, in the Hôtel des Anglais, at the second breakfast, he exclaimed:

'Quick! Cast your eye on the man going out at the door. Take in every detail of him.'

'Why?'

'Do you know who he is?'

'Yes. He spent several days here before you came. He is an old, retired, and very rich silk manufacturer from Lyons, they say, and I guess he is alone in the world, for he always looks sad and dreamy, and doesn't talk with anybody. His name is Théophile Magnan.'

I supposed that Smith would now proceed to justify the large interest which he had shown in Monsieur Magnan; but instead he dropped into a brown study, and was apparently lost to me and to the rest of the world during some minutes. Now and then he passed his fingers through his flossy white hair, to assist his thinking, and meantime he allowed his breakfast to go on cooling. At last he said:

'No, it's gone; I can't call it back.'

'Can't call what back?'

'It's one of Hans Andersen's beautiful little stories. But it's gone from me. Part of it is like this: A child has a caged bird, which it loves, but thoughtlessly neglects. The bird pours out its song unheard and unheeded; but in time, hunger and thirst assail the creature, and its song grows plaintive and feeble and finally ceases – the bird dies. The child comes, and is smitten to the heart with remorse; then, with bitter tears and lamentations, it calls its mates, and they bury the bird with elaborate pomp and the tenderest grief, without knowing, poor things, that it isn't children only who starve poets to death and then spend enough on their funerals and monuments to have kept them alive and made them easy and comfortable. Now – '

But here we were interrupted. About ten that evening I ran across Smith, and he asked me up to his parlour to help him smoke and drink hot Scotch. It was a cosy place, with its comfortable chairs, its cheerful lamps, and its friendly open fire of seasoned olive-wood. To make everything perfect, there was the muffled booming of the surf outside. After the second Scotch and much lazy and contented chat, Smith said:

'Now we are properly primed – I to tell a curious history, and you to listen to it. It has been a secret for many years – a secret between me and three others; but I am going to break the seal now. Are you comfortable?'

'Perfectly. Go on.'

Here follows what he told me:

'A long time ago I was a young artist – a very young artist, in fact – and I wandered about the country parts of France, sketching here and sketching there, and was presently joined by a couple of darling young Frenchmen who were at the same kind of thing that I was doing. We were as happy as we were poor, or as poor as we were happy – phrase it to suit yourself. Claude Frère and Carl Boulanger – these are the names of those boys; dear, dear fellows, and the sunniest spirits that ever laughed at poverty and had a noble good time in all weathers.

'At last we ran hard aground in a Breton village, and an artist as poor as ourselves took us in and literally saved us from starving – François Millet – '

'What! the *great* François Millet?'

'Great? He wasn't any greater than we were, then. He hadn't any fame, even in his own village; and he was so poor that he hadn't anything to feed us on but turnips, and even the turnips failed us sometimes. We four became fast friends, doting friends, inseparables. We painted away together with all our might, piling up stock, piling up stock, but very seldom getting rid of any of it. We had lovely times together; but, O my soul! how we were pinched now and then!

'For a little over two years this went on. At last, one day, Claude said:

' "Boys, we've come to the end. Do you understand that? – absolutely to the end. Everybody has struck – there's a league formed against us. I've been all around the village and it's just as I tell you. They refuse to credit us for another centime until all the odds and ends are paid up."

'This struck us cold. Every face was blank with dismay. We realised that our circumstances were desperate, now. There was a long silence. Finally, Millet said with a sigh:

' "Nothing occurs to me – nothing. Suggest something, lads."

'There was no response, unless a mournful silence may be called a response. Carl got up, and walked nervously up and down awhile, then said:

' "It's a shame! Look at these canvases: stacks and stacks of as good pictures as anybody in Europe paints – I don't care who he is. Yes, and plenty of lounging strangers have said the same – or nearly that, anyway."

' "But didn't buy," Millet said.

' "No matter, they said it; and it's true, too. Look at your 'Angelus' there! Will anybody tell me – "

' "Pah, Carl – my 'Angelus'! I was offered five francs for it."

' "When?"

' "Who offered it?"

' "Where is he?"

' "Why didn't you take it?"

' "Come – don't all speak at once. I thought he would give more – I was sure of it – he looked it – so I asked him eight."

' "Well – and then?"

' "He said he would call again."

' "Thunder and lightning! Why, François – "

' "Oh, I know – I know! It was a mistake, and I was a fool. Boys, I meant for the best; you'll grant me that, and I – "

' "Why, certainly, we know that, bless your dear heart; but don't you be a fool again."

' "I? I wish somebody would come along and offer us a cabbage for it – you'd see!"

' "A cabbage! Oh, don't name it – it makes my mouth water. Talk of things less trying."

' "Boys," said Carl, "*do* these pictures lack merit? Answer me that."

' "No!"

' "Aren't they of very great and high merit? Answer me that."

' "Yes!"

' "Of such great and high merit that, if an illustrious name were attached to them, they would sell at splendid prices. Isn't it so?"

' "Certainly it is. Nobody doubts that."

' "But – I'm not joking – *isn't* it so?"

' "Why, of course it's so – and *we* are not joking. But what of it? What of it? How does that concern us?"

' "In this way, comrades – we'll *attach* an illustrious name to them!"

'The lively conversation stopped. The faces were turned inquiringly upon Carl. What sort of riddle might this be? Where was an illustrious name to be borrowed? And who was to borrow it?

'Carl sat down, and said:

' "Now, I have a perfectly serious thing to propose. I think it is the only way to keep us out of the almshouse, and I believe it to be a perfectly sure way. I base this opinion upon certain multitudinous and long-established facts in human history. I believe my project will make us all rich."

' "Rich! You've lost your mind."

' "No, I haven't."

' "Yes, you have – you've lost your mind. What do you *call* rich?"

' "A hundred thousand francs apiece."

' "He *has* lost his mind. I knew it."

' "Yes, he has. Carl, privation has been too much for you, and – "

' "Carl, you want to take a pill and get right to bed."

' "Bandage him first – bandage his head, and then – "

' "No, bandage his heels; his brains have been settling for weeks – I've noticed it."

' "Shut up!" said Millet, with ostensible severity, "and let the boy say his say. Now, then – come out with your project, Carl. What is it?"

' "Well, then, by way of preamble I will ask you to note this fact in human history: that the merit of many a great artist has never been acknowledged until after he was starved and dead. This has happened so often that I make bold to found a law upon it. This law: that the merit of *every* great unknown and neglected artist must and will be recognised, and his pictures climb to high prices after his death. My project is this: we must cast lots – one of us must die."

'The remark fell so calmly and so unexpectedly that we almost forgot to jump. Then there was a wild chorus of advice again – medical advice – for the help of Carl's brain; but he waited patiently for the hilarity to calm down, then went on again with his project:

' "Yes, one of us must die, to save the others – and himself. We will cast lots. The one chosen shall be illustrious, all of us shall be rich. Hold still, now – hold still; don't interrupt – I tell you I know what I am talking about. Here is the idea. During the next three months the one who is to die shall paint with all his might, enlarge his stock all he can – not pictures, *no!* skeleton sketches, studies, parts of studies, fragments of studies, a dozen dabs of the brush on each – meaningless, of course, but *his* with his cipher on them; turn out fifty a day, each to contain some peculiarity or mannerism easily detectable as his – *they're* the things that sell, you know, and are collected at fabulous prices for the world's museums, after the great man is gone; we'll have a ton of them ready – a ton! And all that time the rest of us will be busy supporting the moribund, and working Paris and the dealers – preparations for the coming event, you know; and when everything is hot and just right, we'll spring the death on them and have the notorious funeral. You get the idea?"

' "N-o; at least, not qu – "

' "Not quite? Don't you see? The man doesn't really die; he changes his name and vanishes; we bury a dummy, and cry over it, with all the world to help. And I – "

'But he wasn't allowed to finish. Everybody broke out into a rousing hurrah of applause; and all jumped up and capered about the room and fell on each other's necks in transports of gratitude and joy. For hours we talked over the great plan, without ever feeling hungry; and at last, when all the details had been arranged satisfactorily, we cast lots and Millet was elected – elected to die, as we called it. Then we scraped together those things which one never parts with until he is betting them against future wealth – keepsake trinkets and suchlike – and these we pawned for enough to furnish us a frugal farewell supper and breakfast, and leave us a few francs over for travel, and a stake of turnips and such for Millet to live on for a few days.

'Next morning, early, the three of us cleared out, straightway after breakfast – on foot, of course. Each of us carried a dozen of Millet's small pictures, purposing to market them. Carl struck for Paris, where he would start the work of building up Millet's fame against the coming great day. Claude and I were to separate, and scatter abroad over France.

'Now, it will surprise you to know what an easy and comfortable thing we had. I walked two days before I began business. Then I began to sketch a villa in the outskirts of a big town – because I saw the proprietor standing on an upper veranda. He came down to look on – I thought he would. I worked swiftly, intending to keep him interested. Occasionally he fired off a little ejaculation of approbation, and by and by he spoke up with enthusiasm, and said I was a master!

'I put down my brush, reached into my satchel, fetched out a Millet, and pointed to the cipher in the corner. I said, proudly:

' "I suppose you recognise *that*? Well, he taught me! I should *think* I ought to know my trade!"

'The man looked guiltily embarrassed, and was silent. I said, sorrowfully:

' "You don't mean to intimate that you don't know the cipher of François Millet!"

'Of course he didn't know that cipher; but he was the gratefulest man you ever saw, just the same, for being let out of an uncomfortable place on such easy terms. He said:

' "No! Why, it *is* Millet's, sure enough! I don't know what I could have been thinking of. Of course I recognise it now."

'Next, he wanted to buy it; but I said that although I wasn't rich I wasn't *that* poor. However, at last, I let him have it for eight hundred francs.'

'Eight hundred!'

'Yes. Millet would have sold it for a pork chop. Yes, I got eight hundred francs for that little thing. I wish I could get it back for eighty thousand. But that time's gone by. I made a very nice picture of that man's house, and I wanted to offer it to him for ten francs, but that wouldn't answer, seeing I was the pupil of such a master, so I sold it to him for a hundred. I sent the eight hundred francs straight back to Millet from that town and struck out again next day.

'But I didn't walk – no. I rode. I have ridden ever since. I sold one picture every day, and never tried to sell two. I always said to my customer:

' "I am a fool to sell a picture of François Millet's at all, for that man is not going to live three months, and when he dies his pictures can't be had for love or money."

'I took care to spread that little fact as far as I could, and prepare the world for the event.

'I take credit to myself for our plan of selling the pictures – it was mine. I suggested it that last evening when we were laying out our campaign, and all three of us agreed to give it a good fair trial before giving it up for some other. It succeeded with all of us. I walked only two days, Claude walked two – both of us afraid to make Millet celebrated too close to home – but Carl walked only half a day, the bright, conscienceless rascal, and after that he travelled like a duke.

'Every now and then we got in with a country editor and started an item around through the press; not an item announcing that a new painter had been discovered, but an item which let on that everybody knew François Millet; not an item praising him in any way, but merely a word concerning the present condition of the "master" – sometimes hopeful, sometimes despondent, but always tinged with fears for the worst. We always marked these paragraphs, and sent the papers to all the people who had bought pictures of us.

'Carl was soon in Paris, and he worked things with a high hand. He made friends with the correspondents, and got Millet's condition reported to England and all over the continent, and America, and everywhere.

'At the end of six weeks from the start, we three met in Paris and called a halt, and stopped sending back to Millet for additional pictures. The boom was so high, and everything so ripe, that we saw that it would be a mistake not to strike now, right away, without waiting any longer. So we wrote Millet to go to bed and begin to waste away pretty fast, for we should like him to die in ten days if he could get ready.

'Then we figured up and found that among us we had sold eighty-five small pictures and studies, and had sixty-nine thousand francs to show for it. Carl had made the last sale and the most brilliant one of all. He sold the "Angelus" for twenty-two hundred francs. How we did glorify him! – not foreseeing that a day was coming by and by when France would struggle to own it and a stranger would capture it for five hundred and fifty thousand, cash.

'We had a wind-up champagne supper that night, and next day Claude and I packed up and went off to nurse Millet through his last days and keep busybodies out of the house and send daily bulletins to Carl in Paris for publication in the papers of several continents for the information of a waiting world. The sad end came at last, and Carl was there in time to help in the final mournful rites.

'You remember that great funeral, and what a stir it made all over the globe, and how the illustrious of two worlds came to attend it and testify their sorrow. We four – still inseparable – carried the coffin, and would allow none to help. And we were right about that, because it hadn't anything in it but a wax figure, and any other coffin-bearers would have found fault with the weight. Yes, we same old four, who had lovingly shared privation together in the old hard times now gone forever, carried the cof – '

'Which four?'

'*We* four – for Millet helped to carry his own coffin. In disguise, you know. Disguised as a relative – distant relative.'

'Astonishing!'

'But true, just the same. Well, you remember how the pictures went up. Money? We didn't know what to do with it. There's a man in Paris today who owns seventy Millet pictures. He paid us two million francs for them. And as for the bushels of sketches and studies which Millet shovelled out during the six weeks that we were on the road, well, it would astonish you to know the figure we sell them at nowadays – that is, when we consent to let one go!'

'It is a wonderful history, perfectly wonderful!'

'Yes – it amounts to that.'

'Whatever became of Millet?'

'Can you keep a secret?'

'I can.'

'Do you remember the man I called your attention to in the dining-room today? *That was François Millet.*'

'Great – '

'Scott! Yes. For once they didn't starve a genius to death and then put into other pockets the rewards he should have had himself. *This* songbird was not allowed to pipe out its heart unheard and then be paid with the cold pomp of a big funeral. We looked out for that.'

My Boyhood Dreams

The dreams of my boyhood? No, they have not been realised. For all who are old, there is something infinitely pathetic about the subject which you have chosen, for in no grey-head's case can it suggest any but one thing – disappointment. Disappointment is its own reason for its pain: the quality or dignity of the hope that failed is a matter aside. The dreamer's valuation of a thing lost – not another man's – is the only standard to measure it by, and his grief for it makes it large and great and fine, and is worthy of our reverence in all cases. We should carefully remember that. There are sixteen hundred million people in the world. Of these there is but a trifling number – in fact, only thirty-eight million – who can understand why a person should have an ambition to belong to the French army; and why, belonging to it, he should be proud of that; and why, having got down that far, he should want to go on down, down, down till he struck bottom and got on the General Staff; and why, being stripped of his livery, or set free and reinvested with his self-respect by any other quick and thorough process, let it be what it might, he should wish to return to his strange serfage. But no matter: the estimate put upon these things by the fifteen hundred and sixty millions is no proper measure of their value: the proper measure, the just measure, is that which is put upon them by Dreyfus, and is cipherable merely upon the littleness or the vastness of the *disappointment* which their loss cost him.

There you have it: the measure of the magnitude of a dream-failure is the measure of the disappointment the failure cost the dreamer; the value, in others' eyes, of the thing lost, has nothing to do with the matter. With this straightening-out and classification of the dreamer's position to help us, perhaps we can put ourselves in his place and respect his dream – Dreyfus's, and the dreams our friends have cherished and reveal to us. Some that I call to mind, some that have been revealed to me, are curious enough; but we may not smile at them, for they were precious to the dreamers, and their failure has left scars which give them dignity and pathos. With this theme in my mind, dear heads that were brown when they and mine were young together rise old and white before me now, beseeching me to speak for them, and most lovingly will I do it.

Howells, Hay, Aldrich, Matthews, Stockton, Cable, Remus – how their young hopes and ambitions come flooding back to my memory now, out of the vague far past, the beautiful past, the lamented past! I remember it so well – that night we met together – it was in Boston, and Mr Fields was there, and Mr Osgood, and Ralph Keeler, and Boyle O'Reilly, lost to us now these many years – and under the seal of confidence revealed to each other what our boyhood dreams had been: dreams which had not as yet been blighted, but over which was stealing the grey of the night that was to come – a night which we prophetically *felt*, and this feeling oppressed us and made us sad. I remember that Howells's voice broke twice, and it was only with great difficulty that he was able to go on; in the end he wept. For he had hoped to be an auctioneer. He told of his early struggles to climb to his goal, and how at last he attained to within a single step of the coveted summit. But there misfortune after misfortune assailed him, and he went down, and down, and down, until now at last, weary and disheartened, he had for the present given up the struggle and become editor of the *Atlantic Monthly*. This was in 1830. Seventy years are gone since, and where now is his dream? It will never be fulfilled. And it is best so; he is no longer fitted for the position; no one would take him now; even if he got it, he would not be able to do himself credit in it, on account of his deliberateness of speech and lack of trained professional vivacity; he would be put on real estate, and would have the pain of seeing younger and abler men entrusted with the furniture and other such goods – goods which draw a mixed and intellectually low order of customers, who must be beguiled of their bids by a vulgar and specialised humour and sparkle, accompanied with antics.

But it is not the thing lost that counts, but only the *disappointment* the loss brings to the dreamer that had coveted that thing and had set his heart of hearts upon it; and when we remember this, a great wave of sorrow for Howells rises in our breasts, and we wish for his sake that his fate could have been different.

At that time Hay's boyhood dream was not yet past hope of realisation, but it was fading, dimming, wasting away, and the wind of a growing apprehension was blowing cold over the perishing summer of his life. In the pride of his young ambition he had aspired to be a steamboat mate; and in fancy saw himself dominating a forecastle someday on the Mississippi and dictating terms to roustabouts in high and wounding tones. I look back now, from this far distance of seventy years, and note with sorrow the stages of that dream's destruction. Hay's history is but Howells's, with differences of detail. Hay climbed high toward his ideal; when success seemed almost sure, his foot upon the very gangplank, his eye upon the capstan, misfortune came and his fall began. Down – down – down – ever down: Private Secretary to the President; Colonel in the field; Chargé d'Affaires in Paris; Chargé d'Affaires in Vienna; Poet; Editor of the *Tribune*; Biographer of Lincoln; Ambassador to England; and now at last there he lies – Secretary of State, Head of Foreign Affairs. And he has fallen like Lucifer, never to rise again. And his dream – where now is his dream? Gone down in blood and tears with the dream of the auctioneer.

And the young dream of Aldrich – where is that? I remember yet how he sat there that night fondling it, petting it; seeing it recede and ever recede; trying to be reconciled and give it up, but not able yet to bear the thought; for it had been his hope to be a horse-doctor. He also climbed high, but, like the others, fell; then fell again, and yet again, and again and again. And now at last he can fall no further. He is old now, he has ceased to struggle, and is only a poet. No one would risk a horse with him now. His dream is over.

Has *any* boyhood dream ever been fulfilled? I must doubt it. Look at Brander Matthews. He wanted to be a cowboy. What is he today? Nothing but a professor in a university. Will he ever be a cowboy? It is hardly conceivable.

Look at Stockton. What was Stockton's young dream? He hoped to be a barkeeper. See where *he* has landed.

Is it better with Cable? What was Cable's young dream? To be ring-master in the circus, and swell around and crack the whip. What is he today? Nothing but a theologian and novelist.

And Uncle Remus – what was his young dream? To be a buccaneer. Look at him now.

Ah, the dreams of our youth, how beautiful they are, and how perishable! The ruins of these might-have-beens, how pathetic! The heart-secrets that were revealed that night now so long vanished, how they touch me as I give them voice! Those sweet privacies, how they endeared us to each other! We were under oath never to tell any of these things, and I have always kept that oath inviolate when speaking with persons whom I thought not worthy to hear them.

Oh, our lost Youth – God keep its memory green in our hearts! for Age is upon us, with the indignity of its infirmities, and Death beckons!

TO THE ABOVE OLD PEOPLE

Sleep! for the Sun that scores another Day
Against the Tale allotted You to stay,
   Reminding You, is Risen, and now
Serves Notice – ah, ignore it while You may!

The chill Wind blew, and those who stood before
The Tavern murmured, 'Having drunk his Score,
   Why tarries He with empty Cup? Behold,
The Wine of Youth once poured, is poured no more.

'Come leave the Cup, and on the Winter's Snow
Your Summer Garment of Enjoyment throw:
   Your Tide of Life is ebbing fast, and it,
Exhausted once, for You no more shall flow.'

While yet the Phantom of false Youth was mine,
I heard a Voice from out the Darkness whine,
   'O Youth, O whither gone? Return,
And bathe my Age in thy reviving Wine.'

In this subduing Draught of tender green
And kindly Absinthe, with its wimpling Sheen
   Of dusky half-lights, let me drown
The haunting Pathos of the Might-Have-Been.

For every nickeled Joy, marred and brief,
We pay someday its Weight in golden Grief
   Mined from our Hearts. Ah, murmur not –
From this one-sided Bargain dream of no Relief!

The Joy of Life, that streaming through their Veins
Tumultuous swept, falls slack – and wanes
   The Glory in the Eye – and one by one
Life's Pleasures perish and make place for Pains.

Whether one hide in some secluded Nook –
Whether at Liverpool or Sandy Hook –
   'Tis one. Old Age will search him out – and He –
He – He – when ready will know where to look.

From Cradle unto Grave I keep a House
Of Entertainment where may drowse

Bacilli and kindred Germs – or feed – or breed
Their festering Species in a deep Carouse.

Think – in this battered Caravanserai,
Whose Portals open stand all Night and Day,
   How Microbe after Microbe with his Pomp
Arrives unasked, and comes to stay.

Our ivory Teeth, confessing to the Lust
Of masticating, once, now own Disgust
   Of Clay-plug'd Cavities – full soon our Snags
Are emptied, and our Mouths are filled with Dust.

Our Gums forsake the Teeth and tender grow,
And fat, like over-ripened Figs – we know
   The Sign – the Riggs Disease is ours, and we
Must list this Sorrow, add another Woe.

Our Lungs begin to fail and soon we Cough,
And chilly Streaks play up our Backs, and off
   Our fever'd Foreheads drips an icy Sweat –
We scoffed before, but now we may not scoff.

Some for the Bunions that afflict us prate
Of Plasters unsurpassable, and hate
   To cut a Corn – ah cut, and let the Plaster go,
Nor murmur if the Solace come too late.

Some for the Honours of Old Age, and some
Long for its Respite from the Hum
   And Clash of sordid Strife – O Fools,
The Past should teach them what's to Come:

Lo, for the Honours, cold Neglect instead!
For Respite, disputatious Heirs a Bed
   Of Thorns for them will furnish. Go,
Seek not Here for Peace – but Yonder – with the Dead.

For whether Zal and Rustam heed this Sign,
And even smitten thus, will not repine,
   Let Zal and Rustam shuffle as they may,
The Fine once levied they must Cash the Fine.

O Voices of the Long Ago that were so dear!
Fall'n Silent, now, for many a Mould'ring Year,

O whither are ye flown? Come back,
And break my Heart, but bless my grieving ear.

Some happy Day my Voice will Silent fall,
And answer not when some that love it call:
   Be glad for Me when this you note – and think
I've found the Voices lost, beyond the Pall.

So let me grateful drain the Magic Bowl
That medicines hurt Minds and on the Soul
   The Healing of its Peace doth lay – if then
Death claim me – Welcome be his Dole!

SANNA, SWEDEN, *September 15th*

Private – If you don't know what Riggs's Disease of the Teeth is, the dentist will tell you. I've had it – and it is more than interesting. S. L. C.

EDITORIAL NOTE

Fearing that there might be some mistake, we submitted a proof of this article to the (American) gentlemen named in it, and asked them to correct any errors of detail that might have crept in among the facts. They reply with some asperity that errors cannot creep in among facts where there are no facts for them to creep in among; and that none are discoverable in this article, but only baseless aberrations of a disordered mind. They have no recollection of any such night in Boston, nor elsewhere; and in their opinion there was never any such night. They have *met* Mr Twain, but have had the prudence not to entrust any privacies to him – particularly under oath; and they think they now see that this prudence was justified, since he has been untrustworthy enough to even betray privacies which had no existence. Further they think it a strange thing that Mr Twain, who was never invited to meddle with anybody's boyhood dreams but his own, has been so gratuitously anxious to see that other people's are placed before the world that he has quite lost his head in his zeal and forgotten to make any mention of his own at all. Provided we insert this explanation, they are willing to let his article pass; otherwise they must require its suppression in the interest of truth.

PS – These replies having left us in some perplexity, and also in some fear lest they might distress Mr Twain if published without his privity, we judged it but fair to submit them to him and give him an opportunity to defend himself. But he does not seem to be troubled, or even aware that he is in a delicate situation. He merely says:

'Do not worry about those former young people. They can write good literature, but when it comes to speaking the truth, they have not had my training. – MARK TWAIN.'

The last sentence seems obscure, and liable to an unfortunate construction. It plainly needs refashioning, but we cannot take the responsibility of doing it. – EDITOR

The Austrian Edison
Keeping School Again

By a paragraph in the *Freie Presse* it appears that Jan Szczepanik, the youthful inventor of the 'telelectroscope' (for seeing at great distances) and some other scientific marvels, has been having an odd adventure, by help of the state.

Vienna is hospitably ready to smile whenever there is an opportunity, and this seems to be a fair one. Three or four years ago, when Szczepanik was nineteen or twenty years old, he was a schoolmaster in a Moravian village, on a salary of – I forget the amount, but no matter; there was not enough of it to remember. His head was full of inventions, and in his odd hours he began to plan them out. He soon perfected an ingenious invention for applying photography to pattern-designing as used in the textile industries, whereby he proposed to reduce the customary outlay of time, labour, and money expended on that department of loom-work to next to nothing. He wanted to carry his project to Vienna and market it; and as he could not get leave of absence, he made his trip without leave. This lost him his place, but did not gain him his market. When his money ran out he went back home, and was presently reinstated. By and by he deserted once more, and went to Vienna, and this time he made some friends who assisted him, and his invention was sold to England and Germany for a great sum. During the past three years he has been experimenting and investigating in velvety comfort. His most picturesque achievement is his telelectroscope, a device which a number of able men – including Mr Edison, I think – had already tried their hands at, with prospects of eventual success. A Frenchman came near to solving the difficult and intricate problem fifteen years ago, but an essential detail was lacking which he could not master, and he suffered defeat. Szczepanik's experiments with his pattern-designing project revealed to him the secret of the lacking detail. He perfected his invention, and a French syndicate has bought it, and saved it for exhibition and fortune-making at the Paris world's fair.

As a schoolmaster Szczepanik was exempt from military duty. When he ceased from teaching, being an educated man he could have had himself enrolled as a one-year volunteer; but he forgot to do it, and this exposed him to the privilege, and also the necessity, of serving *three* years in the army. In the course of duty, the other day, an official discovered the inventor's indebtedness to the state, and took the proper measures to collect. At first there seemed to be no way for the inventor (and the state) out of the difficulty. The authorities were loath to take the young man out of his great laboratory, where he was helping to shove the whole human race along on its road to new prosperities and scientific conquests, and suspend operations in his mental Klondike three years, while he punched the empty air with a bayonet in a time of peace; but there was the law, and how was it to be helped? It was a difficult puzzle, but the authorities laboured at it until they found a forgotten law somewhere which furnished a loophole – a large one, and a long one, too, as it looks to me. By this piece of good luck Szczepanik is saved from soldiering, but he becomes a schoolmaster again; and it is a sufficiently picturesque billet, when you examine it. He must go back to his village every two months, and teach his school half a day – from early in the morning until noon; and, to the best of my understanding of the published terms, he must keep this up the rest of his life! I hope so, just for the romantic poeticalness of it. He is twenty-four, strongly and compactly built, and comes of an ancestry accustomed to waiting to see its great-grandchildren married. It is almost certain that he will live to be ninety. I hope so. This promises him sixty-six years of useful school service. Dissected, it gives him a chance to teach school 396 half-days, make 396 railway trips going and 396 back, pay bed and board 396 times in the village, and lose possibly 1,200 days from his laboratory work – that is to say, three years and three months or so. And he already owes three years to this same account. This has been overlooked; I shall call the attention of the authorities to it. It may be possible for him to get a compromise on this compromise by doing his three years in the army, and saving one; but I think it can't happen. This government 'holds the age' on him; it has what is technically called a 'good thing' in financial circles, and knows a good thing when it sees it. I know the inventor very well, and he has my sympathy. This is friendship. But I am throwing my influence with the government. This is politics.

Szczepanik left for his village in Moravia the day before yesterday to 'do time' for the first time under his sentence. Early yesterday morning he started for the school in a fine carriage, which was stocked with fruits, cakes, toys, and all sorts of knick-knacks, rarities, and surprises for the children, and was met on the road by the school and a body of schoolmasters from the neighbouring districts, marching in column, with the village authorities at the head, and was received with the enthusiastic welcome proper to the man who had made their village's name celebrated, and conducted in state to the humble doors which had been shut against him as a deserter three years before. It is out of materials like these that romances are woven; and when the romancer has done his best, he has not improved upon the unpainted facts. Szczepanik put the sapless school-books aside, and led the children a holiday dance through the enchanted lands of science and invention, explaining to them some of the curious things which he had contrived, and the laws which governed their construction and performance, and illustrating these matters with pictures and models and other helps to a clear understanding of their fascinating mysteries. After this there was play and a distribution of the fruits and toys and things; and after this, again, some more science, including the story of the invention of the telephone, and an explanation of its character and laws, for the convict had brought a telephone along. The children saw that wonder for the first time, and they also personally tested its powers and verified them. Then school 'let out'; the teacher got his certificate, all signed, stamped, taxed, and so on, said goodbye, and drove off in his carriage under a storm of '*Do widzenia!*' ('*Au revoir!*') from the children, who will resume their customary sobrieties until he comes in August and uncorks his flask of scientific fire-water again.

Extracts from Adam's Diary

Monday. This new creature with the long hair is a good deal in the way. It is always hanging around and following me about. I don't like this; I am not used to company. I wish it would stay with the other animals . . . Cloudy today, wind in the east; think we shall have rain . . . *We?* Where did I get that word? – I remember now – the new creature uses it.

Tuesday. Been examining the great waterfall. It is the finest thing on the estate, I think. The new creature calls it Niagara Falls – why, I am sure I do not know. Says it *looks* like Niagara Falls. That is not a reason, it is mere waywardness and imbecility. I get no chance to name anything myself. The new creature names everything that comes along, before I can get in a protest. And always that same pretext is offered – it *looks* like the thing. There is the dodo, for instance. Says the moment one looks at it one sees at a glance that it 'looks like a dodo'. It will have to keep that name, no doubt. It wearies me to fret about it, and it does no good, anyway. Dodo! It looks no more like a dodo than I do.

Wednesday. Built me a shelter against the rain, but could not have it to myself in peace. The new creature intruded. When I tried to put it out, it shed water out of the holes it looks with, and wiped it away with the back of its paws, and made a noise such as some of the other animals make when they are in distress. I wish it would not talk; it is always talking. That sounds like a cheap fling at the poor creature, a slur; but I do not mean it so. I have never heard the human voice before, and any new and strange sound intruding itself here upon the solemn hush of these dreaming solitudes offends my ear and seems a false note. And this new sound is so close to me; it is right at my shoulder, right at my ear, first on one side and then on the other, and I am used only to sounds that are more or less distant from me.

Friday. The naming goes recklessly on, in spite of anything I can do. I had a very good name for the estate, and it was musical and pretty – 'Garden of Eden'. Privately, I continue to call it that, but not any longer publicly. The new creature says it is all woods and rocks and scenery, and therefore has no resemblance to a garden. Says it *looks* like a park, and does not look like anything *but* a park. Consequently, without consulting me, it has been new-named – 'Niagara Falls Park'. This is sufficiently high-handed, it seems to me. And already there is a sign up:

KEEP OFF

THE GRASS

My life is not as happy as it was.

Saturday.   The new creature eats too much fruit. We are going to run short, most likely. 'We' again – that is *its* word; mine, too, now, from hearing it so much. Good deal of fog this morning. I do not go out in the fog myself. The new creature does. It goes out in all weathers, and stumps right in with its muddy feet. And talks. It used to be so pleasant and quiet here.

Sunday.   Pulled through. This day is getting to be more and more trying. It was selected and set apart last November as a day of rest. I had already six of them per week before. This morning found the new creature trying to clod apples out of that forbidden tree.

Monday.   The new creature says its name is Eve. That is all right, I have no objections. Says it is to call it by, when I want it to come. I said it was superfluous, then. The word evidently raised me in its respect; and indeed it is a large, good word and will bear repetition. It says it is not an It, it is a She. This is probably doubtful; yet it is all one to me; what she is were nothing to me if she would but go by herself and not talk.

Tuesday.   She has littered the whole estate with execrable names and offensive signs:

THIS WAY TO THE WHIRLPOOL.

THIS WAY TO THE ISLAND.

CAVE OF THE WINDS THIS WAY.

She says this park would make a tidy summer resort if there was any custom for it. Summer resort – another invention of hers – just words, without any meaning. What is a summer resort? But it is best not to ask her, she has such a rage for explaining.

Friday.   She has taken to beseeching me to stop going over the Falls. What harm does it do? Says it makes her shudder. I wonder why; I have always done it – always liked the plunge, and the excitement and the coolness. I supposed it was what the Falls were for. They have no other use that I can see, and they must have been made for something. She says they were only made for scenery – like the rhinoceros and the mastodon.

I went over the Falls in a barrel – not satisfactory to her. Went over in a tub – still not satisfactory. Swam the Whirlpool and the Rapids in a fig-leaf suit. It got much damaged. Hence, tedious complaints about my extravagance. I am too much hampered here. What I need is change of scene.

Saturday.   I escaped last Tuesday night, and travelled two days, and built me another shelter in a secluded place, and obliterated my tracks as well as I could, but she hunted me out by means of a beast which she has tamed and calls a wolf, and came making that pitiful noise again, and shedding that water out of the places she looks with. I was obliged to return with her, but will presently emigrate again when occasion offers. She engages herself in many foolish things; among others, to study out why the animals called lions and tigers live on grass and flowers, when, as she says, the sort of teeth they wear would indicate that they were intended to eat each other. This is foolish, because to do that would be to kill each other, and that would introduce what, as I understand it, is called 'death'; and death, as I have been told, has not yet entered the Park. Which is a pity, on some accounts.

Sunday.   Pulled through.

Monday.   I believe I see what the week is for: it is to give time to rest up from the weariness of Sunday. It seems a good idea . . . She has been climbing that tree again. Clodded her out of it. She said nobody was looking. Seems to consider that a sufficient justification for chancing any dangerous thing. Told her that. The word justification moved her admiration – and envy, too, I thought. It is a good word.

Tuesday.   She told me she was made out of a rib taken from my body. This is at least doubtful, if not more than that. I have not missed any rib. . . She is in much trouble about the buzzard; says grass does not agree with it; is afraid she can't raise it; thinks it was intended to live on decayed flesh. The buzzard must get along the best it can with what it is provided. We cannot overturn the whole scheme to accommodate the buzzard.

Saturday.   She fell in the pond yesterday when she was looking at herself in it, which she is always doing. She nearly strangled, and said it was most uncomfortable. This made her sorry for the creatures which live in there, which she calls fish, for she continues to fasten names on to things that don't need them and don't come when they are called by them, which is a matter of no consequence to her, she is such a numskull, anyway; so she got a lot of them out and brought them in last night and put them in my bed to keep warm, but I have noticed them now and then all day and I don't see that they are any happier there than they were before, only quieter. When night comes I shall throw them outdoors. I will not sleep with them again, for I find them clammy and unpleasant to lie among when a person hasn't anything on.

Sunday. Pulled through.

Tuesday. She has taken up with a snake now. The other animals are glad, for she was always experimenting with them and bothering them; and I am glad because the snake talks, and this enables me to get a rest.

Friday. She says the snake advises her to try the fruit of that tree, and says the result will be a great and fine and noble education. I told her there would be another result, too – it would introduce death into the world. That was a mistake – it had been better to keep the remark to myself; it only gave her an idea – she could save the sick buzzard, and furnish fresh meat to the despondent lions and tigers. I advised her to keep away from the tree. She said she wouldn't. I foresee trouble. Will emigrate.

Wednesday. I have had a variegated time. I escaped last night, and rode a horse all night as fast as he could go, hoping to get clear out of the Park and hide in some other country before the trouble should begin; but it was not to be. About an hour after sun-up, as I was riding through a flowery plain where thousands of animals were grazing, slumbering, or playing with each other, according to their wont, all of a sudden they broke into a tempest of frightful noises, and in one moment the plain was a frantic commotion and every beast was destroying its neighbour. I knew what it meant – Eve had eaten that fruit, and death was come into the world . . . The tigers ate my horse, paying no attention when I ordered them to desist, and they would have eaten me if I had stayed – which I didn't, but went away in much haste . . . I found this place, outside the Park, and was fairly comfortable for a few days, but she has found me out. Found me out, and has named the place Tonawanda – says it *looks* like that. In fact I was not sorry she came, for there are but meagre pickings here, and she brought some of those apples. I was obliged to eat them, I was so hungry. It was against my principles, but I

find that principles have no real force except when one is well fed . . .
She came curtained in boughs and bunches of leaves, and when I asked
her what she meant by such nonsense, and snatched them away and
threw them down, she tittered and blushed. I had never seen a person
titter and blush before, and to me it seemed unbecoming and idiotic.
She said I would soon know how it was myself. This was correct.
Hungry as I was, I laid down the apple half-eaten – certainly the best
one I ever saw, considering the lateness of the season – and arrayed
myself in the discarded boughs and branches, and then spoke to her
with some severity and ordered her to go and get some more and not
make such a spectacle of herself. She did it, and after this we crept down
to where the wild-beast battle had been, and collected some skins, and I
made her patch together a couple of suits proper for public occasions.
They are uncomfortable, it is true, but stylish, and that is the main point
about clothes . . . I find she is a good deal of a companion. I see I should
be lonesome and depressed without her, now that I have lost my
property. Another thing, she says it is ordered that we work for our
living hereafter. She will be useful. I will superintend.

Ten Days Later.   She accuses *me* of being the cause of our disaster! She
says, with apparent sincerity and truth, that the Serpent assured her
that the forbidden fruit was not apples, it was chestnuts. I said I was
innocent, then, for I had not eaten any chestnuts. She said the Serpent
informed her that 'chestnut' was a figurative term meaning an aged and
mouldy joke. I turned pale at that, for I have made many jokes to pass
the weary time, and some of them could have been of that sort, though
I had honestly supposed that they were new when I made them. She
asked me if I had made one just at the time of the catastrophe. I was
obliged to admit that I had made one to myself, though not aloud. It
was this. I was thinking about the Falls, and I said to myself, 'How
wonderful it is to see that vast body of water tumble down there!' Then
in an instant a bright thought flashed into my head, and I let it fly,
saying, 'It would be a deal more wonderful to see it tumble *up* there!' –
and I was just about to kill myself with laughing at it when all nature
broke loose in war and death and I had to flee for my life. 'There,' she
said, with triumph, 'that is just it; the Serpent mentioned that very jest,
and called it the First Chestnut, and said it was coeval with the
creation.' Alas, I am indeed to blame. Would that I were not witty; oh,
that I had never had that radiant thought!

Next Year.   We have named it Cain. She caught it while I was up
country trapping on the North Shore of the Erie; caught it in the

timber a couple of miles from our dug-out – or it might have been four, she isn't certain which. It resembles us in some ways, and may be a relation. That is what she thinks, but this is an error, in my judgment. The difference in size warrants the conclusion that it is a different and new kind of animal – a fish, perhaps, though when I put it in the water to see, it sank, and she plunged in and snatched it out before there was opportunity for the experiment to determine the matter. I still think it is a fish, but she is indifferent about what it is, and will not let me have it to try. I do not understand this. The coming of the creature seems to have changed her whole nature and made her unreasonable about experiments. She thinks more of it than she does of any of the other animals, but is not able to explain why. Her mind is disordered – everything shows it. Sometimes she carries the fish in her arms half the night when it complains and wants to get to the water. At such times the water comes out of the places in her face that she looks out of, and she pats the fish on the back and makes soft sounds with her mouth to soothe it, and betrays sorrow and solicitude in a hundred ways. I have never seen her do like this with any other fish, and it troubles me greatly. She used to carry the young tigers around so, and play with them, before we lost our property, but it was only play; she never took on about them like this when their dinner disagreed with them.

Sunday.   She doesn't work, Sundays, but lies around all tired out, and likes to have the fish wallow over her; and she makes fool noises to amuse it, and pretends to chew its paws, and that makes it laugh. I have not seen a fish before that could laugh. This makes me doubt . . . I have come to like Sunday myself. Superintending all the week tires a body so. There ought to be more Sundays. In the old days they were tough, but now they come handy.

Wednesday.   It isn't a fish. I cannot quite make out what it is. It makes curious devilish noises when not satisfied, and says 'goo-goo' when it is. It is not one of us, for it doesn't walk; it is not a bird, for it doesn't fly; it is not a frog, for it doesn't hop; it is not a snake, for it doesn't crawl; I feel sure it is not a fish, though I cannot get a chance to find out whether it can swim or not. It merely lies around, and mostly on its back, with its feet up. I have not seen any other animal do that before. I said I believed it was an enigma; but she only admired the word without understanding it. In my judgment it is either an enigma or some kind of a bug. If it dies, I will take it apart and see what its arrangements are. I never had a thing perplex me so.

Three Months Later.   The perplexity augments instead of diminishing. I sleep but little. It has ceased from lying around, and goes about on its four legs now. Yet it differs from the other four-legged animals, in that its front legs are unusually short, consequently this causes the main part of its person to stick up uncomfortably high in the air, and this is not attractive. It is built much as we are, but its method of travelling shows that it is not of our breed. The short front legs and long hind ones indicate that it is of the kangaroo family, but it is a marked variation of the species, since the true kangaroo hops, whereas this one never does. Still it is a curious and interesting variety, and has not been catalogued before. As I discovered it, I have felt justified in securing the credit of the discovery by attaching my name to it, and hence have called it *Kangaroorum Adamiensis* . . . It must have been a young one when it came, for it has grown exceedingly since. It must be five times as big, now, as it was then, and when discontented it is able to make from twenty-two to thirty-eight times the noise it made at first. Coercion does not modify this, but has the contrary effect. For this reason I discontinued the system. She reconciles it by persuasion, and by giving it things which she had previously told it she wouldn't give it. As already observed, I was not at home when it first came, and she told me she found it in the woods. It seems odd that it should be the only one, yet it must be so, for I have worn myself out these many weeks trying to find another one to add to my collection, and for this one to play with; for surely then it would be quieter and we could tame it more easily. But I find none, nor any vestige of any; and strangest of all, no tracks. It has to live on the ground, it cannot help itself; therefore, how does it get about without leaving a track? I have set a dozen traps, but they do no good. I catch all small animals except that one; animals that merely go into the trap out of curiosity, I think, to see what the milk is there for. They never drink it.

Three Months Later.   The Kangaroo still continues to grow, which is very strange and perplexing. I never knew one to be so long getting its growth. It has fur on its head now; not like kangaroo fur, but exactly like our hair except that it is much finer and softer, and instead of being black is red. I am like to lose my mind over the capricious and harassing developments of this unclassifiable zoological freak. If I could catch another one – but that is hopeless; it is a new variety, and the only sample; this is plain. But I caught a true kangaroo and brought it in, thinking that this one, being lonesome, would rather have that for company than have no kin at all, or any animal it could feel a nearness to or get sympathy from in its forlorn condition here among strangers who do not know its ways or habits, or what to do to make it feel that it is among friends; but it was a mistake – it went into such fits at the sight of the kangaroo that I was convinced it had never seen one before. I pity the poor noisy little animal, but there is nothing I can do to make it happy. If I could tame it – but that is out of the question; the more I try the worse I seem to make it. It grieves me to the heart to see it in its little storms of sorrow and passion. I wanted to let it go, but she wouldn't hear of it. That seemed cruel and not like her; and yet she may be right. It might be lonelier than ever; for since I cannot find another one, how could *it*?

Five Months Later.   It is not a kangaroo. No, for it supports itself by holding to her finger, and thus goes a few steps on its hind legs, and then falls down. It is probably some kind of a bear; and yet it has no tail – as yet – and no fur, except on its head. It still keeps on growing – that is a curious circumstance, for bears get their growth earlier than this. Bears are dangerous – since our catastrophe – and I shall not be satisfied to have this one prowling about the place much longer without a muzzle on. I have offered to get her a kangaroo if she would let this one go, but it did no good – she is determined to run us into all sorts of foolish risks, I think. She was not like this before she lost her mind.

A Fortnight Later.   I examined its mouth. There is no danger yet: it has only one tooth. It has no tail yet. It makes more noise now than it ever did before – and mainly at night. I have moved out. But I shall go over, mornings, to breakfast, and see if it has more teeth. If it gets a mouthful of teeth it will be time for it to go, tail or no tail, for a bear does not need a tail in order to be dangerous.

Four Months Later.   I have been off hunting and fishing a month, up in the region that she calls Buffalo; I don't know why, unless it is because there are not any buffaloes there. Meantime the bear has learned to paddle around all by itself on its hind legs, and says 'poppa' and 'momma'. It is certainly a new species. This resemblance to words may be purely accidental, of course, and may have no purpose or meaning; but even in that case it is still extraordinary, and is a thing which no other bear can do. This imitation of speech, taken together with general absence of fur and entire absence of tail, sufficiently indicates that this is a new kind of bear. The further study of it will be exceedingly interesting. Meantime I will go off on a far expedition among the forests of the north and make an exhaustive search. There must certainly be another one somewhere, and this one will be less dangerous when it has company of its own species. I will go straightway; but I will muzzle this one first.

Three Months Later.   It has been a weary, weary hunt, yet I have had no success. In the meantime, without stirring from the home estate, she has caught another one! I never saw such luck. I might have hunted these woods a hundred years, I never would have run across that thing.

Next Day.   I have been comparing the new one with the old one, and it is perfectly plain that they are the same breed. I was going to stuff one of them for my collection, but she is prejudiced against it for some reason or other; so I have relinquished the idea, though I think it is a mistake. It would be an irreparable loss to science if they should get away. The old one is tamer than it was and can laugh and talk like the parrot, having learned this, no doubt, from being with the parrot so much, and having the imitative faculty in a highly developed degree. I shall be astonished if it turns out to be a new kind of parrot; and yet I ought not to be astonished, for it has already been everything else it could think of since those first days when it was a fish. The new one is as ugly now as the old one was at first; has the same sulphur-and-raw-meat complexion and the same singular head without any fur on it. She calls it Abel.

Ten Years Later.   They are *boys*; we found it out long ago. It was their coming in that small, immature shape that puzzled us; we were not used to it. There are some girls now. Abel is a good boy, but if Cain had stayed a bear it would have improved him. After all these years, I see that I was mistaken about Eve in the beginning; it is better to live outside the Garden with her than inside it without her. At first I thought she talked too much; but now I should be sorry to have that voice fall silent and pass out of my life. Blessed be the chestnut that brought us near together and taught me to know the goodness of her heart and the sweetness of her spirit!

The Death Disk[*]

This was in Oliver Cromwell's time. Colonel Mayfair was the youngest officer of his rank in the armies of the Commonwealth, he being but thirty years old. But young as he was, he was a veteran soldier, and tanned and warworn, for he had begun his military life at seventeen; he had fought in many battles, and had won his high place in the service and in the admiration of men, step by step, by valour in the field. But he was in deep trouble now; a shadow had fallen upon his fortunes.

The winter evening was come, and outside were storm and darkness; within, a melancholy silence; for the Colonel and his young wife had talked their sorrow out, had read the evening chapter and prayed the evening prayer, and there was nothing more to do but sit hand in hand and gaze into the fire, and think – and wait. They would not have to wait long; they knew that, and the wife shuddered at the thought.

They had one child – Abby, seven years old, their idol. She would be coming presently for the good-night kiss, and the Colonel spoke now, and said:

'Dry away the tears and let us seem happy, for her sake. We must forget, for the time, that which is to happen.'

'I will. I will shut them up in my heart, which is breaking.'

'And we will accept what is appointed for us, and bear it in patience, as knowing that whatsoever He doeth is done in righteousness and meant in kindness – '

'Saying, His will be done. Yes, I can say it with all my mind and soul – I would I could say it with my heart. Oh, if I could! if this dear hand which I press and kiss for the last time – '

' 'Sh! sweetheart, she is coming!'

[*] The text for this story is a touching incident mentioned in Carlyle's *Letters and Speeches of Oliver Cromwell* – M. T.

A curly-headed little figure in nightclothes glided in at the door and ran to the father, and was gathered to his breast and fervently kissed once, twice, three times.

'Why, papa, you mustn't kiss me like that: you rumple my hair.'

'Oh, I am so sorry – so sorry: do you forgive me, dear?'

'Why, of course, papa. But *are* you sorry? – not pretending, but real, right down sorry?'

'Well, you can judge for yourself, Abby,' and he covered his face with his hands and made believe to sob. The child was filled with remorse to see this tragic thing which she had caused, and she began to cry herself, and to tug at the hands, and say:

'Oh, don't, papa, please don't cry; Abby didn't mean it; Abby wouldn't ever do it again. Please, papa!' Tugging and straining to separate the fingers, she got a fleeting glimpse of an eye behind them, and cried out: 'Why, you naughty papa, you are not crying at all! You are only fooling! And Abby is going to mamma, now: you don't treat Abby right.'

She was for climbing down, but her father wound his arms about her and said: 'No, stay with me, dear: papa *was* naughty, and confesses it, and is sorry – there, let him kiss the tears away – and he begs Abby's forgiveness, and will do anything Abby says he must do, for a punishment; they're all kissed away now, and not a curl rumpled – and whatever Abby commands – '

And so it was made up; and all in a moment the sunshine was back again and burning brightly in the child's face, and she was patting her father's cheeks and naming the penalty – 'A story! a story!'

Hark!

The elders stopped breathing, and listened. Footsteps! faintly caught between the gusts of wind. They came nearer, nearer – louder, louder – then passed by and faded away. The elders drew deep breaths of relief, and the papa said: 'A story, is it? A gay one?'

'No, papa: a dreadful one.'

Papa wanted to shift to the gay kind, but the child stood by her rights – as per agreement, she was to have anything she commanded. He was a good Puritan soldier and had passed his word – he saw that he must make it good. She said:

'Papa, we mustn't always have gay ones. Nurse says people don't always have gay times. Is that true, papa? She *says* so.'

The mamma sighed, and her thoughts drifted to her troubles again. The papa said, gently: 'It is true, dear. Troubles have to come; it is a pity, but it is true.'

'Oh, then tell a story about them, papa – a dreadful one, so that we'll

shiver, and feel just as if it was *us*. Mamma, you snuggle up close, and
hold one of Abby's hands, so that if it's too dreadful it'll be easier for us
to bear it if we are all snuggled up together, you know. Now you can
begin, papa.'

'Well, once there were three Colonels – '

'Oh, goody! *I* know Colonels, just as easy! It's because you are one,
and I know the clothes. Go on, papa.'

'And in a battle they had committed a breach of discipline.'

The large words struck the child's ear pleasantly, and she looked up,
full of wonder and interest, and said:

'Is it something good to eat, papa?'

The parents almost smiled, and the father answered:

'No, quite another matter, dear. They exceeded their orders.'

'Is *that* someth – '

'No; it's as uneatable as the other. They were ordered to feign an
attack on a strong position in a losing fight, in order to draw the
enemy about and give the Commonwealth's forces a chance to retreat;
but in their enthusiasm they overstepped their orders, for they turned
the feint into a fact, and carried the position by storm, and won the day
and the battle. The Lord General was very angry at their disobedi-
ence, and praised them highly, and ordered them to London to be
tried for their lives.'

'Is it the great General Cromwell, papa?'

'Yes.'

'Oh, I've seen *him*, papa! and when he goes by our house so grand on
his big horse, with the soldiers, he looks so – so – well, I don't know just
how, only he looks as if he isn't satisfied, and you can see the people are
afraid of him; but *I'm* not afraid of him, because he didn't look like that
at me.'

'Oh, you dear prattler! Well, the Colonels came prisoners to
London, and were put upon their honour, and allowed to go and see
their families for the last – '

Hark!

They listened. Footsteps again; but again they passed by. The mamma
leaned her head upon her husband's shoulder to hide her paleness.

'They arrived this morning.'

The child's eyes opened wide.

'Why, papa! is it a *true* story?'

'Yes, dear.'

'Oh, how good! Oh, it's ever so much better! Go on, papa. Why,
mamma! – *dear* mamma, are you crying?'

'Never mind me, dear – I was thinking of the – of the – the poor families.'

'But *don't* cry, mamma: it'll all come out right – you'll see; stories always do. Go on, papa, to where they lived happy ever after; then she won't cry any more. You'll see, mamma. Go on, papa.'

'First, they took them to the Tower before they let them go home.'

'Oh, *I* know the Tower! We can see it from here. Go on, papa.'

'I am going on as well as I can, in the circumstances. In the Tower the military court tried them for an hour, and found them guilty, and condemned them to be shot.'

'*Killed*, papa?'

'Yes.'

'Oh, how naughty! *Dear* mamma, you are crying again. Don't, mamma; it'll soon come to the good place – you'll see. Hurry, papa, for mamma's sake; you don't go fast enough.'

'I know I don't, but I suppose it is because I stop so much to reflect.'

'But you mustn't *do* it, papa; you must go right on.'

'Very well, then. The three Colonels – '

'Do you know them, papa?'

'Yes, dear.'

'Oh, I wish I did! I love Colonels. Would they let me kiss them, do you think?' The Colonel's voice was a little unsteady when he answered –

'*One* of them would, my darling! There – kiss me for him.'

'There, papa – and these two are for the others. I think they would let me kiss them, papa; for I would say, "My papa is a Colonel, too, and brave, and he would do what you did; so it *can't* be wrong, no matter what those people say, and you needn't be the least bit ashamed;" then they would let me – wouldn't they, papa?'

'God knows they would, child!'

'Mamma! – oh, mamma, you mustn't. He's soon coming to the happy place; go on, papa.'

'Then, some were sorry – they all were; that military court, I mean; and they went to the Lord General, and said they had done their duty – for it *was* their duty, you know – and now they begged that two of the Colonels might be spared, and only the other one shot. One would be sufficient for an example for the army, they thought. But the Lord General was very stern, and rebuked them forasmuch as, having done *their* duty and cleared their consciences, they would beguile him to do less, and so smirch his soldierly honour. But they answered that they were asking nothing of him that they would not do themselves if they stood in his great place and held in their hands the noble prerogative of mercy. That struck him, and he paused and stood thinking, some of the sternness passing out of his face. Presently he bid them wait, and he retired to his closet to seek counsel of God in prayer; and when he came again, he said: "They shall cast lots. That shall decide it, and two of them shall live." '

'And did they, papa, did they? And which one is to die? – ah, that poor man!'

'No. They refused.'

'They wouldn't do it, papa?'

'No.'

'Why?'

'They said that the one that got the fatal bean would be sentencing himself to death by his own voluntary act, and it would be but suicide, call it by what name one might. They said they were Christians, and the Bible forbade men to take their own lives. They sent back that word, and said they were ready – let the court's sentence be carried into effect.'

'What does that mean, papa?'

'They – they will all be shot.'

Hark!

The wind? No. Tramp – tramp – tramp – r–r–r–umble-dumdum, r–r–rumble-dumdum –

'Open – in the Lord General's name!'

'Oh, goody, papa, it's the soldiers! – I love the soldiers! Let *me* let them in, papa, let *me!*'

She jumped down, and scampered to the door and pulled it open, crying joyously: 'Come in! come in! Here they are, papa! Grenadiers! *I* know the Grenadiers!'

The file marched in and straightened up in line at shoulder arms; its officer saluted, the doomed Colonel standing erect and returning the courtesy, the soldier wife standing at his side, white, and with features drawn with inward pain, but giving no other sign of her misery, the child gazing on the show with dancing eyes . . .

One long embrace, of father, mother, and child; then the order, 'To the Tower – forward!' Then the Colonel marched forth from the house with military step and bearing, the file following; then the door closed.

'Oh, mamma, didn't it come out beautiful! I *told* you it would; and they're going to the Tower, and he'll *see* them! He – '

'Oh, come to my arms, you poor innocent thing!'. . .

❦ 2 ❦

The next morning the stricken mother was not able to leave her bed; doctors and nurses were watching by her, and whispering together now and then; Abby could not be allowed in the room; she was told to run and play – mamma was very ill. The child, muffled in winter wraps, went out and played in the street awhile; then it struck her as strange, and also wrong, that her papa should be allowed to stay at the Tower in ignorance at such a time as this. This must be remedied; she would attend to it in person.

An hour later the military court were ushered into the presence of the Lord General. He stood grim and erect, with his knuckles resting upon the table, and indicated that he was ready to listen. The spokesman said: 'We have urged them to reconsider; we have implored them: but they persist. They will not cast lots. They are willing to die, but not to defile their religion.'

The Protector's face darkened, but he said nothing. He remained a time in thought, then he said: 'They shall not all die; the lots shall be cast *for* them.' Gratitude shone in the faces of the court. 'Send for them. Place them in that room there. Stand them side by side with their faces to the wall and their wrists crossed behind them. Let me have notice when they are there.'

When he was alone he sat down, and presently gave this order to an attendant: 'Go, bring me the first little child that passes by.'

The man was hardly out at the door before he was back again – leading Abby by the hand, her garments lightly powdered with snow. She went straight to the Head of the State, that formidable personage at the mention of whose name the principalities and powers of the earth trembled, and climbed up in his lap, and said:

'I know *you*, sir: you are the Lord General; I have seen you; I have seen you when you went by my house. Everybody was afraid; but *I* wasn't afraid, because you didn't look cross at *me*; you remember, don't you? I had on my red frock – the one with the blue things on it down the front. Don't you remember that?'

A smile softened the austere lines of the Protector's face, and he began to struggle diplomatically with his answer:

'Why, let me see – I – '

'I was standing right by the house – *my* house, you know.'

'Well, you dear little thing, I ought to be ashamed, but you know – '

The child interrupted, reproachfully:

'Now you *don't* remember it. Why, I didn't forget *you*.'

'Now I *am* ashamed: but I will never forget you again, dear; you have my word for it. You will forgive me now, won't you, and be good friends with me, always and forever?'

'Yes, indeed I will, though I don't know how you came to forget it; you must be very forgetful: but I am too, sometimes. I can forgive you without any trouble, for I think you *mean* to be good and do right, and I think you are just as kind – but you must snuggle me better, the way papa does – it's cold.'

'You shall be snuggled to your heart's content, little new friend of mine, always to be *old* friend of mine hereafter, isn't it? You mind me of my little girl – not little any more, now – but she was dear, and sweet, and daintily made, like you. And she had your charm, little witch – your all-conquering sweet confidence in friend and stranger alike, that wins to willing slavery any upon whom its precious compliment falls. She used to lie in my arms, just as you are doing now; and charm the weariness and care out of my heart and give it peace, just as you are doing now; and we were comrades, and equals, and playfellows together. Ages ago it was, since that pleasant heaven faded away and vanished, and you have brought it back again; take a burdened man's blessing for it, you tiny creature, who are carrying the weight of England while I rest!'

'Did you love her very, very, *very* much?'

'Ah, you shall judge by this: she commanded and I obeyed!'

'I think you are lovely! Will you kiss me?'

'Thankfully – and hold it a privilege, too. There – this one is for you; and there – this one is for her. You made it a request; and you could have made it a command, for you are representing her, and what you command I must obey.'

The child clapped her hands with delight at the idea of this grand promotion – then her ear caught an approaching sound: the measured tramp of marching men.

'Soldiers! – soldiers, Lord General! Abby wants to see them!'

'You shall, dear; but wait a moment, I have a commission for you.'

An officer entered and bowed low, saying, 'They are come, your Highness,' bowed again, and retired.

The Head of the Nation gave Abby three little disks of sealing-wax: two white, and one a ruddy red – for this one's mission was to deliver death to the Colonel who should get it.

'Oh, what a lovely red one! Are they for me?'

'No, dear; they are for others. Lift the corner of that curtain, there, which hides an open door; pass through, and you will see three men standing in a row, with their backs toward you and their hands behind their backs – so – each with one hand open, like a cup. Into each of the open hands drop one of those things, then come back to me.'

Abby disappeared behind the curtain, and the Protector was alone. He said, reverently: 'Of a surety that good thought came to me in my perplexity from Him who is an ever present help to them that are in doubt and seek His aid. He knoweth where the choice should fall, and has sent His sinless messenger to do His will. Another would err, but He cannot err. Wonderful are His ways, and wise – blessed be His holy Name!'

The small fairy dropped the curtain behind her and stood for a moment conning with alert curiosity the appointments of the chamber of doom, and the rigid figures of the soldiery and the prisoners; then her face lighted merrily, and she said to herself: 'Why, one of them is papa! I know his back. He shall have the prettiest one!' She tripped gayly forward and dropped the disks into the open hands, then peeped around under her father's arm and lifted her laughing face and cried out:

'Papa! papa! look what you've got. *I* gave it to you!'

He glanced at the fatal gift, then sunk to his knees and gathered his innocent little executioner to his breast in an agony of love and pity. Soldiers, officers, released prisoners, all stood paralysed, for a moment, at the vastness of this tragedy, then the pitiful scene smote their hearts, their eyes filled, and they wept unashamed. There was deep and reverent silence during some minutes, then the officer of the guard moved reluctantly forward and touched his prisoner on the shoulder, saying, gently:

'It grieves me, sir, but my duty commands.'

'Commands what?' said the child.

'I must take him away. I am so sorry.'

'Take him away? Where?'

'To – to – God help me! – to another part of the fortress.'

'Indeed you can't. My mamma is sick, and I am going to take him home.' She released herself and climbed upon her father's back and put her arms around his neck. 'Now Abby's ready, papa – come along.'

'My poor child, I can't. I must go with them.'

The child jumped to the ground and looked about her, wondering. Then she ran and stood before the officer and stamped her small foot indignantly and cried out:

'I told you my mamma is sick, and you might have listened. Let him go – you *must*!'

'Oh, poor child, would God I could, but indeed I must take him away. Attention, guard! . . . fall in! . . . shoulder arms!' . . .

Abby was gone – like a flash of light. In a moment she was back, dragging the Lord Protector by the hand. At this formidable apparition all present straightened up, the officers saluting and the soldiers presenting arms.

'Stop them, sir! My mamma is sick and wants my papa, and I *told* them so, but they never even listened to me, and are taking him away.'

The Lord General stood as one dazed.

'*Your* papa, child? Is he your papa?'

'Why, of course – he was *always* it. Would I give the pretty red one to any other, when I love him so? No!'

A shocked expression rose in the Protector's face, and he said:

'Ah, God help me! through Satan's wiles I have done the cruellest thing that ever man did – and there is no help, no help! What can I do?'

Abby cried out, distressed and impatient: 'Why, you can make them let him go,' and she began to sob. 'Tell them to do it! You told me to command, and now the very first time I tell you to do a thing you don't do it!'

A tender light dawned in the rugged old face, and the Lord General laid his hand upon the small tyrant's head and said: 'God be thanked for the saving accident of that unthinking promise; and you, inspired by Him, for reminding me of my forgotten pledge, O incomparable child! Officer, obey her command – she speaks by my mouth. The prisoner is pardoned; set him free!'

A Double-Barrelled Detective Story

We ought never to do wrong when people are looking

I

The first scene is in the country, in Virginia; the time, 1880. There has been a wedding, between a handsome young man of slender means and a rich young girl – a case of love at first sight and a precipitate marriage; a marriage bitterly opposed by the girl's widowed father.

Jacob Fuller, the bridegroom, is twenty-six years old, is of an old but unconsidered family which had by compulsion emigrated from Sedgemoor, and for King James's purse's profit, so everybody said – some maliciously, the rest merely because they believed it. The bride is nineteen and beautiful. She is intense, high-strung, romantic, immeasurably proud of her Cavalier blood, and passionate in her love for her young husband. For its sake she braved her father's displeasure, endured his reproaches, listened with loyalty unshaken to his warning predictions, and went from his house without his blessing, proud and happy in the proofs she was thus giving of the quality of the affection which had made its home in her heart.

The morning after the marriage there was a sad surprise for her. Her husband put aside her proffered caresses, and said:

'Sit down. I have something to say to you. I loved you. That was before I asked your father to give you to me. His refusal is not my grievance – I could have endured that. But the things he said of me to you – that is a different matter. There – you needn't speak; I know quite well what they were; I got them from authentic sources. Among other things he said that my character was written in my face; that I was treacherous, a dissembler, a coward, and a brute without sense of pity or compassion: the 'Sedgemoor trademark', he called it – and 'white-sleeve badge'. Any other man in my place would have gone to his house and shot him down like a dog. I wanted to do it, and was minded to do it, but a better thought came to me: to put him to shame; to break his heart; to kill him by inches. How to do it? Through my treatment of you, his idol! I would marry you; and then – Have patience. You will see.'

From that moment onward, for three months, the young wife suffered all the humiliations, all the insults, all the miseries that the diligent and inventive mind of the husband could contrive, save physical injuries only. Her strong pride stood by her, and she kept the secret of her troubles. Now and then the husband said, 'Why don't you go to your father and tell him?' Then he invented new tortures, applied them, and asked again. She always answered, 'He shall never know by my mouth,' and taunted him with his origin; said she was the lawful slave of a scion of slaves, and must obey, and would – up to that point, but no further; he could kill her if he liked, but he could not break her; it was not in the Sedgemoor breed to do it. At the end of the three months he said, with a dark significance in his manner, 'I have tried all things but one' – and waited for her reply. 'Try that,' she said, and curled her lip in mockery.

That night he rose at midnight and put on his clothes, then said to her, 'Get up and dress!'

She obeyed – as always, without a word. He led her half a mile from the house, and proceeded to lash her to a tree by the side of the public road; and succeeded, she screaming and struggling. He gagged her then, struck her across the face with his cowhide, and set his blood-hounds on her. They tore the clothes off her, and she was naked. He called the dogs off, and said:

'You will be found – by the passing public. They will be dropping along about three hours from now, and will spread the news – do you hear? Goodbye. You have seen the last of me.'

He went away then. She moaned to herself:

'I shall bear a child – to *him*! God grant it may be a boy!'

The farmers released her by and by – and spread the news, which was natural. They raised the country with lynching intentions, but the bird had flown. The young wife shut herself up in her father's house; he shut himself up with her, and thenceforth would see no one. His pride was broken, and his heart; so he wasted away, day by day, and even his daughter rejoiced when death relieved him.

Then she sold the estate and disappeared.

❦ 2 *❦*

In 1886 a young woman was living in a modest house near a secluded New England village, with no company but a little boy about five years old. She did her own work, she discouraged acquaintanceships, and had none. The butcher, the baker, and the others that served her could tell the villagers nothing about her further than that her name was Stillman, and that she called the child Archy. Whence she came they had not been able to find out, but they said she talked like a Southerner. The child had no playmates and no comrade, and no teacher but the mother. She taught him diligently and intelligently, and was satisfied with the results – even a little proud of them. One day Archy said,

'Mamma, am I different from other children?'

'Well, I suppose not. Why?'

'There was a child going along out there and asked me if the postman had been by and I said yes, and she said how long since I saw him and I said I hadn't seen him at all, and she said how did I know he'd been by, then, and I said because I smelt his track on the sidewalk, and she said I was a dumb fool and made a mouth at me. What did she do that for?'

The young woman turned white, and said to herself, 'It's a birthmark! The gift of the bloodhound is in him.' She snatched the boy to her breast and hugged him passionately, saying, 'God has appointed the way!' Her eyes were burning with a fierce light and her breath came short and quick with excitement. She said to herself: 'The puzzle is solved now; many a time it has been a mystery to me, the impossible things the child has done in the dark, but it is all clear to me now.'

She set him in his small chair, and said,

'Wait a little till I come, dear; then we will talk about the matter.'

She went up to her room and took from her dressing-table several small articles and put them out of sight: a nail-file on the floor under the bed; a pair of nail-scissors under the bureau; a small ivory paper-knife under the wardrobe. Then she returned, and said:

'There! I have left some things which I ought to have brought down.' She named them, and said, 'Run up and bring them, dear.'

The child hurried away on his errand and was soon back again with the things.

'Did you have any difficulty, dear?'

'No, mamma; I only went where you went.'

During his absence she had stepped to the book case, taken several books from the bottom shelf, opened each, passed her hand over a page, noting its number in her memory, then restored them to their places. Now she said:

'I have been doing something while you have been gone, Archy. Do you think you can find out what it was?'

The boy went to the bookcase and got out the books that had been touched, and opened them at the pages which had been stroked.

The mother took him in her lap, and said:

'I will answer your question now, dear. I have found out that in one way you are quite different from other people. You can see in the dark, you can smell what other people cannot, you have the talents of a bloodhound. They are good and valuable things to have, but you must keep the matter a secret. If people found it out, they would speak of you as an odd child, a strange child, and children would be disagreeable to you, and give you nicknames. In this world one must be like everybody else if he doesn't want to provoke scorn or envy or jealousy. It is a great and fine distinction which has been born to you, and I am glad; but you will keep it a secret, for mamma's sake, won't you?'

The child promised, without understanding.

All the rest of the day the mother's brain was busy with excited thinkings; with plans, projects, schemes, each and all of them uncanny, grim, and dark. Yet they lit up her face; lit it with a fell light of their own; lit it with vague fires of hell. She was in a fever of unrest; she could not sit, stand, read, sew; there was no relief for her but in movement. She tested her boy's gift in twenty ways, and kept saying to herself all the time, with her mind in the past: 'He broke my father's heart, and night and day all these years I have tried, and all in vain, to think out a way to break his. I have found it now – I have found it now.'

When night fell, the demon of unrest still possessed her. She went on with her tests; with a candle she traversed the house from garret to cellar, hiding pins, needles, thimbles, spools, under pillows, under carpets, in cracks in the walls, under the coal in the bin; then sent the little fellow in the dark to find them; which he did, and was happy and proud when she praised him and smothered him with caresses.

From this time forward life took on a new complexion for her. She said, 'The future is secure – I can wait, and enjoy the waiting.' The most of her lost interests revived. She took up music again, and languages, drawing, painting, and the other long-discarded delights of her maidenhood. She was happy once more, and felt again the zest of life. As the years drifted by she watched the development of her boy, and was contented with it. Not altogether, but nearly that. The soft side of his heart was larger than the other side of it. It was his only defect, in her eyes. But she considered that his love for her and worship of her made up for it. He was a good hater – that was well; but it was a question if the materials of his hatreds were of as tough and enduring a quality as those of his friendships – and that was not so well.

The years drifted on. Archy was become a handsome, shapely, athletic youth, courteous, dignified, companionable, pleasant in his ways, and looking perhaps a trifle older than he was, which was sixteen. One evening his mother said she had something of grave importance to say to him, adding that he was old enough to hear it now, and old enough and possessed of character enough and stability enough to carry out a stern plan which she had been for years contriving and maturing. Then she told him her bitter story, in all its naked atrociousness. For a while the boy was paralysed; then he said:

'I understand. We are Southerners; and by our custom and nature there is but one atonement. I will search him out and kill him.'

'Kill him? No! Death is release, emancipation; death is a favour. Do I owe him favours? You must not hurt a hair of his head.'

The boy was lost in thought awhile; then he said:

'You are all the world to me, and your desire is my law and my pleasure. Tell me what to do and I will do it.'

The mother's eyes beamed with satisfaction, and she said:

'You will go and find him. I have known his hiding-place for eleven years; it cost me five years and more of inquiry, and much money, to locate it. He is a quartz-miner in Colorado, and well-to-do. He lives in Denver. His name is Jacob Fuller. There – it is the first time I have spoken it since that unforgettable night. Think! That name could have been yours if I had not saved you that shame and furnished you a cleaner one. You will drive him from that place; you will hunt him down and drive him again; and yet again, and again, and again, persistently, relentlessly, poisoning his life, filling it with mysterious terrors, loading it with weariness and misery, making him wish for death, and that he had a suicide's courage; you will make of him another wandering Jew; he shall know no rest any more, no peace of mind, no placid sleep; you shall shadow him, cling to him, persecute him, till you break his heart, as he broke my father's and mine.'

'I will obey, mother.'

'I believe it, my child. The preparations are all made; everything is ready. Here is a letter of credit; spend freely, there is no lack of money. At times you may need disguises. I have provided them; also some other conveniences .' She took from the drawer of the typewriter table several squares of paper. They all bore these typewritten words:

$10,000 REWARD

It is believed that a certain man who is wanted in an Eastern State is sojourning here. In 1880, in the night, he tied his young wife to a tree by the public road, cut her across the face with a cowhide, and made his dogs tear her clothes from her, leaving her naked. He left her there, and fled the country. A blood-relative of hers has searched for him for seventeen years. Address . . . . Post-office. The above reward will be paid in cash to the person who will furnish the seeker, in a personal interview, the criminal's address.

'When you have found him and acquainted yourself with his scent, you will go in the night and placard one of these upon the building he occupies, and another one upon the post-office or in some other prominent place. It will be the talk of the region. At first you must give him several days in which to force a sale of his belongings at something approaching their value. We will ruin him by and by, but gradually; we must not impoverish him at once, for that could bring him to despair and injure his health, possibly kill him.'

She took three or four more typewritten forms from the drawer – duplicates – and read one:

. . . . 18 . . .

To JACOB FULLER – You have . . . . . .days in which to settle your affairs. You will not be disturbed during that limit, which will expire at . . . . . . on the . . . . . . of . . . . . . You must then MOVE ON. If you are still in the place after the named hour, I will placard you on all the dead walls, detailing your crime once more, and adding the date, also the scene of it, with all names concerned, including your own. Have no fear of bodily injury – it will in no circumstances ever be inflicted upon you. You brought misery upon an old man, and ruined his life and broke his heart. What he suffered, you are to suffer.

'You will add no signature. He must receive this before he learns of the reward placard – before he rises in the morning – lest he lose his head and fly the place penniless.'

'I shall not forget.'

'You will need to use these forms only in the beginning – once may be enough. Afterward, when you are ready for him to vanish out of a place, see that he gets a copy of *this* form, which merely says:

MOVE ON. You have . . . . . . days.

'He will obey. That is sure.'

❧ 3 ❧

Extracts from letters to the mother:

Denver, April 3, 1897
I have now been living several days in the same hotel with Jacob Fuller. I have his scent; I could track him through ten divisions of infantry and find him. I have often been near him and heard him talk. He owns a good mine, and has a fair income from it; but he is not rich. He learned mining in a good way – by working at it for wages. He is a cheerful creature, and his forty-three years sit lightly upon him; he could pass for a younger man – say thirty-six or thirty-seven. He has never married again – passes himself off for a widower. He stands well, is liked, is popular, and has many friends. Even I feel a drawing toward him – the paternal blood in me making its claim. How blind and unreasoning and arbitrary are some of the laws of nature – the most of them, in fact! My task is become hard now – you realise it? you comprehend, and make allowances? – and the fire of it has cooled, more than I like to confess to myself. But I will carry it out. Even with the pleasure paled, the duty remains, and I will not spare him.

And for my help, a sharp resentment rises in me when I reflect that he who committed that odious crime is the only one who has not suffered by it. The lesson of it has manifestly reformed his character, and in the change he is happy. He, the guilty party, is absolved from all suffering; you, the innocent, are borne down with it. But be comforted – he shall harvest his share.

Silver Gulch, May 19
I placarded Form No. 1 at midnight of April 3; an hour later I dipped Form No. 2 under his chamber door, notifying him to leave Denver at or before 11.50 the night of the 14th.

Some late bird of a reporter stole one of my placards, then hunted the town over and found the other one, and stole that. In this manner he accomplished what the profession calls a 'scoop' – that is, he got a valuable item, and saw to it that no other paper got it. And so his paper – the principal one in the town – had it in glaring type on the editorial page in the morning, followed by a Vesuvian opinion of our wretch a column long, which wound up by adding a thousand dollars to our reward on the *paper's* account! The journals out here know how to do the noble thing – when there's business in it.

At breakfast I occupied my usual seat – selected because it afforded a view of papa Fuller's face, and was near enough for me to hear the talk that went on at his table. Seventy-five or a hundred people were in the room, and all discussing that item, and saying they hoped the seeker would find that rascal and remove the pollution of his presence from the town – with a rail, or a bullet, or something.

When Fuller came in he had the Notice to Leave – folded up – in one hand, and the newspaper in the other; and it gave me more than half a pang to see him. His cheerfulness was all gone, and he looked old and pinched and ashy. And then – only think of the things he had to listen to! Mamma, he heard his own unsuspecting friends describe him with epithets and characterisations drawn from the very dictionaries and phrase-books of Satan's own authorised editions down below. And more than that, he had to *agree* with the verdicts and applaud them. His applause tasted bitter in his mouth, though; he could not disguise that from me; and it was observable that his appetite was gone; he only nibbled; he couldn't eat. Finally a man said:

'It is quite likely that that relative is ill the room and hearing what this town thinks of that unspeakable scoundrel. I hope so.'

Ah, dear, it was pitiful the way Fuller winced, and glanced around scared! He couldn't endure any more, and got up and left.

During several days he gave out that he had bought a mine in Mexico, and wanted to sell out and go down there as soon as he could, and give the property his personal attention. He played his cards well; said he would take $40,000 – a quarter in cash, the rest in safe notes; but that as he greatly needed money on account of his new purchase, he would diminish his terms for cash in full. He sold out for $30,000. And then, what do you think he did? He asked for *greenbacks*, and took them, saying the man in Mexico was a New-Englander, with a head full of crotchets, and preferred greenbacks to gold or drafts. People thought it queer, since a draft on New York could produce greenbacks quite conveniently. There was talk of this odd thing, but only for a day; that is as long as any topic lasts in Denver.

I was watching, all the time. As soon as the sale was completed and the money paid – which was on the 11th – I began to stick to Fuller's track without dropping it for a moment. That night – no, 12th, for it was a little past midnight – I tracked him to his room, which was four doors from mine in the same hall; then I went back and put on my muddy day-labourer disguise, darkened my complexion, and sat down in my room in the gloom, with a gripsack handy, with a change in it, and my door ajar. For I suspected that the bird would take wing now. In half an hour an old woman passed by, carrying a grip: I caught the familiar whiff, and followed with my grip, for it was Fuller. He left the hotel by a side entrance, and at the corner he turned up an unfrequented street and walked three blocks in a light rain and a heavy darkness, and got into a two-horse hack, which of course was waiting for him by appointment. I took a seat (uninvited) on the trunk platform behind, and we drove briskly off. We drove ten miles, and the hack stopped at a way-station and was discharged. Fuller got out and took a seat on a barrow under the awning, as far as he could get from the light; I went inside, and watched the ticket-office. Fuller bought no ticket; I bought none. Presently the train came along, and he boarded a car; I entered the same car at the other end, and came down the aisle and took the seat behind him. When he paid the conductor and named his objective point, I dropped back several seats, while the conductor was changing a bill, and when he came to me I paid to the same place – about a hundred miles westward.

From that time for a week on end he led me a dance. He travelled here and there and yonder – always on a general westward trend – but he was not a woman after the first day. He was a labourer, like myself, and wore bushy false whiskers. His outfit was perfect, and he could do the character without thinking about it, for he had served the trade for wages. His nearest friend could not have recognised him. At last he located himself here, the obscurest little mountain camp in Montana; he has a shanty, and goes out prospecting daily; is gone all day, and avoids society. I am living at a miner's boarding-house, and it is an awful place: the bunks, the food, the dirt – everything.

We have been here four weeks, and in that time I have seen him but once; but every night I go over his track and post myself. As soon as he engaged a shanty here I went to a town fifty miles away and telegraphed that Denver hotel to keep my baggage till I should send for it. I need nothing here but a change of army shirts, and I brought that with me.

Silver Gulch, June 12
The Denver episode has never found its way here, I think. I know the

most of the men in camp, and they have never referred to it, at least in my hearing. Fuller doubtless feels quite safe in these conditions. He has located a claim, two miles away, in an out-of-the-way place in the mountains; it promises very well, and he is working it diligently. Ah, but the change in him! He never smiles, and he keeps quite to himself, consorting with no one – he who was so fond of company and so cheery only two months ago. I have seen him passing along several times recently – drooping, forlorn, the spring gone from his step, a pathetic figure. He calls himself David Wilson.

I can trust him to remain here until we disturb him. Since you insist, I will banish him again, but I do not see how he can be unhappier than he already is. I will go back to Denver and treat myself to a little season of comfort, and edible food, and endurable beds, and bodily decency; then I will fetch my things, and notify poor papa Wilson to move on.

Denver, June 19

They miss him here. They all hope he is prospering in Mexico, and they do not say it just with their mouths, but out of their hearts. You know you can always tell. I am loitering here overlong, I confess it. But if you were in my place you would have charity for me. Yes, I know what you will say, and you are right: if I were in *your* place, and carried your scalding memories in my heart –

I will take the night train back tomorrow.

Denver, June 20

God forgive us, mother, we are hunting the *wrong man!* I have not slept any all night. I am now waiting, at dawn, for the *morning* train – and how the minutes drag, how they drag!

This Jacob Fuller is a *cousin* of the guilty one. How stupid we have been not to reflect that the guilty one would never again wear his own name after that fiendish deed! The Denver Fuller is four years younger than the other one; he came here a young widower in '79, aged twenty-one – a year before you were married; and the documents to prove it are innumerable. Last night I talked with familiar friends of his who have known him from the day of his arrival. I said nothing, but a few days from now I will land him in this town again, with the loss upon his mine made good; and there will be a banquet, and a torch-light procession, and there will not be any expense on anybody but me. Do you call this 'gush'? I am only a boy, as you well know; it is my privilege. By and by I shall not be a boy any more.

Silver Gulch, July 3

Mother, he is gone! Gone, and left no trace. The scent was cold when I came. Today I am out of bed for the first time since. I wish I were not a boy; then I could stand shocks better. They all think he went west. I start tonight, in a wagon – two or three hours of that, then I get a train. I don't know where I'm going, but I must go; to try to keep still would be torture.

Of course he has effaced himself with a new name and a disguise. This means that *I may have to search the whole globe to find him*. Indeed it is what I expect. Do you see, mother? It is *I* that am the Wandering Jew. The irony of it! We arranged that for another.

Think of the difficulties! And there would be none if I only could advertise for him. But if there is any way to do it that would not frighten him, I have not been able to think it out, and I have tried till my brains are addled. 'If the gentleman who lately bought a mine in Mexico and sold one in Denver will send his address to' (to whom, mother!), 'it will be explained to him that it was all a mistake; his forgiveness will be asked, and full reparation made for a loss which he sustained in a certain matter.' Do you see? He would think it a trap. Well, anyone would. If I should say, 'It is now known that he was not the man wanted, but another man – a man who once bore the same name, but discarded it for good reasons' – would that answer? But the Denver people would wake up then and say 'Oho!' and they would remember about the suspicious greenbacks, and say, 'Why did he run away if he wasn't the right man? – it is too thin.' If I failed to find him he would be ruined there – there where there is no taint upon him now. You have a better head than mine. Help me.

I have one clue, and only one. I know his handwriting. If he puts his new false name upon a hotel register and does not disguise it too much, it will be valuable to me if I ever run across it.

San Francisco, June 28, 1898

You already know how well I have searched the States from Colorado to the Pacific, and how nearly I came to getting him once. Well, I have had another close miss. It was here, yesterday. I struck his trail, *hot*, on the street, and followed it on a run to a cheap hotel. That was a costly mistake; a dog would have gone the other way. But I am only part dog, and can get very humanly stupid when excited. He had been stopping in that house ten days; I almost know, now, that he stops long nowhere, the past six or eight months, but is restless and has to keep moving. I understand that feeling! and I know what it is to feel it. He still uses the name he had registered when I came so near catching him nine months ago – 'James Walker' ; doubtless the same he adopted when he fled from Silver Gulch. An unpretending man, and has small taste for fancy names. I recognised the hand easily, through its slight disguise. A square man, and not good at shams and pretences.

They said he was just gone, on a journey; left no address; didn't say where he was going; looked frightened when asked to leave his address; had no baggage but a cheap valise; carried it off on foot – a 'stingy old person, and not much loss to the house.' '*Old!*' I suppose he is, now. I hardly heard; I was there but a moment. I rushed along his trail, and it led me to a wharf. Mother, the smoke of the steamer he had taken was just fading out on the horizon! I should have saved half an hour if I had gone in the right direction at first. I could have taken a fast tug, and should have stood a chance of catching that vessel. She is bound for Melbourne.

Hope Canyon, California, October 3, 1900
You have a right to complain. 'A letter a year' *is* a paucity; I freely acknowledge it; but how can one write when there is nothing to write about but failures? No one can keep it up; it breaks the heart.

I told you – it seems ages ago, now – how I missed him at Melbourne, and then chased him all over Australasia for months on end.

Well, then, after that I followed him to India; almost *saw* him in Bombay; traced him all around – to Baroda, Rawal-Pindi, Lucknow, Lahore, Cawnpore, Allahabad, Calcutta, Madras – oh, everywhere; week after week, month after month, through the dust and swelter – always approximately on his track, sometimes close upon him, yet never catching him. And down to Ceylon, and then to – Never mind; by and by I will write it all out.

I chased him home to California, and down to Mexico, and back again to California. Since then I have been hunting him about the State from the first of last January down to a month ago. I feel almost sure he is not far from Hope Canyon; I traced him to a point thirty miles from here, but there I lost the trail; someone gave him a lift in a wagon, I suppose.

I am taking a rest, now – modified by searchings for the lost trail. I was tired to death, mother, and low-spirited, and sometimes coming uncomfortably near to losing hope; but the miners in this little camp are good fellows, and I am used to their sort this long time back; and their breezy ways freshen a person up and make him forget his troubles. I have been here a month. I am cabining with a young fellow named 'Sammy' Hillyer, about twenty-five, the only son of his mother – like me – and loves her dearly, and writes to her every week – part of which is like me. He is a timid body, and in the matter of intellect – well, he cannot be depended upon to set a river on fire; but no matter, he is well liked; he is good and fine, and it is meat and bread and rest and luxury to sit and talk with him and have a comradeship again. I wish 'James Walker' could have it. He had friends; he liked company. That brings up that picture of him, the time that I saw him last. The pathos of it! It comes before me often and often. At that very time, poor thing, I was girding up my conscience to make him move on again!

Hillyer's heart is better than mine, better than anybody's in the community, I suppose, for he is the one friend of the black sheep of the camp – Flint Buckner – and the only man Flint ever talks with or allows to talk with him. He says he knows Flint's history, and that it is trouble that has made him what he is, and so one ought to be as charitable toward him as one can. Now none but a pretty large heart could find space to accommodate a lodger like Flint Buckner, from all I hear about him outside. I think that this one detail will give you a better idea of Sammy's character than any laboured-out description I could furnish you of him. In one of our talks he said something about like this: 'Flint is a kinsman of mine, and he pours out all his troubles to me – empties his breast from time to time, or I reckon it would burst. There couldn't be any unhappier man, Archy Stillman; his life has been made up of misery of mind – he isn't near as old as he looks. He has lost the feel of reposefulness and peace – oh, years and years ago! He doesn't know what good luck is – never has had any; often says he wishes he was in the other hell, he is so tired of this one.'

❧ 4 ☙

No real gentleman will tell the naked truth in the presence of ladies

It was a crisp and spicy morning in early October. The lilacs and laburnums, lit with the glory-fires of autumn, hung burning and flashing in the upper air, a fairy bridge provided by kind Nature for the wingless wild things that have their homes in the tree-tops and would visit together; the larch and the pomegranate flung their purple and yellow flames in brilliant broad splashes along the slanting sweep of the woodland; the sensuous fragrance of innumerable deciduous flowers rose upon the swooning atmosphere; far in the empty sky a solitary œsophagus* slept upon motionless wing; everywhere brooded stillness, serenity, and the peace of God.

October is the time – 1900; Hope Canyon is the place, a silver-mining camp away down in the Esmeralda region. It is a secluded spot,

*From the *Springfield Republican*, April 12, 1902

To the Editor of the Republican –
One of your citizens has asked me a question about the 'œsophagus', and I wish to answer him through you. This in the hope that the answer will get around, and save me some penmanship, for I have already replied to the same question more than several times, and am not getting as much holiday as I ought to have.

I published a short story lately, and it was in that that I put the œsophagus. I will say privately that I expected it to bother some people – in fact, that was the intention – but the harvest has been larger than I was calculating upon. The œsophagus has gathered in the guilty and the innocent alike, whereas I was only fishing for the innocent – the innocent and confiding. I knew a few of these would write and ask me; that would give me but little trouble; but I was not expecting that the wise and the learned would call upon me for succour. However, that has happened, and it is time for me to speak up and stop the inquiries if I can, for letter-writing is not restful to me, and I am not having so much fun out of this thing as I counted on. That you may understand the situation, I will insert a couple of sample inquiries. The first is from a public instructor in the Philippines:

Santa Cruz, Ilocos Sur, PI, February 13, 1902
MY DEAR SIR – I have just been reading the first part of your latest story, entitled 'A Double-Barrelled Detective Story', and am very much delighted with it. In Part IV, page 264, *Harper's Magazine* for January, occurs this passage: 'Far in the empty sky a solitary "œsophagus" slept, upon motionless wing; everywhere brooded stillness, serenity, and the peace of God.' Now, there is one word I do not understand, namely, 'œsophagus'. My only work of reference is the *Standard Dictionary*, but that fails to explain the meaning. If you can spare the time, I would be glad to have the meaning cleared up, as I consider the passage a very touching and beautiful one. It may seem foolish to you, but consider my lack of means away out in the northern part of Luzon.
Yours very truly . . .

Do you notice? Nothing in the paragraph disturbed him but that one word. It shows that that paragraph was most ably constructed for the deception it was intended to put upon the reader. It was my intention that it should read plausibly, and it is now plain that it does; it was my intention that it should be emotional and touching, and you see, yourself, that it fetched this public high and remote; recent as to discovery; thought by its occupants to be rich in metal – a year or two's prospecting will decide that matter one way or the other. For inhabitants, the camp has about two hundred miners, one white woman and child, several Chinese washermen, five squaws, and a dozen vagrant buck Indians in rabbit-skin robes, battered plug hats, and tin-can necklaces. There are no mills as yet; no church, no newspaper. The camp has existed but two years; it has made no big strike; the world is ignorant of its name and place.

On both sides of the canyon the mountains rise wall-like, three thousand feet, and the long spiral of straggling huts down in its narrow bottom gets a kiss from the sun only once a day, when he sails over at noon. The village is a couple of miles long; the cabins stand well apart

---

instructor. Alas, if I had but left that one treacherous word out, I should have scored! scored everywhere; and the paragraph would have slidden through every reader's sensibilities like oil, and left not a suspicion behind.

The other sample inquiry is from a professor in a New England university. It contains one naughty word (which I cannot bear to suppress), but he is not in the theological department, so it is no harm –

DEAR MR CLEMENS –
'*Far in the empty sky a solitary œsophagus slept upon motionless wing.*'
It is not often I get a chance to read much periodical literature, but I have just gone through at this belated period, with much gratification and edification, your 'Double-Barrelled Detective Story'.
But what in hell is an œsophagus? I keep one myself, but it never sleeps in the air or anywhere else. My profession is to deal with words, and œsophagus interested me the moment I lighted upon it. But as a companion of my youth used to say, 'I'll be eternally, co-eternally cussed' if I can make it out. Is it a joke, or I an ignoramus?

Between you and me, I was almost ashamed of having fooled that man, but for pride's sake I was not going to say so. I wrote and told him it was a joke – and that is what I am now saying to my Springfield inquirer. And I told him to carefully read the whole paragraph, and he would find not a vestige of sense in any detail of it. This also I commend to my Springfield inquirer.

I have confessed. I am sorry – partially. I will not do so any more – for the present. Don't ask me any more questions; let the œsophagus have a rest – on his same old motionless wing.

MARK TWAIN

New York City, April 20, 1902
(EDITORIAL)
The 'Double-Barrelled Detective Story', which appeared in *Harper's Magazine* for January and February last, is the most elaborate of burlesques on detective fiction, with striking melodramatic passages in which it is difficult to detect the

from each other. The tavern is the only 'frame' house – the only house, one might say. It occupies a central position, and is the evening resort of the population. They drink there, and play seven-up and dominoes; also billiards, for there is a table, crossed all over with torn places repaired with court-plaster; there are some cues, but no leathers; some chipped balls which clatter when they run, and do not slow up gradually, but stop suddenly and sit down; there is a part of a cube of chalk, with a projecting jag of flint in it; and the man who can score six on a single break can set up the drinks at the bar's expense.

Flint Buckner's cabin was the last one of the village, going south; his silver claim was at the other end of the village, northward, and a little beyond the last hut in that direction. He was a sour creature, unsociable, and had no companionships. People who had tried to get acquainted with him had regretted it and dropped him. His history was not known.

––––––––––––––

deception, so ably is it done. But the illusion ought not to endure even the first incident in the February number. As for the paragraph which has so admirably illustrated the skill of Mr Clemens's ensemble and the carelessness of readers, here it is –

> It was a crisp and spicy morning in early October. The lilacs and laburnums, lit with the glory-fires of autumn, hung burning and flashing in the upper air, a fairy bridge provided by kind nature for the wingless wild things that have their home in the tree-tops and would visit together; the larch and the pomegranate flung their purple and yellow flames in brilliant broad splashes along the slanting sweep of the woodland; the sensuous fragrance of innumerable deciduous flowers rose upon the swooning atmosphere; far in the empty sky a solitary œsophagus slept upon motionless wing; everywhere brooded stillness, serenity, and the peace of God.

The success of Mark Twain's joke recalls to mind his story of the petrified man in the cavern, whom he described most punctiliously, first giving a picture of the scene, its impressive solitude, and all that; then going on to describe the majesty of the figure, casually mentioning that the thumb of his right hand rested against the side of his nose; then after further description observing that the fingers of the right hand were extended in a radiating fashion; and, recurring to the dignified attitude and position of the man, incidentally remarked that the thumb of the left hand was in contact with the little finger of the right – and so on. But it was so ingeniously written that Mark, relating the history years later in an article which appeared in that excellent magazine of the past, the *Galaxy*, declared that no one ever found out the joke, and, if we remember aright, that that astonishing old mockery was actually looked for in the region where he, as a Nevada newspaper editor, had located it. It is certain that Mark Twain's jumping frog has a good many more 'pints' than any other frog.

Some believed that Sammy Hillyer knew it; others said no. If asked, Hillyer said no, he was not acquainted with it. Flint had a meek English youth of sixteen or seventeen with him, whom he treated roughly, both in public and in private; and of course this lad was applied to for information, but with no success. Fetlock Jones – name of the youth – said that Flint picked him up on a prospecting tramp, and as he had neither home nor friends in America, he had found it wise to stay and take Buckner's hard usage for the sake of the salary, which was bacon and beans. Further than this he could offer no testimony.

Fetlock had been in this slavery for a month now, and under his meek exterior he was slowly consuming to a cinder with the insults and humiliations which his master had put upon him. For the meek suffer bitterly from these hurts; more bitterly, perhaps, than do the manlier sort, who can burst out and get relief with words or blows when the limit of endurance has been reached. Good-hearted people wanted to help Fetlock out of his trouble, and tried to get him to leave Buckner; but the boy showed fright at the thought, and said he 'dasn't'. Pat Riley urged him, and said:

'You leave the damned hunks and come with me; don't you be afraid. I'll take care of *him*.'

The boy thanked him with tears in his eyes, but shuddered and said he 'dasn't risk it'; he said Flint would catch him alone, some time, in the night, and then – 'Oh, it makes me sick, Mr Riley, to think of it.'

Others said, 'Run away from him; we'll stake you; skip out for the coast some night.' But all these suggestions failed; he said Flint would hunt him down and fetch him back, just for meanness.

The people could not understand this. The boy's miseries went steadily on, week after week. It is quite likely that the people would have understood if they had known how he was employing his spare time. He slept in an out-cabin near Flint's; and there, nights, he nursed his bruises and his humiliations, and studied and studied over a single problem – how he could murder Flint Buckner and not be found out. It was the only joy he had in life; these hours were the only ones in the twenty-four which he looked forward to with eagerness and spent in happiness.

He thought of poison. No – that would not serve; the inquest would reveal where it was procured and who had procured it. He thought of a shot in the back in a lonely place when Flint would be homeward bound at midnight – his unvarying hour for the trip. No – somebody might be near, and catch him. He thought of stabbing him in his sleep. No – he might strike an inefficient blow, and Flint would seize him. He examined a hundred different ways – none of them would answer; for in even the very obscurest and secretest of them there was always the fatal defect of a *risk*, a chance, a possibility that he might be found out. He would have none of that.

But he was patient, endlessly patient. There was no hurry, he said to himself. He would never leave Flint till he left him a corpse; there was no hurry – he would find the way. It was somewhere, and he would endure shame and pain and misery until he found it. Yes, somewhere there was a way which would leave not a trace, not even the faintest clue to the murderer – there was no hurry – he would find that way, and then – oh, then, it would just be good to be alive! Meantime he would diligently keep up his reputation for meekness; and also, as always theretofore, he would allow no one to hear him say a resentful or offensive thing about his oppressor.

Two days before the before-mentioned October morning Flint had bought some things, and he and Fetlock had brought them home to Flint's cabin: a fresh box of candles, which they put in the corner; a tin can of blasting-powder, which they placed upon the candle-box; a keg of blasting-powder, which they placed under Flint's bunk; a huge coil of fuse, which they hung on a peg. Fetlock reasoned that Flint's mining operations had outgrown the pick, and that blasting was about to begin now. He had seen blasting done, and he had a notion of the process, but he had never helped in it. His conjecture was right – blasting-time had come. In the morning the pair carried fuse, drills, and the powder-can to the shaft; it was now eight feet deep, and to get into it and out of it a short ladder was used. They descended, and by command Fetlock held the drill – without any instructions as to the right way to hold it – and Flint proceeded to strike. The sledge came down; the drill sprang out of Fetlock's hand, almost as a matter of course.

'You mangy son of a nigger, is that any way to hold a drill? Pick it up! Stand it up! There – hold fast. Damn you! *I'll* teach you!'

At the end of an hour the drilling was finished.

'Now, then, charge it.'

The boy started to pour in the powder.

'Idiot!'

A heavy bat on the jaw laid the lad out.

'Get up! You can't lie snivelling there. Now then, stick in the fuse *first. Now* put in the powder. Hold on, hold on! Are you going to fill the hole *all* up? Of all the sap-headed milksops! – Put in some dirt! Put in some gravel! Tamp it down! Hold on, hold on! Oh, great Scott! get out of the way!' He snatched the iron and tamped the charge himself, meantime cursing and blaspheming like a fiend. Then he fired the fuse, climbed out of the shaft, and ran fifty yards away, Fetlock following. They stood waiting a few minutes, then a great volume of smoke and rocks burst high into the air with a thunderous explosion; after a little there was a shower of descending stones; then all was serene again.

'I wish to God you'd been in it!' remarked the master.

They went down the shaft, cleaned it out, drilled another hole, and put in another charge.

'Look here! How much fuse are you proposing to waste? Don't you know how to time a fuse?'

'No, sir.'

'You *don't*! Well, if you don't beat anything *I* ever saw!'

He climbed out of the shaft and spoke down:

'Well, idiot, are you going to be all day? Cut the fuse and light it!'

The trembling creature began,

'If you please, sir, I – '

'You talk back to *me*? Cut it and light it!'

The boy cut and lit.

'Ger-reat Scott! a one-minute fuse! I wish you were in – '

In his rage he snatched the ladder out of the shaft and ran. The boy was aghast.

'Oh, my God! Help! Help! Oh, save me!' he implored. 'Oh what can I do! What *can* I do!'

He backed against the wall as tightly as he could; the sputtering fuse frightened the voice out of him; his breath stood still; he stood gazing and impotent; in two seconds, three seconds, four he would be flying toward the sky torn to fragments. Then he had an inspiration. He sprang at the fuse; severed the inch of it that was left above ground, and was saved.

He sank down limp and half lifeless with fright, his strength gone; but he muttered with a deep joy:

'He has learnt me! I knew there was a way, if I would wait.'

After a matter of five minutes Buckner stole to the shaft, looking worried and uneasy, and peered down into it. He took in the situation; he saw what had happened. He lowered the ladder, and the boy dragged himself weakly up it. He was very white. His appearance added something to Buckner's uncomfortable state, and he said, with a show of regret and sympathy which sat upon him awkwardly from lack of practice:

'It was an accident, you know. Don't say anything about it to anybody; I was excited, and didn't notice what I was doing. You're not looking well; you've worked enough for today; go down to my cabin and eat what you want, and rest. It's just an accident, you know, on account of my being excited.'

'It scared me,' said the lad, as he started away; 'but I learnt something, so I don't mind it.'

'Damned easy to please!' muttered Buckner, following him with his eye. 'I wonder if he'll tell? Mightn't he? . . . I wish it *had* killed him.'

The boy took no advantage of his holiday in the matter of resting; he employed it in work, eager and feverish and happy work. A thick growth of chaparral extended down the mountain-side clear to Flint's cabin; the most of Fetlock's labour was done in the dark intricacies of that stubborn growth; the rest of it was done in his own shanty. At last all was complete, and he said:

'If he's got any suspicions that I'm going to tell on him, he won't keep them long, tomorrow. He will see that I am the same milksop as I always was – all day and the next. And the day after tomorrow night there'll be an end of him; nobody will ever guess who finished him up nor how it was done. He dropped me the idea his own self, and that's odd.'

❦ 5 ❦

The next day came and went.

It is now almost midnight, and in five minutes the new morning will begin. The scene is in the tavern billiard-room. Rough men in rough clothing, slouch hats, breeches stuffed into boot-tops, some with vests, none with coats, are grouped about the boiler-iron stove, which has ruddy cheeks and is distributing a grateful warmth; the billiard balls are clacking; there is no other sound – that is, within; the wind is fitfully moaning without. The men look bored; also expectant. A hulking broad-shouldered miner, of middle age, with grizzled whiskers, and an unfriendly eye set in an unsociable face, rises, slips a coil of fuse upon his arm, gathers up some other personal properties, and departs without word or greeting to anybody. It is Flint Buckner. As the door closes behind him a buzz of talk breaks out.

'The regularest man that ever was,' said Jake Parker, the blacksmith: 'you can tell when it's twelve just by him leaving, without looking at your Waterbury.'

'And it's the only virtue he's got, as fur as I know,' said Peter Hawes, miner.

'He's just a blight on this society,' said Wells-Fargo's man, Ferguson. 'If I was running this shop I'd make him say something, *some*time or other, or vamoos the ranch.' This with a suggestive glance at the barkeeper, who did not choose to see it, since the man under discussion was a good customer, and went home pretty well set up, every night, with refreshments furnished from the bar.

'Say,' said Ham Sandwich, miner, 'does any of you boys ever recollect of him asking you to take a drink?'

'*Him*? Flint *Buckner*? Oh, Laura!'

This sarcastic rejoinder came in a spontaneous general outburst in one form of words or another from the crowd. After a brief silence, Pat Riley, miner, said:

'He's the 15-puzzle, that cuss. And his boy's another one. *I* can't make them out.'

'Nor anybody else,' said Ham Sandwich; 'and if they are 15-puzzles, how are you going to rank up that other one? When it comes to A1 right-down solid mysteriousness, he lays over both of them. *Easy* – don't he?'

'You bet!'

Everybody said it. Every man but one. He was the newcomer – Peterson. He ordered the drinks all round, and asked who No. 3 might be. All answered at once, 'Archy Stillman!'

'Is he a mystery?' asked Peterson.

'Is *he* a mystery? Is Archy *Stillman* a mystery?' said Wells-Fargo's man, Ferguson. 'Why, the fourth dimension's foolishness to *him*.'

For Ferguson was learned.

Peterson wanted to hear all about him; everybody wanted to tell him; everybody began. But Billy Stevens, the barkeeper, called the house to order, and said one at a time was best. He distributed the drinks, and appointed Ferguson to lead. Ferguson said:

'Well, he's a boy. And that is just about all we know about him. You can pump him till you are tired; it ain't any use; you won't get anything. At least about his intentions, or line of business, or where he's from, and such things as that. And as for getting at the nature and get-up of his main big chief mystery, why, he'll just change the subject, that's all. You can *guess* till you're black in the face – it's your privilege – but suppose you do, where do you arrive at? Nowhere, as near as I can make out.'

'What *is* his big chief one?'

'Sight, maybe. Hearing, maybe. Instinct, maybe. Magic, maybe. Take your choice – grown-ups, twenty-five; children and servants, half price.

Now I'll tell you what he can do. You can start here, and just disappear; you can go and hide wherever you want to, I don't care where it is, nor how far – and he'll go straight and put his finger on you.'

'You don't mean it!'

'I just do, though. Weather's nothing to him – elemental conditions is nothing to him – he don't even take notice of them.'

'Oh, come! Dark? Rain? Snow? Hey?'

'It's all the same to him. He don't give a damn.'

'Oh, *say* – including *fog*, per'aps?'

'*Fog!* he's got an eye't can plunk through it like a bullet.'

'Now, boys, honour bright, what's he giving me?'

'It's a fact!' they all shouted. 'Go on, Wells-Fargo.'

'Well, sir, you can leave him here, chatting with the boys, and you can slip out and go to any cabin in this camp and open a book – yes, sir, a dozen of them – and take the page in your memory, and he'll start out and go straight to that cabin and open every one of them books at the right page, and call it off, and never make a mistake.'

'He must be the devil!'

'More than one has thought it. Now I'll tell you a perfectly wonderful thing that he done. The other night he – '

There was a sudden great murmur of sounds outside, the door flew open, and an excited crowd burst in, with the camp's one white woman in the lead and crying:

'My child! my child! she's lost and gone! For the love of God help me to find Archy Stillman; we've hunted everywhere!'

Said the barkeeper:

'Sit down, sit down, Mrs. Hogan, and don't worry. He asked for a bed three hours ago, tuckered out tramping the trails the way he's always doing, and went upstairs. Ham Sandwich, run up and roust him out; he's in No. 14.'

The youth was soon downstairs and ready. He asked Mrs Hogan for particulars.

'Bless you, dear, there ain't any; I wish there was. I put her to sleep at seven in the evening, and when I went in there an hour ago to go to bed myself, she was gone. I rushed for your cabin, dear, and you wasn't there, and I've hunted for you ever since, at every cabin down the gulch, and now I've come up again, and I'm that distracted and scared and heart-broke; but, thanks to God, I've found you at last, dear heart, and you'll find my child. Come on! come quick!'

'Move right along; I'm with you, madam. Go to your cabin first.'

The whole company streamed out to join the hunt. All the southern half of the village was up, a hundred men strong, and waiting outside, a vague dark mass sprinkled with twinkling lanterns. The mass fell into columns by threes and fours to accommodate itself to the narrow road, and strode briskly along southward in the wake of the leaders. In a few minutes the Hogan cabin was reached.

'There's the bunk,' said Mrs Hogan; 'there's where she was; it's where I laid her at seven o'clock; but where she is now, God only knows.'

'Hand me a lantern,' said Archy. He set it on the hard earth floor and knelt by it, pretending to examine the ground closely. 'Here's her track,' he said, touching the ground here and there and yonder with his finger. 'Do you see?'

Several of the company dropped upon their knees and did their best to see. One or two thought they discerned something like a track; the others shook their heads and confessed that the smooth hard surface had no marks upon it which their eyes were sharp enough to discover. One said, 'Maybe a child's foot could make a mark on it, but *I* don't see how.'

Young Stillman stepped outside, held the light to the ground, turned leftward, and moved three steps, closely examining; then said, 'I've got the direction – come along; take the lantern, somebody.'

He strode off swiftly southward, the files following, swaying and bending in and out with the deep curves of the gorge. Thus a mile, and the mouth of the gorge was reached; before them stretched the sage-brush plain, dim, vast, and vague. Stillman called a halt, saying, 'We mustn't start wrong, now; we must take the direction again.'

He took a lantern and examined the ground for a matter of twenty yards; then said, 'Come on; it's all right,' and gave up the lantern. In and out among the sage bushes he marched, a quarter of a mile, bearing gradually to the right; then took a new direction and made another great semicircle; then changed again and moved due west nearly half a mile – and stopped.

'She gave it up, here, poor little chap. Hold the lantern. You can see where she sat.'

But this was in a slick alkali flat which was surfaced like steel, and no person in the party was quite hardy enough to claim an eyesight that could detect the track of a cushion on a veneer like that. The bereaved mother fell upon her knees and kissed the spot, lamenting.

'But where is she, then?' someone said. 'She didn't stay here. We can see *that* much, anyway.'

Stillman moved about in a circle around the place, with the lantern, pretending to hunt for tracks.

'Well!' he said presently, in an annoyed tone, 'I don't understand it.' He examined again. 'No use. She was here – that's certain; she never *walked* away from here – and that's certain. It's a puzzle; I can't make it out.'

The mother lost heart then.

'Oh, my God! oh, blessed Virgin! some flying beast has got her. I'll never see her again!'

'Ah, *don't* give up,' said Archy. 'We'll find her – don't give up.'

'God bless you for the words, Archy Stillman!' and she seized his hand and kissed it fervently.

Peterson, the newcomer, whispered satirically in Ferguson's ear:

'Wonderful performance to find this place, wasn't it? Hardly worth while to come so far, though; any other supposititious place would have answered just as well – hey?'

Ferguson was not pleased with the innuendo. He said, with some warmth:

'Do you mean to insinuate that the child hasn't been here? I tell you the child *has* been here! Now if you want to get yourself into as tidy a little fuss as – '

'All right!' sang out Stillman. 'Come, everybody, and look at this! It was right under our noses all the time, and we didn't see it.'

There was a general plunge for the ground at the place where the child was alleged to have rested, and many eyes tried hard and hopefully to see the thing that Archy's finger was resting upon. There was a pause, then a several-barrelled sigh of disappointment. Pat Riley and Ham Sandwich said, in the one breath:

'What is it, Archy? There's nothing here.'

'Nothing? Do you call *that* nothing?' and he swiftly traced upon the ground a form with his finger. 'There – don't you recognise it now? It's Injun Billy's track. He's got the child.'

'God be praised!' from the mother.

'Take away the lantern. I've got the direction. Follow!'

He started on a run, racing in and out among the sage bushes a matter of three hundred yards, and disappeared over a sand-wave; the others struggled after him, caught him up, and found him waiting. Ten steps away was a little wickieup, a dim and formless shelter of rags and old horse-blankets, a dull light showing through its chinks.

'You lead, Mrs Hogan,' said the lad. 'It's your privilege to be first.'

All followed the sprint she made for the wickieup, and saw, with her, the picture its interior afforded. Injun Billy was sitting on the ground; the child was asleep beside him. The mother hugged it with a wild embrace, which included Archy Stillman, the grateful tears running down her face, and in a choked and broken voice she poured out a golden stream of that wealth of worshipping endearments which has its home in full richness nowhere but in the Irish heart.

'I find her bymeby it is ten o'clock,' Billy explained. 'She 'sleep out yonder, ve'y tired – face wet, been cryin', 'spose; fetch her home, feed her, she heap much hungry – go 'sleep 'gin.'

In her limitless gratitude the happy mother waived rank and hugged him too, calling him 'the angel of God in disguise.' And he probably was in disguise if he was that kind of an official. He was dressed for the character.

At half-past one in the morning the procession burst into the village singing, 'When Johnny Comes Marching Home', waving its lanterns, and swallowing the drinks that were brought out all along its course. It concentrated at the tavern, and made a night of what was left of the morning.

❧ 6 ☙

The next afternoon the village was electrified with an immense sensation. A grave and dignified foreigner of distinguished bearing and appearance had arrived at the tavern, and entered this formidable name upon the register:

SHERLOCK HOLMES

The news buzzed from cabin to cabin, from claim to claim; tools were dropped, and the town swarmed toward the centre of interest. A man passing out at the northern end of the village shouted it to Pat Riley, whose claim was the next one to Flint Buckner's. At that time Fetlock Jones seemed to turn sick. He muttered to himself:

'Uncle *Sherlock*! The mean luck of it! – that *he* should come just when . . . .' He dropped into a reverie, and presently said to himself: 'But what's the use of being afraid of *him*? Anybody that knows him the way I do knows he can't detect a crime except where he plans it all out beforehand and arranges the clues and hires some fellow to commit it according to instructions . . . Now there ain't going to *be* any clues this time – so, what show has he got? None at all. No, sir; everything's ready. If I was to risk putting it off . . . No, I won't run any risk like that. Flint Buckner goes out of this world tonight, for sure.'

Then another trouble presented itself. 'Uncle Sherlock'll be wanting to talk home matters with me this evening, and how am I going to get rid of him? for I've *got* to be at my cabin a minute or two about eight o'clock.' This was an awkward matter, and cost him much thought. But he found a way to beat the difficulty. 'We'll go for a walk, and I'll leave him in the road a minute, so that he won't see what it is I do: the best way to throw a detective off the track, anyway, is to have him along when you are preparing the thing. Yes, that's the safest – I'll take him with me.'

Meantime the road in front of the tavern was blocked with villagers waiting and hoping for a glimpse of the great man. But he kept his room, and did not appear. None but Ferguson, Jake Parker the blacksmith, and Ham Sandwich had any luck. These enthusiastic admirers of the great scientific detective hired the tavern's detained-baggage lockup, which looked into the detective's room across a little alleyway ten or twelve feet wide, ambushed themselves in it, and cut some peep-holes in the window-blind. Mr Holmes's blinds were down; but by and by he raised them. It gave the spies a hair-lifting but pleasurable thrill to find themselves face to face with the Extraordinary Man who had filled the world with the fame of his more than human ingenuities. There he sat – not a myth, not a shadow, but real, alive, compact of substance, and almost within touching distance with the hand.

'Look at that head!' said Ferguson, in an awed voice. 'By gracious! *that's* a head!'

'You bet!' said the blacksmith, with deep reverence. 'Look at his nose! look at his eyes! Intellect? Just a battery of it!'

'And that paleness,' said Ham Sandwich. 'Comes from thought – that's what it comes from. Hell! duffers like us don't know what real thought *is*.'

'No more we don't,' said Ferguson. 'What we take for thinking is just blubber-and-slush.'

'Right you are, Wells-Fargo. And look at that frown – that's *deep* thinking – away down, down, forty fathom into the bowels of things. He's on the track of something.'

'Well, he is, and don't you forget it. Say – look at that awful gravity – look at that pallid solemnness – there ain't any corpse can lay over it.'

'No, sir, not for dollars! And it's his'n by hereditary rights, too; he's been dead four times a'ready, and there's history for it. Three times natural, once by accident. I've heard say he smells damp and cold, like a grave. And he – '

' 'Sh! Watch him! There – he's got his thumb on the bump on the near corner of his forehead, and his forefinger on the off one. His think-works is just a-*grinding* now, you bet your other shirt.'

'That's so. And now he's gazing up toward heaven and stroking his moustache slow, and – '

'Now he has rose up standing, and is putting his clues together on his left fingers with his right finger. See? he touches the forefinger – now middle finger – now ring-finger – '

'Stuck!'

'Look at him scowl! He can't seem to make out *that* clue. So he – '

'See him smile! – like a tiger – and tally off the other fingers like nothing! He's got it, boys; he's got it sure!'

'Well, I should *say*! I'd hate to be in that man's place that he's after.'

Mr Holmes drew a table to the window, sat down with his back to the spies, and proceeded to write. The spies withdrew their eyes from the peep-holes, lit their pipes, and settled themselves for a comfortable smoke and talk. Ferguson said, with conviction:

'Boys, it's no use talking, he's a wonder! He's got the signs of it all over him.'

'You hain't ever said a truer word than that, Wells-Fargo,' said Jake Parker. 'Say, wouldn't it 'a' been nuts if he'd a-been here last night?'

'Oh, by George, but wouldn't it!' said Ferguson. 'Then we'd have seen *scientific* work. Intellect – just pure intellect – away up on the upper levels, dontchuknow. Archy is all right, and it don't become anybody to belittle *him*, I can tell you. But his gift is only just eyesight, sharp as an owl's, as near as I can make it out just a grand natural animal talent, no more, no less, and prime as far as it goes, but no intellect in it, and for awfulness and marvellousness no more to be compared to what this man does than – than – Why, let me tell you what *he'd* have done. He'd have stepped over to Hogan's and glanced – just *glanced*, that's all – at the premises, and that's enough . See everything? Yes, sir, to the last little *d*etail; and he'd know more about that place than the Hogans would know in seven years. Next, he would sit down on the bunk, just as ca'm, and say to Mrs Hogan – *Say*, Ham, consider that you are Mrs Hogan. I'll ask the questions; you answer them.'

'All right; go on.'

' "Madam, if you please – attention – do not let your mind wander. Now, then – sex of the child?"

' "Female, your Honour."

' "Um – female. Very good, very good. Age?"

' "Turned six, your Honour."

' "Um – young, weak – two miles. Weariness will overtake it then. It will sink down and sleep. We shall find it two miles away, or less. Teeth?"

' "Five, your Honour, and one a-coming."

' "Very good, very good, *very* good, indeed." You see, boys, *he* knows a clue when he sees it, when it wouldn't mean a dern thing to anybody else. "Stockings, madam? Shoes?"

' "Yes, your Honour – both."

' "Yarn, perhaps? Morocco?"

' "Yarn, your Honour. And kip."

' "Um – kip. This complicates the matter. However, let it go – we shall manage. Religion?"

' "Catholic, your Honour."

' "Very good. Snip me a bit from the bed blanket, please. Ah, thanks. Part wool – foreign make. Very well. A snip from some garment of the child's, please. Thanks. Cotton. Shows wear. An excellent clue, excellent. Pass me a pellet of the floor dirt, if you'll be so kind. Thanks, many thanks. Ah, admirable, admirable! *Now* we know where we are, I think.' You see, boys, he's got all the clues he wants now; he don't need anything more. Now, then, what does this Extraordinary Man do? He lays those snips and that dirt out on the table and leans over them on his elbows, and puts them together side by side and studies them – mumbles to himself, "Female"; changes them around – mumbles, "Six years old"; changes them this way and that – again mumbles: "Five teeth – one a-coming – Catholic – yarn – cotton – kip – damn that kip." Then he straightens up and gazes toward heaven, and plows his hands through his hair – plows and plows, muttering, "Damn that kip!" Then he stands up and frowns, and begins to tally off his clues on his fingers – and gets stuck at the ring-finger. But only just a minute – then his face glares all up in a smile like a house afire, and he straightens up stately and majestic, and says to the crowds, "Take a lantern, a couple of you, and go down to Injun Billy's and fetch the child – the rest of you go 'long home to bed; good-night, madam; good-night, gents." And he bows like the Matterhorn, and pulls out for the tavern. That's *his* style, and the *Only* – scientific, intellectual – all over in fifteen minutes – no poking around all over the sage-brush range an hour and a half in a mass-meeting crowd for *him*, boys – you hear *me*!'

'By Jackson, it's grand!' said Ham Sandwich. 'Wells-Fargo, you've got him down to a dot. He ain't painted up any exacter to the life in the books. By George, I can just *see* him – can't you, boys?'

'You bet you! It's just a photograft, that's what it is.'

Ferguson was profoundly pleased with his success, and grateful. He sat silently enjoying his happiness a little while, then he murmured, with a deep awe in his voice,

'I wonder if God made him?'

There was no response for a moment; then Ham Sandwich said, reverently,

'Not all at one time, I reckon.'

❦ 7 ❧

At eight o'clock that evening two persons were groping their way past Flint Buckner's cabin in the frosty gloom. They were Sherlock Holmes and his nephew.

'Stop here in the road a moment, uncle,' said Fetlock, 'while I run to my cabin; I won't be gone a minute.'

He asked for something – the uncle furnished it – then he disappeared in the darkness, but soon returned, and the talking-walk was resumed. By nine o'clock they had wandered back to the tavern. They worked their way through the billiard-room, where a crowd had gathered in the hope of getting a glimpse of the Extraordinary Man. A royal cheer was raised. Mr Holmes acknowledged the compliment with a series of courtly bows, and as he was passing out his nephew said to the assemblage,

'Uncle Sherlock's got some work to do, gentlemen, that'll keep him till twelve or one; but he'll be down again then, or earlier if he can, and hopes some of you'll be left to take a drink with him.'

'By George, he's just a duke, boys! Three cheers for Sherlock Holmes, the greatest man that ever lived!' shouted Ferguson. 'Hip, hip, hip – '

'Hurrah! hurrah! hurrah! Tiger!'

The uproar shook the building, so hearty was the feeling the boys put into their welcome. Upstairs the uncle reproached the nephew gently, saying,

'What did you get me into that engagement for?'

'I reckon you don't want to be unpopular, do you, uncle? Well, then, don't you put on any exclusiveness in a mining-camp, that's all. The boys admire you; but if you was to leave without taking a drink with them, they'd set you down for a snob. And besides, you said you had home talk enough in stock to keep us up and at it half the night.'

The boy was right, and wise – the uncle acknowledged it. The boy was wise in another detail which he did not mention – except to himself: 'Uncle and the others will come handy – in the way of nailing an *alibi* where it can't be budged.'

He and his uncle talked diligently about three hours. Then, about midnight, Fetlock stepped downstairs and took a position in the dark a dozen steps from the tavern, and waited. Five minutes later Flint Buckner came rocking out of the billiard-room and almost brushed him as he passed.

'I've *got* him!' muttered the boy. He continued to himself, looking after the shadowy form: 'Goodbye – goodbye for good, Flint Buckner; you called my mother a – well, never mind what: it's all right, now; you're taking your last walk, friend.'

He went musing back into the tavern. 'From now till one is an hour. We'll spend it with the boys: it's good for the *alibi*.'

He brought Sherlock Holmes to the billiard room, which was jammed with eager and admiring miners; the guest called the drinks, and the fun began. Everybody was happy; everybody was complimentary; the ice was soon broken, songs, anecdotes, and more drinks followed, and the pregnant minutes flew. At six minutes to one, when the jollity was at its highest –

Boom!

There was silence instantly. The deep sound came rolling and rumbling from peak to peak up the gorge, then died down, and ceased. The spell broke, then, and the men made a rush for the door, saying,

'Something's blown up!'

Outside, a voice in the darkness said,

'It's away down the gorge; I saw the flash.'

The crowd poured down the canyon – Holmes, Fetlock, Archy Stillman, everybody. They made the mile in a few minutes. By the light of a lantern they found the smooth and solid dirt floor of Flint Buckner's cabin; of the cabin itself not a vestige remained, not a rag nor a splinter. Nor any sign of Flint. Search parties sought here and there and yonder, and presently a cry went up.

'Here he is!'

It was true. Fifty yards down the gulch they had found him – that is, they had found a crushed and lifeless mass which represented him. Fetlock Jones hurried thither with the others and looked.

The inquest was a fifteen-minute affair. Ham Sandwich, foreman of the jury, handed up the verdict, which was phrased with a certain unstudied literary grace, and closed with this finding, to wit: that 'deceased came to his death by his own act or some other person or persons unknown to this jury not leaving any family or similar effects behind but his cabin which was blown away and God have mercy on his soul amen'.

Then the impatient jury rejoined the main crowd, for the storm-centre of interest was there – Sherlock Holmes. The miners stood silent and reverent in a half-circle, enclosing a large vacant space which included the front exposure of the site of the late premises. In this considerable space the Extraordinary Man was moving about, attended by his nephew with a lantern. With a tape he took measurements of the cabin site; of the distance from the wall of chaparral to the road; of the height of the chaparral bushes; also various other measurements. He gathered a rag here, a splinter there, and a pinch of earth yonder, inspected them profoundly, and preserved them. He took the 'lay' of the place with a pocket compass, allowing two seconds for magnetic variation. He took the time (Pacific) by his watch, correcting it for local time. He paced off the distance from the cabin site to the corpse, and corrected that for tidal differentiation. He took the altitude with a pocket-aneroid, and the temperature with a pocket-thermometer. Finally he said, with a stately bow:

'It is finished. Shall we return, gentlemen?'

He took up the line of march for the tavern, and the crowd fell into his wake, earnestly discussing and admiring the Extraordinary Man, and interlarding guesses as to the origin of the tragedy and who the author of it might be.

'My, but it's grand luck having him here – hey, boys?' said Ferguson.

'It's the biggest thing of the century,' said Ham Sandwich. 'It'll go all over the world; you mark my words.'

'*You* bet!' said Jake Parker the blacksmith. 'It'll boom this camp. Ain't it so, Wells-Fargo?'

'Well, as you want my opinion – if it's any sign of how *I* think about it, I can tell you this: yesterday I was holding the Straight Flush claim at two dollars a foot; I'd like to see the man that can get it at sixteen today.'

'Right you are, Wells-Fargo! It's the grandest luck a new camp ever struck. Say, did you see him collar them little rags and dirt and things? What an eye! He just can't overlook a clue – 'tain't *in* him.'

'That's so. And they wouldn't mean a thing to anybody else; but to him, why, they're just a book – large print at that.'

'Sure's you're born! Them odds and ends have got their little old secret, and they think there ain't anybody can pull it; but, land! when he sets his grip there they've got to squeal, and don't you forget it.'

'Boys, I ain't sorry, now, that he wasn't here to roust out the child; this is a bigger thing, by a long sight. Yes, sir, and more tangled up and scientific and intellectual.'

'I reckon we're all of us glad it's turned out this way. Glad? 'George! it ain't any name for it. Dontchuknow, Archy could've *learnt* something if he'd had the nous to stand by and take notice of how that man works the system. But no; he went poking up into the chaparral and just missed the whole thing.'

'It's true as gospel; I seen it myself. Well, Archy's young. He'll know better one of these days.'

'Say, boys, who do you reckon done it?'

That was a difficult question, and brought out a world of unsatisfying conjecture. Various men were mentioned as possibilities, but one by one they were discarded as not being eligible. No one but young Hillyer had been intimate with Flint Buckner; no one had really had a quarrel with him; he had affronted every man who had tried to make up to him, although not quite offensively enough to require bloodshed. There was one name that was upon every tongue from the start, but it was the last to get utterance – Fetlock Jones's. It was Pat Riley that mentioned it.

'Oh, well,' the boys said, 'of course we've all thought of him, because he had a million rights to kill Flint Buckner, and it was just his plain duty to do it. But all the same there's two things we can't get around: for one thing, he hasn't got the sand; and for another, he wasn't anywhere near the place when it happened.'

'I know it,' said Pat. 'He was there in the billiard-room with us when it happened.'

'Yes, and was there all the time for an hour *before* it happened.'

'It's so. And lucky for him, too. He'd have been suspected in a minute if it hadn't been for that.'

⌘ 8 ⌘

The tavern dining-room had been cleared of all its furniture save one six-foot pine table and a chair. This table was against one end of the room; the chair was on it; Sherlock Holmes, stately, imposing, impressive, sat in the chair. The public stood. The room was full. The tobacco smoke was dense, the stillness profound.

The Extraordinary Man raised his hand to command additional silence; held it in the air a few moments; then, in brief, crisp terms he put forward question after question, and noted the answers with 'Um-ums', nods of the head, and so on. By this process he learned all about Flint Buckner, his character, conduct, and habits, that the people were able to tell him. It thus transpired that the Extraordinary Man's nephew was the only person in the camp who had a killing-grudge against Flint Buckner. Mr Holmes smiled compassionately upon the witness, and asked, languidly –

'Do any of you gentlemen chance to know where the lad Fetlock Jones was at the time of the explosion?'

A thunderous response followed –

'In the billiard-room of this house!'

'Ah. And had he just come in?'

'Been there all of an hour!'

'Ah. It is about – about – well, about how far might it be to the scene of the explosion?'

'All of a mile!'

'Ah. It isn't *much* of an alibi, 'tis true, but – '

A storm-burst of laughter, mingled with shouts of 'By jiminy, but he's chain-lightning!' and 'Ain't you sorry you spoke, Sandy?' shut off the rest of the sentence, and the crushed witness drooped his blushing face in pathetic shame. The inquisitor resumed:

'The lad Jones's somewhat *distant* connection with the case' (laughter) 'having been disposed of, let us now call the *eye*-witnesses of the tragedy, and listen to what they have to say.'

He got out his fragmentary clues and arranged them on a sheet of cardboard on his knee. The house held its breath and watched.

'We have the longitude and the latitude, corrected for magnetic variation, and this gives us the exact location of the tragedy. We have the altitude, the temperature, and the degree of humidity prevailing – inestimably valuable, since they enable us to estimate with precision the degree of influence which they would exercise upon the mood and disposition of the assassin at that time of the night.'

(Buzz of admiration; muttered remark, 'By George, but he's deep!') He fingered his clues.

'And now let us ask these mute witnesses to speak to us.

'Here we have an empty linen shotbag. What is its message? This: that robbery was the motive, not revenge. What is its further message? This: that the assassin was of inferior intelligence – shall we say light-witted, or perhaps approaching that? How do we know this? Because a person of sound intelligence would not have proposed to rob the man Buckner, who never had much money with him. But the assassin might have been a stranger? Let the bag speak again. I take from it this article. It is a bit of silver-bearing quartz. It is peculiar. Examine it, please – you – and you – and you. Now pass it back, please. There is but one lode on this coast which produces just that character and colour of quartz; and that is a lode which crops out for nearly two miles on a stretch, and in my opinion is destined, at no distant day, to confer upon its locality a globe-girdling celebrity, and upon its two hundred owners riches beyond the dreams of avarice. Name that lode, please.'

'The Consolidated Christian Science and Mary Ann!' was the prompt response.

A wild crash of hurrahs followed, and every man reached for his neighbour's hand and wrung it, with tears in his eyes; and Wells-Fargo Ferguson shouted, 'The Straight Flush is on the lode, and up she goes to a hundred and fifty a foot – you hear *me*!'

When quiet fell, Mr Holmes resumed:

'We perceive, then, that three facts are established, to wit: the assassin was approximately light-witted; he was not a stranger; his motive was robbery, not revenge. Let us proceed. I hold in my hand a small fragment of fuse, with the recent smell of fire upon it. What is its testimony? Taken with the corroborative evidence of the quartz, it reveals to us that the assassin was a miner. What does it tell us further? This, gentlemen: that the assassination was consummated by means of an explosive. What else does it say? This: that the explosive was located against the side of the cabin nearest the road – the front side – for within six feet of that spot I found it.

'I hold in my fingers a burnt Swedish match – the kind one rubs on a safety-box. I found it in the road, 622 feet from the abolished cabin. What does it say? This: that the train was fired from that point. What further does it tell us? This: that the assassin was left-handed. How do I know this? I should not be able to explain to you, gentlemen, how I know it, the signs being so subtle that only long experience and deep study can enable one to detect them. But the signs are here, and they are reinforced by a fact which you must have often noticed in the great detective narratives – that *all* assassins are left-handed.'

'By Jackson, *that's* so!' said Ham Sandwich, bringing his great hand down with a resounding slap upon his thigh; 'blamed if I ever thought of it before.'

'Nor I!' 'Nor I!' cried several. 'Oh, there can't anything escape *him* – look at his eye!'

'Gentlemen, distant as the murderer was from his doomed victim, he did not wholly escape injury. This fragment of wood which I now exhibit to you struck him. It drew blood. Wherever he is, he bears the telltale mark. I picked it up where he stood when he fired the fatal train.' He looked out over the house from his high perch, and his countenance began to darken; he slowly raised his hand, and pointed –

'There stands the assassin!'

For a moment the house was paralysed with amazement; then twenty voices burst out with:

'Sammy Hillyer? Oh, *hell*, no! *Him?* It's pure foolishness!'

'Take care, gentlemen – be not hasty. Observe – he has the blood-mark on his brow.'

Hillyer turned white with fright. He was near to crying. He turned this way and that, appealing to every face for help and sympathy; and held out his supplicating hands toward Holmes and began to plead:

'*Don't*, oh, don't! I never did it; I give my word I never did it. The way I got this hurt on my forehead was – '

'Arrest him, constable!' cried Holmes. 'I will swear out the warrant.'

The constable moved reluctantly forward – hesitated – stopped.

Hillyer broke out with another appeal. 'Oh, Archy, don't let them do it; it would kill mother! *You* know how I got the hurt. Tell them, and save me, Archy; save me!'

Stillman worked his way to the front, and said:

'Yes, I'll save you. Don't be afraid.' Then he said to the house, 'Never mind how he got the hurt; it hasn't anything to do with this case, and isn't of any consequence.'

'God bless you, Archy, for a true friend!'

'Hurrah for Archy! Go in, boy, and play 'em a knock-down flush to their two pair 'n' a jack!' shouted the house, pride in their home talent and a patriotic sentiment of loyalty to it rising suddenly in the public heart and changing the whole attitude of the situation.

Young Stillman waited for the noise to cease; then he said,

'I will ask Tom Jeffries to stand by that door yonder, and Constable Harris to stand by the other one here, and not let anybody leave the room.'

'Said and done. Go on, old man!'

'The criminal is present, I believe. I will show him to you before long, in case I am right in my guess. Now I will tell you all about the tragedy, from start to finish. The motive *wasn't* robbery; it was revenge. The murderer *wasn't* light-witted. He *didn't* stand 622 feet away. He *didn't* get hit with a piece of wood. He *didn't* place the explosive against the cabin. He *didn't* bring a shot-bag with him, and he *wasn't* left-handed. With the exception of these errors, the distinguished guest's statement of the case is substantially correct.'

A comfortable laugh rippled over the house; friend nodded to friend, as much as to say, 'That's the word, with the bark *on* it. Good lad, good boy. *He* ain't lowering his flag any!'

The guest's serenity was not disturbed. Stillman resumed:

'I also have some witnesses; and I will presently tell you where you can find some more.' He held up a piece of coarse wire; the crowd craned their necks to see. 'It has a smooth coating of melted tallow on it. And here is a candle which is burned half-way down. The remaining half of it has marks cut upon it an inch apart. Soon I will tell you where I found these things. I will now put aside reasonings, guesses, the impressive hitchings of odds and ends of clues together, and the other showy theatricals of the detective trade, and tell you in a plain, straightforward way just how this dismal thing happened.'

He paused a moment, for effect – to allow silence and suspense to intensify and concentrate the house's interest; then he went on:

'The assassin studied out his plan with a good deal of pains. It was a good plan, very ingenious, and showed an intelligent mind, not a feeble one. It was a plan which was well calculated to ward off all suspicion from its inventor. In the first place, he marked a candle into spaces an inch apart, and lit it and timed it. He found it took three hours to burn four inches of it. I tried it myself for half an hour, awhile ago, upstairs here, while the inquiry into Flint Buckner's character and ways was being conducted in this room, and I arrived in that way at the rate of a candle's consumption when sheltered from the wind. Having proved his trial-candle's rate, he blew it out – I have already shown it to you – and put his inch-marks on a fresh one.

'He put the fresh one into a tin candlestick. Then at the five-hour mark he bored a hole through the candle with a red-hot wire. I have already shown you the wire, with a smooth coat of tallow on it – tallow that had been melted and had cooled.

'With labour – very hard labour, I should say – he struggled up through the stiff chaparral that clothes the steep hillside back of Flint Buckner's place, tugging an empty flour-barrel with him. He placed it in that absolutely secure hiding-place, and in the bottom of it he set the candlestick. Then he measured off about thirty-five feet of fuse – the barrel's distance from the back of the cabin. He bored a hole in the side of the barrel – here is the large gimlet he did it with. He went on and finished his work; and when it was done, one end of the fuse was in

Buckner's cabin, and the other end, with a notch chipped in it to expose the powder, was in the hole in the candle – timed to blow the place up at one o'clock this morning, provided the candle was lit about eight o'clock yesterday evening – which I am betting it was – and provided there was an explosive in the cabin and connected with that end of the fuse – which I am also betting there was, though I can't prove it. Boys, the barrel is there in the chaparral, the candle's remains are in it in the tin stick; the burnt-out fuse is in the gimlet-hole, the other end is down the hill where the late cabin stood. I saw them all an hour or two ago, when the Professor here was measuring off unimplicated vacancies and collecting relics that hadn't anything to do with the case.'

He paused. The house drew a long, deep breath, shook its strained cords and muscles free and burst into cheers. 'Dang him!' said Ham Sandwich, 'that's why he was snooping around in the chaparral, instead of picking up points out of the P'fessor's game. Looky here – *he* ain't no fool, boys.'

'No, sir! Why, great Scott – '

But Stillman was resuming:

'While we were out yonder an hour or two ago, the owner of the gimlet and the trial-candle took them from a place where he had concealed them – it was not a good place – and carried them to what he probably thought was a better one, two hundred yards up in the pine woods, and hid them there, covering them over with pine needles. It was there that I found them. The gimlet exactly fits the hole in the barrel. And now – '

The Extraordinary Man interrupted him. He said, sarcastically:

'We have had a very pretty fairytale, gentlemen – very pretty indeed. Now I would like to ask this young man a question or two.'

Some of the boys winced, and Ferguson said,

'I'm afraid Archy's going to catch it now.'

The others lost their smiles and sobered down. Mr Holmes said:

'Let us proceed to examine into this fairytale in a consecutive and orderly way – by geometrical progression, so to speak – linking detail to detail in a steadily advancing and remorselessly consistent and unassailable march upon this tinsel toy-fortress of error, the dream-fabric of a callow imagination. To begin with, young sir, I desire to ask you but three questions at present – *at present*. Did I understand you to say it was your opinion that the supposititious candle was lighted at about eight o'clock yesterday evening?'

'Yes, sir – about eight.'

'Could you say exactly eight?'

'Well, no, I couldn't be that exact.'

'Um. If a person had been passing along there just about that time, he would have been almost sure to encounter that assassin, do you think?'

'Yes, I should think so.'

'Thank you, that is all. For the present. I say, all *for the present.*'

'Dern him! he's laying for Archy,' said Ferguson.

'It's so,' said Ham Sandwich. 'I don't like the look of it.'

Stillman said, glancing at the guest,

'I was along there myself at half past eight – no, about nine.'

'In-deed? This is interesting – this very interesting. Perhaps you encountered the assassin?'

'No, I encountered no one.'

'Ah. Then – if you will excuse the remark – I do not quite see the relevancy of the information.'

'It has none. At present. I say it has none – at present.'

He paused. Presently he resumed: 'I did not encounter the assassin, but I am on his track, I am sure, for I believe he is in this room. I will ask you all to pass one by one in front of me – here, where there is a good light – so that I can see your feet.'

A buzz of excitement swept the place, and the march began, the guest looking on with an iron attempt at gravity which was not an unqualified success. Stillman stooped, shaded his eyes with his hand, and gazed down intently at each pair of feet as it passed. Fifty men tramped monotonously by – with no result. Sixty. Seventy. The thing was beginning to look absurd. The guest remarked, with suave irony,

'Assassins appear to be scarce this evening.'

The house saw the humour of it, and refreshed itself with a cordial laugh. Ten or twelve more candidates tramped by – no, *danced* by, with airy and ridiculous capers which convulsed the spectators – then suddenly Stillman put out his hand and said,

'This is the assassin!'

'Fetlock Jones, by the great Sanhedrim!' roared the crowd; and at once let fly a pyrotechnic explosion and dazzle and confusion of stirring remarks inspired by the situation.

At the height of the turmoil the guest stretched out his hand, commanding peace. The authority of a great name and a great personality laid its mysterious compulsion upon the house, and it obeyed. Out of the panting calm which succeeded, the guest spoke, saying, with dignity and feeling:

'*This* is serious. It strikes at an innocent life. Innocent beyond suspicion! Innocent beyond peradventure! Hear me *prove* it; observe how simple a fact can brush out of existence this witless lie. Listen. My friends, that lad was never out of my sight yesterday evening at *any* time!'

It made a deep impression. Men turned their eyes upon Stillman with grave inquiry in them. His face brightened, and he said,

'I *knew* there was another one!' He stepped briskly to the table and glanced at the guest's feet, then up at his face, and said: 'You were *with* him! You were not fifty steps from him when he lit the candle that by and by fired the powder!' (Sensation.) 'And what is more, you furnished the matches yourself!'

Plainly the guest seemed hit; it looked so to the public. He opened his mouth to speak; the words did not come freely.

'This – er – this is insanity – this – '

Stillman pressed his evident advantage home. He held up a charred match.

'Here is one of them. I found it in the barrel – and there's *another* one there.'

The guest found his voice at once.

'*Yes* – and put them there yourself!'

It was recognised a good shot. Stillman retorted.

'It is *wax* – a breed unknown to this camp. I am ready to be searched for the box. Are you?'

The guest was staggered this time – the dullest eye could see it. He fumbled with his hands; once or twice his lips moved, but the words did not come. The house waited and watched, in tense suspense, the stillness adding effect to the situation. Presently Stillman said, gently,

'We are waiting for your decision.'

There was silence again during several moments; then the guest answered, in a low voice,

'I refuse to be searched.'

There was no noisy demonstration, but all about the house one voice after another muttered:

'That settles it! He's Archy's meat.'

What to do now? Nobody seemed to know. It was an embarrassing situation for the moment – merely, of course, because matters had taken such a sudden and unexpected turn that these unpractised minds were not prepared for it, and had come to a standstill, like a stopped clock, under the shock. But after a little the machinery began to work again, tentatively, and by twos and threes the men put their heads together and privately buzzed over this and that and the other proposition. One of these propositions met with much favour; it was, to confer upon the assassin a vote of thanks for removing Flint Buckner, and let him go. But the cooler heads opposed it, pointing out that addled brains in the Eastern States would pronounce it a scandal, and make no end of foolish noise about it. Finally the cool heads got the upper hand, and obtained general consent to a proposition of their own; their leader then called the house to order and stated it – to this effect: that Fetlock Jones be jailed and put upon trial.

The motion was carried. Apparently there was nothing further to do now, and the people were glad, for, privately, they were impatient to get out and rush to the scene of the tragedy, and see whether that barrel and the other things were really there or not.

But no – the break-up got a check. The surprises were not over yet. For a while Fetlock Jones had been silently sobbing, unnoticed in the absorbing excitements which had been following one another so persistently for some time; but when his arrest and trial were decreed, he broke out despairingly, and said:

'No! it's no use. I don't want any jail, I don't want any trial; I've had all the hard luck I want, and all the miseries. Hang me now, and let me out! It would all come out, anyway – there couldn't anything save me. He has told it all, just as if he'd been with me and seen it – *I* don't know how he found out; and you'll find the barrel and things, and then I wouldn't have any chance any more. I killed him; and *you'd* have done it too, if he'd treated you like a dog, and you only a boy, and weak and poor, and not a friend to help you.'

'And served him damned well right!' broke in Ham Sandwich. 'Looky here, boys – '

From the constable: 'Order! Order, gentlemen!'

A voice: 'Did your uncle know what you was up to?'

'No, he didn't.'

'Did he give you the matches, sure enough?'

'Yes, he did; but he didn't know what I wanted them for.'

'When you was out on such a business as that, how did you venture to risk having him along – and him a *detective*? How's that?'

The boy hesitated, fumbled with his buttons in an embarrassed way, then said, shyly,

'I know about detectives, on account of having them in the family; and if you don't want them to find out about a thing, it's best to have them around when you do it.'

The cyclone of laughter which greeted this naïve discharge of wisdom did not modify the poor little waif's embarrassment in any large degree.

🍃 9 🍃

From a letter to Mrs Stillman, dated merely 'Tuesday'.

Fetlock Jones was put under lock and key in an unoccupied log cabin, and left there to await his trial. Constable Harris provided him with a couple of days' rations, instructed him to keep a good guard over himself, and promised to look in on him as soon as further supplies should be due.

Next morning a score of us went with Hillyer, out of friendship, and helped him bury his late relative, the unlamented Buckner, and I acted as first assistant pall-bearer, Hillyer acting as chief. Just as we had finished our labours a ragged and melancholy stranger, carrying an old hand-bag, limped by with his head down, and I caught the scent I had chased around the globe! It was the odour of Paradise to my perishing hope!

In a moment I was at his side and had laid a gentle hand upon his shoulder. He slumped to the ground as if a stroke of lightning had withered him in his tracks; and as the boys came running he struggled to his knees and put up his pleading hands to me, and out of his chattering jaws he begged me to persecute him no more, and said,

'You have hunted me around the world, Sherlock Holmes, yet God is my witness I have never done any man harm!'

A glance at his wild eyes showed us that he was insane. That was my work, mother! The tidings of your death can someday repeat the misery I felt in that moment, but nothing else can ever do it. The boys lifted him up, and gathered about him, and were full of pity of him, and said the gentlest and touchingest things to him, and said cheer up and don't be troubled, he was among friends now, and they would take care of him, and protect him, and hang any man that laid a hand on him. They are just like so many mothers, the rough mining-camp boys are, when you wake up the south side of their hearts; yes, and just like so many reckless and unreasoning children when you wake up the opposite side of that muscle. They did everything they could think of to comfort him, but nothing succeeded until Wells-Fargo Ferguson, who is a clever strategist, said,

'If it's only Sherlock Holmes that's troubling you, you needn't worry any more.'

'Why?' asked the forlorn lunatic, eagerly.

'Because he's dead again.'

'Dead! Dead! Oh, don't trifle with a poor wreck like me. *Is* he dead? On honour, now – is he telling me true, boys?'

'True as you're standing there!' said Ham Sandwich, and they all backed up the statement in a body.

'They hung him in San Bernardino last week,' added Ferguson, clinching the matter, 'whilst he was searching around after you. Mistook him for another man. They're sorry, but they can't help it now.'

'They're a-building him a monument,' said Ham Sandwich, with the air of a person who had contributed to it, and knew.

'James Walker' drew a deep sigh – evidently a sigh of relief – and said nothing; but his eyes lost something of their wildness, his countenance cleared visibly, and its drawn look relaxed a little. We all went to our cabin, and the boys cooked him the best dinner the camp could furnish the materials for, and while they were about it Hillyer and I outfitted him from hat to shoe-leather with new clothes of ours, and made a comely and presentable old gentleman of him. 'Old' is the right word, and a pity, too: old by the droop of him, and the frost upon his hair, and the marks which sorrow and distress have left upon his face; though he is only in his prime in the matter of years. While he ate, we smoked and chatted; and when he was finishing he found his voice at last, and of his own accord broke out with his personal history. I cannot furnish his exact words, but I will come as near it as I can.

THE 'WRONG MAN's' STORY

It happened like this: I was in Denver. I had been there many years; sometimes I remember how many, sometimes I don't – but it isn't any matter. All of a sudden I got a notice to leave, or I would be exposed for a horrible crime committed long before – years and years before – in the East.

I knew about that crime, but I was not the criminal; it was a cousin of mine of the same name. What should I better do? My head was all disordered by fear, and I didn't know. I was allowed very little time – only one day, I think it was. I would be ruined if I was published, and the people would lynch me, and not believe what I said. It is always the way with lynchings: when they find out it is a mistake they are sorry, but it is too late – the same as it was with Mr Holmes, you see. So I said I would sell out and get money to live on, and run away until it blew over and I could come back with my proofs. Then I escaped in the night and went a long way off in the mountains somewhere, and lived disguised and had a false name.

I got more and more troubled and worried, and my troubles made me see spirits and hear voices, and I could not think straight and clear on any subject, but got confused and involved and had to give it up, because my head hurt so. It got to be worse and worse; more spirits and more voices. They were about me all the time; at first only in the night, then in the day too. They were always whispering around my bed and plotting against me, and it broke my sleep and kept me fagged out, because I got no good rest.

And then came the worst. One night the whispers said, 'We'll never manage, because we can't *see* him, and so can't point him out to the people.'

They sighed; then one said: 'We must bring Sherlock Holmes. He can be here in twelve days.'

They all agreed, and whispered and gibbered with joy. But my heart broke; for I had read about that man, and knew what it would be to have him upon my track, with his superhuman penetration and tireless energies.

The spirits went away to fetch him, and I got up at once in the middle of the night and fled away, carrying nothing but the hand-bag that had my money in it – thirty thousand dollars; two-thirds of it are in the bag there yet. It was forty days before that man caught up on my track. I just escaped. From habit he had written his real name on a tavern register, but had scratched it out and written 'Dagget Barclay' in the place of it. But fear gives you a watchful eye and keen, and I read the true name through the scratches, and fled like a deer.

He has hunted me an over this world for three years and a half – the Pacific States, Australasia, India – everywhere you can think of; then back to Mexico and up to California again, giving me hardly any rest; but that name on the registers always saved me, and what is left of me is alive yet. And I am *so* tired! A cruel time he has given me, yet I give you my honour I have never harmed him nor any man.

That was the end of the story, and it stirred those boys to blood-heat, be sure of it. As for me – each word burnt a hole in me where it struck.

We voted that the old man should bunk with us, and be my guest and Hillyer's. I shall keep my own counsel, naturally; but as soon as he is well rested and nourished, I shall take him to Denver and rehabilitate his fortunes.

The boys gave the old fellow the bone-mashing good-fellowship handshake of the mines, and then scattered away to spread the news.

At dawn next morning Wells-Fargo Ferguson and Ham Sandwich called us softly out, and said, privately:

'That news about the way that old stranger has been treated has spread all around, and the camps are up. They are piling in from everywhere, and are going to lynch the P'fessor. Constable Harris is in a dead funk, and has telephoned the sheriff. Come along!'

We started on a run. The others were privileged to feel as they chose, but in my heart's privacy I hoped the sheriff would arrive in time; for I had small desire that Sherlock Holmes should hang for my deeds, as you can easily believe. I had heard a good deal about the sheriff, but for reassurance's sake I asked,

'Can he stop a mob?'

'Can *he* stop a mob? Can Jack *Fairfax* stop a mob? Well, I should smile! Ex-desperado – nineteen scalps on his string. Can *he*? Oh, I *say*!'

As we tore up the gulch, distant cries and shouts and yells rose faintly on the still air, and grew steadily in strength as we raced along. Roar after roar burst out, stronger and stronger, nearer and nearer; and at last, when we closed up upon the multitude massed in the open area in front of the tavern, the crash of sound was deafening. Some brutal roughs from Daly's gorge had Holmes in their grip, and he was the calmest man there; a contemptuous smile played about his lips, and if any fear of death was in his British heart, his iron personality was master of it and no sign of it was allowed to appear.

'Come to a vote, men!' This from on of the Daly gang, Shadbelly Higgins. 'Quick! is it hang, or shoot?'

'Neither!' shouted one of his comrades. 'He'd be alive again in a week; burning's the only permanency for *him*.'

The gangs from all the outlying camps burst out in a thunder-crash of approval, and went struggling and surging toward the prisoner, and closed around him, shouting, 'Fire! fire's the ticket!' They dragged him to the horse-post, backed him against it, chained him to it, and piled wood and pine cones around him waist-deep. Still the strong face did not blench, and still the scornful smile played about the thin lips.

'A match! fetch a match!'

Shadbelly struck it, shaded it with his hand, stooped, and held it under a pine cone. A deep silence fell upon the mob. The cone caught, a tiny flame flickered about it a moment or two. I seemed to catch the sound of distant hoofs – it grew more distinct – still more and more distinct, more and more definite, but the absorbed crowd did not appear to notice it. The match went out. The man struck another, stooped, and again the flame rose; this time it took hold and began to spread – here and there men turned away their faces. The executioner stood with the charred match in his fingers, watching his work. The hoof-beats turned a projecting crag, and now they came thundering down upon us. Almost the next moment there was a shout –

'The sheriff!'

And straightway he came tearing into the midst, stood his horse almost on his hind feet, and said,

'Fall back, you guttersnipes!'

He was obeyed. By all but their leader. He stood his ground, and his hand went to his revolver. The sheriff covered him promptly, and said:

'Drop your hand, you parlour-desperado. Kick the fire away. Now unchain the stranger.'

The parlour-desperado obeyed. Then the sheriff made a speech; sitting his horse at martial ease, and not warming his words with any touch of fire, but delivering them in a measured and deliberate way, and in a tone which harmonised with their character and made them impressively disrespectful.

'You're a nice lot – now ain't you? Just about eligible to travel with this bilk here – Shadbelly Higgins – this loud-mouthed sneak that shoots people in the back and calls himself a desperado. If there's anything I do particularly despise, it's a lynching mob; I've never seen one that had a man in it. It has to tally up a hundred against one before it can pump up pluck enough to tackle a sick tailor. It's made up of cowards, and so is the community that breeds it; and ninety-nine times out of a hundred the sheriff's another one.' He paused – apparently to turn that last idea over in his mind and taste the juice of it – then he went on: 'The sheriff that lets a mob take a prisoner away from him is the lowest-down coward there is. By the statistics there was a hundred and eighty-two of them drawing sneak pay in America last year. By the way it's going, pretty soon there'll be a new disease in the doctor books – *sheriff complaint*.' That idea pleased him – anyone could see it. 'People will say, "Sheriff sick again?" "Yes; got the same old thing." And next there'll be a new title. People won't say, "He's running for sheriff of Rapaho County," for instance; they'll say, "He's running for Coward of Rapaho." Lord, the idea of a grown-up person being afraid of a lynch mob!'

He turned an eye on the captive, and said, 'Stranger, who are you, and what have you been doing?'

'My name is Sherlock Holmes, and I have not been doing anything.'

It was wonderful, the impression which the sound of that name made on the sheriff, notwithstanding he must have come posted. He spoke up with feeling, and said it was a blot on the country that a man whose marvellous exploits had filled the world with their fame and their ingenuity, and whose histories of them had won every reader's heart by the brilliancy and charm of their literary setting, should be visited under the Stars and Stripes by an outrage like this. He apologised in the name of the whole nation, and made Holmes a most handsome bow, and told Constable Harris to see him to his quarters, and hold himself personally responsible if he was molested again. Then he turned to the mob and said:

'Hunt your holes, you scum!' which they did; then he said: 'Follow me, Shadbelly; I'll take care of your case myself. No – keep your pop-gun; whenever I see the day that I'll be afraid to have you behind me with that thing, it'll be time for me to join last year's hundred and eighty-two;' and he rode off in a walk, Shadbelly following.

When we were on our way back to our cabin, toward breakfast-time, we ran upon the news that Fetlock Jones had escaped from his lock-up in the night and is gone! Nobody is sorry. Let his uncle track him out if he likes; it is in his line; the camp is not interested.

❧ 10 ☙

Ten days later
'James Walker' is all right in body now, and his mind shows improvement too. I start with him for Denver tomorrow morning.

Next night. Brief note, mailed at a way station
As we were starting, this morning, Hillyer whispered to me: 'Keep this news from Walker until you think it safe and not likely to disturb his mind and check his improvement: the ancient crime he spoke of was really committed – and by his cousin, as he said. *We buried the real criminal* the other day – the unhappiest man that has lived in a century – Flint Buckner. His real name was Jacob Fuller!' There, mother, by help of me, an unwitting mourner, your husband and my father is in his grave. Let him rest.

Wordsworth American Library

IRVING BACHELLER
Eben Holden

AMBROSE BIERCE
Can Such Things Be?

KATE CHOPIN
The Awakening

JAMES FENIMORE COOPER
The Deerslayer

STEPHEN CRANE
The Red Badge of Courage
Maggie: A Girl of the Streets

RICHARD HENRY DANA JR
Two Years Before the Mast

FREDERICK DOUGLASS
The Life and Times of
Frederick Douglass

THEODORE DREISER
Sister Carrie

BENJAMIN FRANKLIN
Autobiography of
Benjamin Franklin

ZANE GREY
Riders of the Purple Sage

EDWARD E. HALE
The Man Without a Country

NATHANIEL HAWTHORNE
The House of the Seven Gables
The Scarlet Letter

HENRY JAMES
Washington Square
The Awkward Age

JACK LONDON
The Iron Heel
Call of the Wild/White Fang

HERMAN MELVILLE
Moby Dick

HARRIET BEECHER STOWE
Uncle Tom's Cabin

MARK TWAIN
The Man That
Corrupted Hadleyburg
The Tragedy of Pudd'nhead
Wilson

HENRY DAVID THOREAU
Walden

EDITH WHARTON
Ethan Frome
The House of Mirth

OWEN WISTER
The Virginian